"I came as soon as I heard the news!"

A voice rang out as the door swung open.

"What is it, Charlotte?"

...here, so I came to take a look!"

Musia
A mage in the service of House Louvent. Quiet and reserved.

Charlotte
The leader of House Louvent's mages. Whimsical and free-spirited.

Wren

Ars's younger sister.

"Yip, yip!"

Rio

A type of fox known as a king blue.

Kreiz

Ars's younger brother.

Rio barked excitedly. The fox seemed to be in a fabulous mood.

"Hee hee! Rio is certainly a spirited one. And it's such a lovely day out today, too! You could hardly ask for a more pleasant temperature,"

Licia said with a smile as she watched the fox frolic. It was fall, at the moment, which was one of the nicer seasons in Missian. I had to agree—it was hard to imagine better weather to take a walk in.

Ars
The head of House Louvent. Bearer of the Eye of Appraisal.

Licia
Ars's wife. Clear-headed and keen-minded.

"Shame. Time for a change of plans, then..."

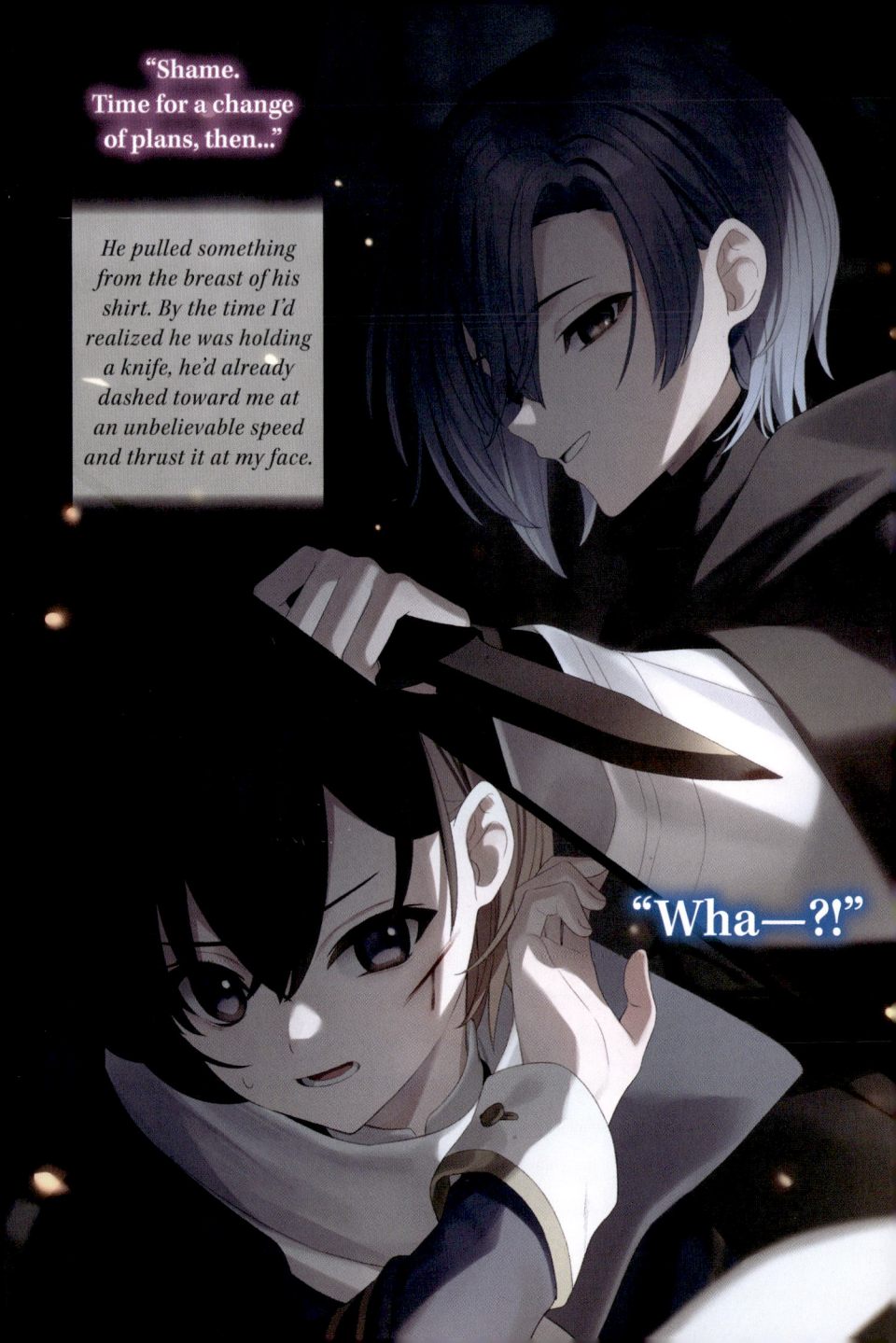

He pulled something from the breast of his shirt. By the time I'd realized he was holding a knife, he'd already dashed toward me at an unbelievable speed and thrust it at my face.

"Wha—?!"

As a Reincarnated Aristocrat,
I'll Use My Appraisal Skill
to Rise in the World

6

By Miraijin A
Illustrations by jimmy

Translated by Tristan K. Hill

KODANSHA

As a Reincarnated Aristocrat, I'll Use My Appraisal Skill to Rise in the World 6

A VERTICAL Book

Translation: Tristan K. Hill
Editor: Maneesh Maganti
Production: Shirley Fang
Proofreading: Kevin Luo

Copyright © 2024 Miraijin A

All rights reserved.

Publication rights for this English edition arranged through Kodansha, Ltd., Tokyo.
English language version produced by Kodansha USA Publishing, LLC, 2025.

Originally published in Japan as *Tensei Kizoku Kantei Sukiru de Nariagaru 6 ~Jakushou Ryouchi o Uketsuidanode, Yuushuuna Jinzai o Fuyashite Itara, Saikyou Ryouchi ni Natteta~* by Kodansha, Tokyo, 2024.

ISBN 978-1-64729-439-7

Printed in the United States of America

The authorized representatives in the EU for product safety and compliance are Marko & Daniel Novkovic; eucomply OÜ; Pärnu mnt 139b-14, 11317; Tallinn, Estonia; hello@eucompliancepartner.com; +33-7569-0241

First Edition

Kodansha USA Publishing, LLC
25 E. 22nd St.
New York, NY 10010

www.kodansha.us

KODANSHA

Design: **AFTERGLOW** Illustrations: **jimmy**

Contents

Prologue... **009**

Chapter 1: A Pet.. **013**

Chapter 2: Proclamation of Independence....... **069**

Chapter 3: An Emergency for House Louvent.... **129**

Chapter 4: An Unexpected Meeting................. **161**

Epilogue... **227**

Prologue

Fourteen years had come and gone since I was reborn in this world as Ars Louvent.

Aside from Appraisal—a power I was born with which allowed me to see other people's talents and capabilities—I was a decidedly average individual. Nevertheless, I wound up inheriting the title of Baron, sallying forth into war, and getting wrapped up in large-scale campaigns of territorial conquest, making it through ordeal after ordeal alive by the skin of my teeth. Oh, and while I'd died alone and unmarried in my previous life, in this world I'd already found myself a bride. You really never knew what's going to be thrown at you next.

My homeland was a nation known as the Summerforth Empire, a tumultuous realm that was rife with conflict and civil war. It was, in fact, more or less an empire in name only in the modern era. One could easily make an argument that the Summerforth Empire had already fallen.

As matters stood, Summerforth was for all intents and purposes a collection of seven nations, each of which was vying for control of the continent at large. I'd met the emperor myself, and had found him to be a man of remarkably little drive and ambition—essentially a puppet controlled by his own vassals. With him on the throne, I had a feeling that there wasn't much hope of the empire regaining its former glory.

Thanks to the state of the empire, it was hard to find a region that hadn't been subjected to some form of armed conflict. My own homeland, however—the County of Canarre, located in the Duchy of Missian—had been blessed with a period of peace ever since the succession war between Couran and Vasmarque's forces drew to a close.

That peace had brought about an economic upsurge in Canarre, and thanks to my newfound surplus of both time and money, I'd been able to get out there and proactively search for new vassals to recruit. Using my Appraisal skill to its fullest potential, I'd managed to bring a number of new, highly capable retainers into my fold. I'd hired a loquacious man named Virge, as well as a trio of siblings from the Fujimiya family. I'd also managed to convince Mireille's younger brother Thomas to do work for House Louvent, though he hadn't formally entered into my service as a retainer just yet.

In addition, I'd found a very talented woman named Enan who I'd recruited to help Shin with the airship project that I was funding. If her help ended up speeding the airship's development along on its way, it could prove tremendously important for the future of the county. I didn't know exactly what sort of airship they were developing, mind you, but no matter how it ended up turning out, I had a feeling they could be handy for all sorts of things. Airships would surely be useful for warfare, and could serve as a means of transportation as well. They might even be helpful for trade.

I found myself naively hoping that the peace we'd won for ourselves would carry on forever, and that Canarre would continue to develop at a steady pace. These, however, were troubled times, and the life of peace and security that I longed for would soon prove itself impossible to attain once again...

Chapter 1:
A Pet

A few months had passed since the Fujimiya siblings entered my service, and the third month of the year had arrived. It was fall, and the weather was a little chilly, but otherwise quite pleasant all around. It was also a celebratory time of the year, thanks in part to a number of large-scale harvest festivals held across the county.

All three of the Fujimiyas had hit the ground running in their new positions as my retainers. They'd made notable contributions to the state of public order in Canarre City, and Maika's way with words had allowed her to secure a source of cheap aqua magia for us as well. I still didn't feel like I could entrust them with any truly important duties, but they had handled the tasks that I had given them with remarkable consistency.

Ultimately, Mireille—who'd been griping about not having enough help for quite some time—had badgered me into sending the Fujimiyas over to assist her. She'd wasted no time in putting them to work, apparently, assigning them task after task. Maika was remarkably smart, Takao was as brawny as they came, and Rikuya was an all-rounder who could take on all sorts of assignments, so between the three of their specialties, there were very few matters that they couldn't resolve.

Mireille herself, as a consequence, quickly ended up without much of any work on her own plate. I made a mental note to threaten that if she slacked off too much when it came to Lamberg's management, I'd be more than happy to give her position to someone who'd take it seriously. There was no telling how much she'd take advantage of the Fujimiyas' help if I didn't keep her in check, after all.

All things considered, the Fujimiya siblings had gradually racked up accomplishment after accomplishment since entering into my service. That wasn't to say, however, that I'd been resting on my recruitment laurels for the past several months. I'd been searching for personnel as actively as ever, and while I'd found plenty of people who were skilled enough to hire, I hadn't managed to come across any truly stand-out talents who were willing to work for me.

Still, I'd found a number of people with a reasonable talent for magic, and Canarre's unit of mages was more well-staffed than ever. Bolstering our magical forces was, at the moment, my top priority. We still didn't have enough recruits with the right talents to form the mounted mage unit that Rosell had proposed, though, since it was very rare for my skill to identify someone as having both decent Mage and Cavalry Aptitudes. I knew that if I did manage to bring the unit up to a functional capacity it would be a force to be reckoned with, so all I could do was keep searching for new hires, working slowly and steadily toward my goal.

Mages aside, I'd recently come across quite a few individuals with high Valor scores. I'd assigned them to Braham's elite squadron, bringing its already impressive capabilities up to even greater heights. Braham himself was currently one of House Louvent's most capable commanders, and considering how much he and his troops seemed to have improved recently, I was confident that they would be invaluable the next time battle broke out.

I WILL USE MY APPRAISAL SKILL TO RISE IN THE WORLD

Although I'd found a reasonable number of high-valor individuals who had the potential to be soldiers, I'd found very few with high Intelligence or Politics scores. Bringing Virge into the fold had taken a lot of weight off Rietz's shoulders, but he was still quite overworked, and I was hoping to find someone else who would be capable enough to help him. Luck hadn't been on my side in that regard, though, which unfortunately was something I couldn't do anything to change. I'd always had the impression that people with high Intelligence and Politics scores were relatively rare, for some reason. I had to wonder: were the people of Missian naturally inclined toward martial pursuits?

I still wasn't satisfied with the number of people I'd managed to recruit, but that being said, the number of new people I had brought in was large enough that hiring anyone else would put a precarious strain on our finances. If Canarre kept growing I'd gain the financial leeway that I needed to start actively hiring again, but until that time came, I knew that I'd have to put my search for new talent on temporary hold.

The neighboring Duchy of Seitz, meanwhile, had been gathering up aqua magia and bolstering the ranks of their army, but had made no attempts to stage another invasion. There was every chance that they were working behind the scenes to set the stage for another assault, but so far, I hadn't found any evidence as to what specifically they could be plotting.

Fortunately, House Louvent had an incredibly skilled band of spies called the Shadows in its employ. They'd done a first-rate job both at figuring out what our enemies were scheming and moving to obstruct those schemes before they could come to fruition. Our foes certainly wouldn't find it easy to engage in subterfuge in the City of Canarre itself, in any case.

We had also been dealing with more bandits than usual lately, and there was a chance that their unusual numbers were part of one of Seitz's schemes. For the moment, however, our troops were putting in the work to keep the brigands subdued. If anything, the county had suffered fewer bandit-related losses in recent times than ever before.

As things stood, Cannare's dedicated military force was stronger than ever before. The unification of Missian also meant that it would be easy for Couran to send us reinforcements, in a pinch. As such, I had to imagine that Seitz wouldn't attack any time soon unless something major happened to upset the status quo. Our economy was booming, our population was gradually growing, and on the whole, my job as Canarre's chief administrator seemed like it was going as smoothly as could be.

○

Early one morning, Licia and I were eating breakfast together in our chambers.

"I'm so excited for the Founding Festival!" Licia cheerfully exclaimed.

"Me too," I said with a nod. "It's just ten days away or so, isn't it?"

The Founding Festival was one of a number of major festivals that occurred around this time of year. It was a longstanding Missian tradition, and commemorated the date on which the Kingdom of Missian first came to be. Even after the Summerforth Empire was founded and the kingdom became a thing of the past, the celebration had carried on as a tradition of its own.

"I'm sure everyone's going to get all dressed up again this year,"

I WILL USE MY APPRAISAL SKILL TO RISE IN THE WORLD

Licia said with an air of excitement.

A rather odd aspect of the Founding Festival tradition in Canarre involved everyone dressing up in costumes to walk around town in. That wasn't a thing in other parts of Missian, it seemed—it was Canarre's own unique spin on the Festival's customs. I'd never heard any compelling explanation for how or why that custom had come about, but my best guess was that at some point in the festival's long history, someone had thought it up as a way to make the event more exciting.

Costumes aside, the festival featured stalls set up on the major streets and in the plazas, where events would be held as well. An incredible number of people participated in the festivities, and the day of the festival was always a bustling, lively affair.

"What sort of outfit will you be wearing, Ars?" asked Licia.

"Me?" I replied. "I haven't decided yet, actually..."

"In that case, allow me to pick out one that would suit you! Hmm... I have a feeling that a woman's outfit would suit you perfectly... A maid's uniform, perhaps...?"

"W-Wait a second! You can't seriously think I'd wear something like that?!"

"Yes, I suppose that's fair... It might not be appropriate for a lord to wear a servant's uniform, when you put it that way..."

"That's actually not the part that I had a problem with," I sighed. I had a terrible feeling that if I left Licia to her own devices, I'd be forced to wear a costume that'd be outrageous in more ways than one. "Y-You know, I think I'll pick out my own outfit after all!"

"Oh, will you? I'd be perfectly happy to help, though," Licia replied, looking a little disappointed.

"It's fine, I have it under control! More importantly, we have to hurry up with all our preparations and make sure the festival can

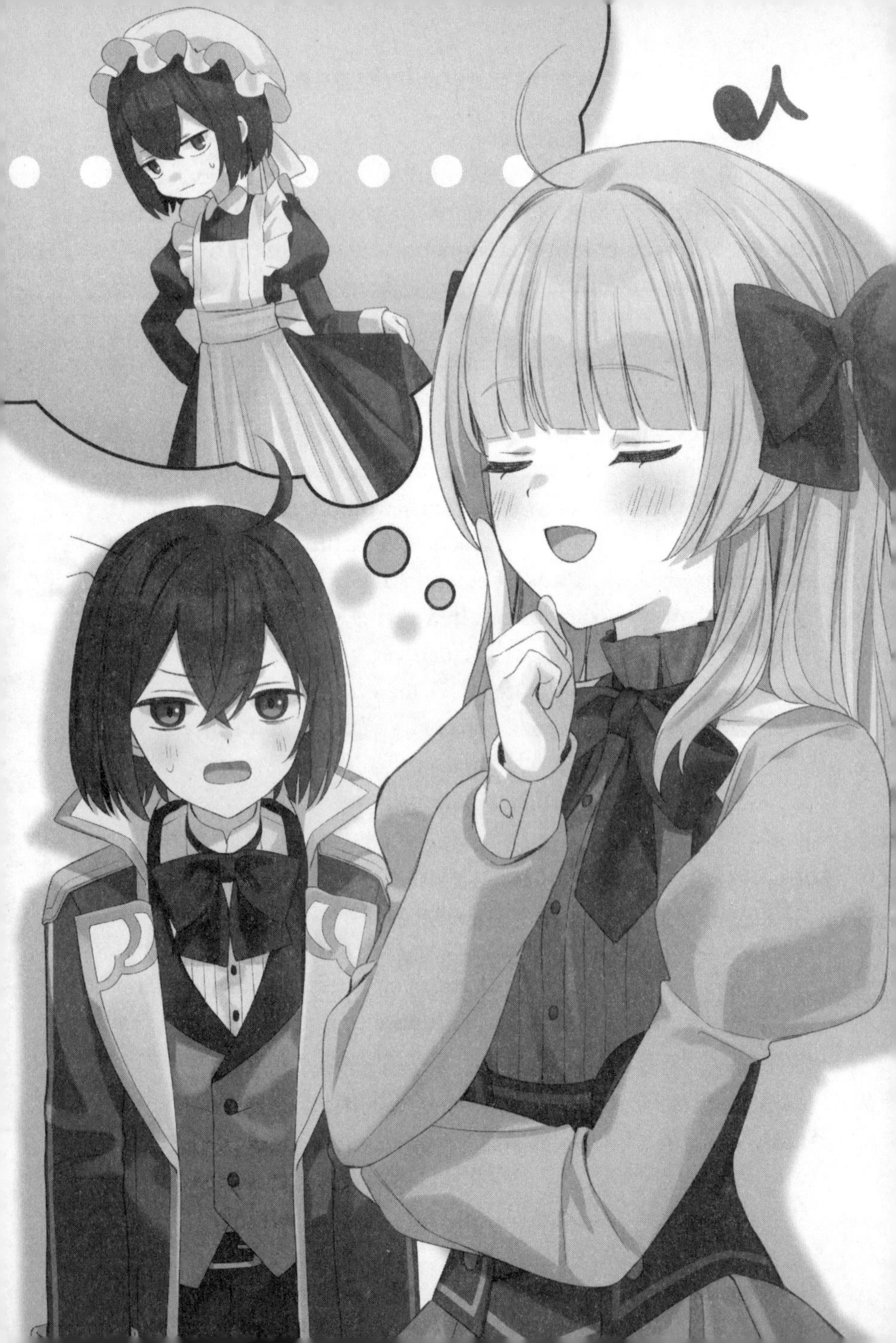

happen in the first place!"

"True indeed!" Licia exclaimed.

I finished breakfast, then headed to my first task of the day: a meeting in which we'd be planning the very same festival that Licia and I had been discussing.

○

Before I knew it, the day of the Founding Festival had arrived. We'd worked our way through all sorts of preparations to make sure the event could happen, and in the end, they seemed to have all paid off—the event was going off without a hitch.

Needless to say, I'd be participating in the festival. Making appearances at events like this was a surefire way for a lord to gain the trust of their subjects, and so Licia, my retainers, and I walked through the streets of Canarre together.

Crowds of costumed people thronged the streets, strolling around and enjoying the festival to the fullest. Stalls lined each side of the roadway, and the air was full of energy. I'd been to Canarre's Founding Festival a number of times before, but I didn't remember it ever being as crowded of an event as it had turned out to be this year. The county's growing population, it seemed, had dramatically raised the number of festival participants.

"It certainly is crowded! And just look at all the lovely costumes everyone's wearing!" Licia exclaimed, her eyes sparkling with glee as we strolled along, taking in the sights. She had dressed up for the occasion as well, and was wearing a black robe that made her look like a witch. She was actually pulling off the outfit quite well, and looked very cute in it.

I, meanwhile, was wearing a long, white coat that made me look like a doctor. I'd chosen the costume out myself, for fear of Licia making me cross-dress if I let her pick one for me. It was a nice, safe outfit that didn't feel at all humiliating to walk around in.

My retainers had dressed up as well. Rietz was wearing an outfit from Yoh—apparently, he'd learned about the country's traditional clothing from the Fujimiya siblings and had decided to try wearing some for himself. He had a sword on hand as well, just in case he needed to defend us at a moment's notice. Charlotte, on the other hand, was wearing a maid uniform, while Mireille was cross-dressing in a butler's outfit. I had to admit: she actually looked pretty dashing in men's clothes.

"Why do I have to walk around dressed like this…?" muttered Rosell, who was walking with us as well…dressed in women's clothing.

"Come on, you're really pulling off the look!" Charlotte said with a smirk.

"If I'm dressing up as a man, then it's only fair for you to dress as a girl," Mireille added.

"How does that make sense?!" Rosell wailed.

Apparently, Mireille had more or less coerced him into cross-dressing for the festival. I felt for him, honestly, but I also had to admit that he really was pulling it off. He'd always looked a little girly, and the clothes genuinely suited him.

"Don't let your guards down," Rietz said, cautioning our more spirited companions. "Remember that part of why we're out here is to keep watch. There's no telling what sort of ruffians will be out and about, considering how much larger the crowds are this year."

The more participants who showed up for the festival, the more chances there would be for trouble to crop up. It was important that we keep a close enough eye out to catch any issues before they spiraled out of control, especially considering my suspicions that Seitz was working to undermine Canarre behind the scenes. If this festival ended up being a disastrous failure, then there was a chance that the citizens would lose faith in House Louvent's leadership. That was something I wanted to avoid at all costs.

We weren't the only group keeping watch in the city. Braham's unit and the Fujimiya siblings were also spread throughout the capital, patrolling their own assigned areas. We'd tasked a large number of soldiers with wandering around the festival too, though considering that having armed guards skulking all over the place ran the risk of alarming the populace, we had them all wear costumes for their patrols.

I had to admit I was a little worried that some of them—or, well, mostly Braham—would get so worked up by the costumes that they'd forget all about keeping watch and just enjoy the festival instead. On the other hand, Braham had matured a lot in recent months, and his second-in-command Zaht would be there to keep him in check as well.

As I walked along, glancing at the street stalls, a voice rang out. "Ah! It's Lord Ars!" a child who'd recognized me shouted, pointing in my direction.

The coat I was wearing was nothing like my usual outfits, but it also didn't do much to hide my appearance. It wasn't too surprising that someone would recognize me, and now that the child had pointed me out, the nearby adults started realizing who I was too.

"Lord Ars!" one of them shouted.

"Thank you for everything you've done for us!"

"Business has been booming lately! My inn's never turned profits like these before!"

The people of Canarre sounded as cheerful and upbeat as could be. I walked around the city on a regular basis, but it was rare for the citizens to talk with me this readily. It wasn't that they didn't notice me so much as that casually chatting up the lord of a territory was usually something of a breach of social protocol. Today was a festival, however, which seemed to mean that those walls had been temporarily lowered.

"We're blessed to have a lord who listens to his people! I hope you'll rule over Canarre forever!" cried out one of the citizens.

"We're living in dangerous times, what with all the wars and all, but you keep winning them for us, which means we get to put on our Founding Festival, just like always! This is all thanks to you, Lord Ars!" said another.

My people were lavishing me with praise, and I certainly wasn't unhappy to hear it. I credited my retainers with our success in the recent wars, so it felt like the people's kind words were really more about them than they were about me, but on the other hand, hearing my retainers be praised for their hard work was nice in its own way. I'd worried that I wouldn't cut it as the lord of a domain, back when the job was first thrust upon me, but now I felt confident that the methods I'd chosen really were effective.

We walked around for some time, and no trouble in particular presented itself. Just when I thought that the day would end without incident, however, a commotion suddenly began to spread through the crowd.

"Did something happen?" I wondered out loud.

We stopped in our tracks and looked around, trying to find the source of the disturbance. It didn't take long for us to pick out a large-bodied man who was laying into one of the stalls with a club, doing his best to destroy it. Rietz reacted immediately, dashing over to the man and grabbing him by the wrist in the blink of an eye.

I WILL USE MY APPRAISAL SKILL TO RISE IN THE WORLD

"Ugh! What the—I-I can't move?!" the man yelped in confusion. Rietz's grip strength alone was enough to completely immobilize his arm. The man's grip, on the other hand, loosened to the point that the club fell from his now limp grasp.

"Don't move a muscle," Rietz said as he held his sword to the man's throat. The man grimaced with frustration, but gave in, kneeling to the ground at Rietz's direction.

For a moment, I thought that was case closed. The next thing I knew, however, I heard a woman let out a sharp scream from somewhere else in the vicinity. Not just one, in fact—several screams rang out in quick succession, and the commotion on the street grew greater still. Something, clearly, was going very wrong.

"Charlotte! Let everyone know that something strange is happening in the main street!" I said.

"You got it," Charlotte replied before casting a sound magic spell to send a signal to Braham and the Fujimiyas, who were patrolling elsewhere. The scale of the disturbance was large enough that I knew we'd need all the help we could get to cope with it.

The sound of Charlotte's spell echoed out across the city. That noise, unfortunately, seemed to raise concerns among the townsfolk, and the commotion grew louder than ever.

"Why were you attacking that stall?" Rietz asked the man he'd apprehended. It seemed very likely that he had a connection to the disturbance, and I figured that Rietz was hoping to get some helpful information out of him.

The man, however, responded only with stony silence. He wasn't interested in talking.

"I'd loosen those lips if I were you. You're in for some serious pain if you don't, trust me," said Mireille. The man stayed silent, and her glare took on a sharp edge. "Oh? Looks like you've got a spine, eh? Leave this guy to me, Rietz. I'll deal with interrogating him, so you can head out and handle whoever else is causing trouble out there."

"Understood," Rietz replied.

Mireille dragged the man Rietz had captured elsewhere. Whatever she was planning on doing to him, she apparently didn't want to do it in public.

"Stay with Ars and the others, Charlotte. Guard them with your life," said Rietz.

"'Kaaay," Charlotte droned.

With that, Rietz charged off to stop whatever was causing the other disturbances.

I was no use whatsoever in a fight, which meant that when trouble actually broke out, I ended up just holding everyone else back. Unfortunately, there wasn't much I could do about that. My only choice was to wait for Rietz and Mireille to report back in with new intel.

"Hmm... Multiple incidents on the main street, all happening at the exact same time...? Someone might have set this up. It could be Seitz trying to undermine us," Rosell muttered. I imagined we'd learn whether or not his analysis was on the mark once Mireille had managed to convince our prisoner to spill the beans to her.

Before long, the commotion began to die down. Charlotte's signal had brought reinforcements rushing in, and they seemed to have gotten the situation under control in short order.

"Okay, all finished," Mireille said as she returned to us with the troublemaking man in tow.

I noticed that the man seemed rather unsteady on his feet, but he didn't have a single visible injury. I wondered what in the world she'd done to him, but I was also way too scared to actually ask her

I WILL USE MY APPRAISAL SKILL TO RISE IN THE WORLD

for any specifics.

"Looks like someone hired him to attack the festival," Mireille explained.

"Someone? Who?" I asked.

"Dunno. He never found out any details about his client, but considering how well they paid, I'm thinking it'd have to be a merchant or a noble."

"Okay, then... In that case, it really does seem likely that this was Seitz's work," Rosell muttered. "Maybe they thought that ruining the festival would destabilize the situation in Canarre?"

"I can't rule that out...but if this was a Seitzan plot, it was a pretty sloppy one. Who'd hire an amateur like this guy for a job like that?"

Mireille and Rosell sank into thought, and soon afterward, Rietz returned to us. We shared the information we'd gained from our captive with him.

"I see," Rietz said when we'd finished. "So someone paid him to cause trouble... In any case, we've apprehended all the other men who were involved in the incidents. There were nine of them—ten in total, counting the one here. Braham and Zaht are questioning the others now. I certainly hope they'll provide enough details to determine who hired them..."

Judging by Rietz's report, it seemed we'd managed to resolve the issue. It had caused a bit of a fuss, but thanks to Rietz's quick response, things hadn't gotten out of control. The only major damage that had been done were a few wrecked street stalls. Their owners were working to repair them, but there was no doubt that their sales would suffer. Thankfully, however, nobody had been injured. It seemed that the troublemakers hadn't attacked any people at all, which led me to believe that they weren't completely irredeemable.

The question remained: just who had organized the attacks, and for what purpose? Was it really a Seitzan plot? I knew that we had to get to the bottom of the issue fast, or we'd run the risk of the same thing happening all over again.

"I'll be heading over to join up with Braham and his men, Lord Ars," Rietz told me.

"Should the rest of us go with you?" I asked.

"Huh?" Rietz said. "There's no need for that. You should stay here and enjoy the festival."

"I'm not so sure about that... I don't think I'd be able to enjoy it at all, with all these questions about what happened still eating at me..."

"Fair enough. And I suppose you will be safer by my side... Very well, then. We'll go together," Rietz agreed with a nod. Licia didn't object to the plan either, so in the end, all of us headed over to where Braham was conducting his interrogation.

Our destination was a guard station located in Canarre's downtown area, where criminals were brought for interrogations on a regular basis. When we arrived, we found nine restrained men being questioned by Braham, Zaht, and the Fujimiya siblings.

"Have they said anything useful?" Rietz asked Braham.

"Nah, not a word! They won't tell me anything, the tight-lipped bastards! I swear, first they crash the festival, and now this?! How dare they?!" Braham shouted, seemingly in a rage. Like Rietz, he'd attended the festival in a traditional outfit from Yoh, though he'd added an ostentatious necklace to the ensemble that I assumed he must have bought at a stall somewhere. I had a funny feeling that he was more upset with the ruffians for spoiling his fun than anything else.

"Sounds like it's my turn, then," said Mireille. "This might be a

I WILL USE MY APPRAISAL SKILL TO RISE IN THE WORLD

little too intense for you kiddos, so I'd wait outside if I were you," she added, glancing at me with a disconcerting smirk.

"R-Right, of course. We'll leave you to it," I said.

"Y-Yes, indeed," Licia agreed.

We stepped outside and waited for Mireille to extract the information we needed. Barely a matter of seconds later, I heard someone wail "I'll talk! I'll tell you everything you want to know, I swear!" from inside.

"'Kay, all finished!" Mireille called out to us. Just like that, we filed right back into the guard station.

"Looks like they were hired by a merchant," Mireille explained. "Guy by the name of Apotta. That ring a bell?"

A look of shock spread across Rietz's face as he heard the name. "Apotta!" he exclaimed. "He's one of the most well-known merchants in Canarre—of course I know him! What in the world would he do something like this for? Could he be in league with Seitz?"

"Seems he didn't tell his cronies what exactly he was after when he hired 'em," said Mireille. "Just means we'll have to find him and hear it straight from the horse's mouth, of course."

So a merchant was behind this? What would someone like that have to gain from sabotaging the festival?

Regardless, I knew that as long as we brought this Apotta to justice, we wouldn't have to worry about any further disruptions.

"So a pocketful of coin is all it takes to make you trash the festival?" Braham fumed, incensed now that he knew the ruffians' motivations. "Well, you'll have plenty of time in jail to think about why that was a bad choice! Everyone was having so much fun until you messed it all up!"

"I-I didn't just do it for the money," one of the men fearfully objected.

"Oh yeah? Well, what did you do it for, then?!"

"I did it because I couldn't take it anymore," the man replied. There was a look of pure hatred in his eyes. "People like us wake up every morning not knowing if we'll manage to have a single bite to eat before we go to bed again. Every damn day's a struggle, and then we have to watch *those* people go setting up for their festival without a care in the world… It made me wanna tear it all down around them."

"Wh-What?! How selfish can you possibly be?!" Braham exclaimed.

"Hmph! You people with your cushy jobs could never know what it's like to not be sure when your next meal is going to come. You'll never understand…" the man said, the hatred in his eyes fading into a look of tired resignation. It felt like he hadn't expected us to understand him from the very start.

I was starting to get a clearer picture of what was going on. All of the men, it seemed, were down on their luck after failing to find work in Canarre for one reason or another. They were all still young, and I could tell by their worn and ragged clothing that they didn't have money to spare.

Needless to say, there was no such thing as a city where literally everyone lived in happiness and comfort. Canarre was no exception to that rule—while some of its residents were blissfully enjoying their festival, others lived in poverty and misery that they couldn't escape from. The more Canarre's population grew, the more of its people would find themselves just barely scraping by.

The men in front of me hadn't hurt anyone, which I believed meant that they hadn't strayed so far from the right path that they couldn't find it again. I wanted to give them a chance to start their lives anew.

I WILL USE MY APPRAISAL SKILL TO RISE IN THE WORLD

I tried appraising them, and found that none of their stats were particularly remarkable. Their current abilities were all quite low—low enough that I could confidently declare that they didn't have any strong points to speak of. That said, that was only true when it came to their current stats. When I looked at their maximum values, all of them had areas in which they could excel in the future. If they only had the chance to nurture those abilities, I was confident they'd be able to find jobs that would make good use of them.

"All of you have broken the law today," I said to the group of men. "You only damaged property, and no one was hurt, so I can't say that your crimes are especially grave. Nevertheless, a crime is still a crime, and you'll have to make up for what you've done."

"Hmph! Make up for it? How?" one of the men grumbled.

"You'll be working to pay for the damage you caused," I replied.

"Huh? How're we supposed to work?! We don't have jobs! We're useless layabouts, remember?!" the man said, bewildered by my answer.

"That's where you're wrong. All of you have strengths and talents, though it seems that you have yet to discover them. You, for example, have the talent to be a capable fighter. You'd make a good soldier."

"A soldier? S-Sure, I'm pretty big, but I'm also slow! No way I'd be any help in a fight!"

"Again, you're mistaken. Speed is something that you can attain through proper training. I think you'll understand that in due time, since starting tomorrow, you'll be joining the army of Canarre as a trainee," I said. The man's eyes widened with shock, and I gestured toward another member of the group. "You, meanwhile, seem like you have a good head on your shoulders. You'd do well training under a merchant's guidance—I'll make some introductions and find you an appropriate employer."

"Y-You're saying I'm smart?! Nobody's ever said that to me before!" the man yelped with surprise. Considering his current Intelligence score was 15, I wasn't shocked to hear that. His maximum score, however, was 60, meaning that with the right education, he could turn out to be reasonably capable.

I went from one man to the next in much the same manner, informing them of the jobs they'd be suited for. In the end, I ordered them to work for the places of employment I introduced them to until their debts were paid.

"You're being pretty soft on them, eh, kiddo? Sure you don't wanna punish them?" asked Mireille.

"But I am, remember?" I replied. "Their punishment is to work until they've paid for the damage they caused. And if they decide to turn a new leaf and stick with their jobs after they've finished, so much the better, since it'll mean more capable workers in Canarre. Don't you think?"

"I think there's no guarantee any of them are gonna turn any leaves at all."

"And if they don't, we'll handle it when the time comes."

The men we were dealing with were still young. It only seemed fair to give them a second chance.

The remainder of the Founding Festival passed by without incident. Apotta was quickly taken into custody, and didn't have the chance to cause any more trouble. As for his motives, it turned out that Seitz hadn't been involved at all—he'd simply known that a business rival of his was due to turn a massive profit thanks to the festival, and had thought that sabotaging it would be a good way to take his competitor's business down a peg.

I WILL USE MY APPRAISAL SKILL TO RISE IN THE WORLD

If Apotta's plan had succeeded, then the festival that the townspeople had been looking forward to for so very long would have been ruined. This was a serious crime, in my eyes, and I made sure that he was punished accordingly.

The men who we'd captured, by the way, had all begun working at their new jobs. There weren't many places that would employ criminals, even with a lord to vouch for them, so many of those workplaces had been reluctant at first, but Virge's silver tongue had saved the day and brought them all around in the end. Now all I could do was pray that they'd take their jobs seriously and put in the effort to turn their lives around.

I'd reached a realization thanks to this incident: if I wanted to make Canarre into a better county than it had ever been before, I'd have to do more than just recruit more and more talented retainers. My skill was good for more than that—it could also let me find new paths and careers for the citizens of my realm who'd lost their way in life.

○

It was the sixteenth day of the third month, and I found myself in Castle Canarre. I'd thought that my talent search being put on hold would mean I'd have some free time for once, but I'd been surprised to find that my schedule was actually quite packed anyway. I'd been receiving an incredible number of letters and messages from other nobles recently, and found myself hopelessly occupied by the sort of diplomatic matters that took a lord to deal with.

I had to assume that our recent victory over Seitz, as well as Canarre's rapid growth, had raised the nearby lords' opinion of House Louvent considerably. Visitors had started to come calling on a regular basis, and whenever they did, I had no choice but to meet with them in person. That sort of affair took a lot of preparations before the meeting as well, and in the end, I wound up with barely a moment to spare for myself.

On that particular day, I'd finally finished with my work and was on my way back to my chambers.

"I can tell you're tired, having to meet with visitors day after day like this," Licia, who was walking beside me, said with a sympathetic smile.

"You're not wrong about that," I agreed with a nod. "Thanks for always coming along with me."

"But of course! It's my responsibility as your wife!" Licia declared.

She'd made a point of accompanying me every time I went to meet with a visitor. She'd always been sharper than me when it came to people, if I'm being honest, and she had a knack for conversation and negotiation as well, which had proven quite helpful on many occasions. Her abilities made me realize just how much I still had to grow as a lord.

"Ars! Big Brother!"

Suddenly, I heard a voice from behind me. I didn't even have to turn around to know that it was my younger brother Kreiz. He was the only one who called me "Big Brother" these days, for one thing—my younger sister, Wren, had taken to referring to me as her "Elder Brother" lately instead.

I turned around to find both Kreiz and Wren standing behind me. The two of them looked troubled, and Kreiz was holding something in his arms. Well, "something" might not be the right expression, actually—it was an animal with blue fur, large ears, and a big, fluffy tail. Its eyes were rather narrow. At a glance, it looked like a fox.

Why would Kreiz be holding a fox, though? And wait, do they even have foxes in this world?

"We found it all huddled up and shivering in a corner of the castle, so we decided to bring it to you!" Kreiz explained, clearing up at least a few of my questions about the fox—or, well, the fox-like animal.

Blue fur aside, it looked almost exactly like the foxes that I knew about. On reflection, it struck me that it was totally possible that we'd had blue foxes back on Earth, and I just hadn't been aware of it. Anyway, I'd seen all sorts of animals since my reincarnation, but this was my first time encountering a fox-like one. I'd been shocked by a winged dog right after my birth, but coloration aside, this fox creature didn't seem to have any features that were nearly that surprising.

"Why, I've never seen anything like it," said Licia. "Do you know what sort of animal this is, Ars?"

"I think it's called a fox, most likely... Have you ever heard of those?" I asked.

"A fox...? No, I can't say I have," Licia said as she studied the creature.

Maybe they really are rare in Canarre, then?

"I have to say, though, it seems oddly comfortable being held for a wild animal," Licia noted.

"When you put it that way, it doesn't look like it's feeling well, does it? Maybe it's sick?" I asked, giving the fox a closer look in turn. It was panting, and seemed to be trembling as well. Something was clearly wrong with it.

"It must be hungry! Don't you think?" suggested Wren.

That seemed reasonable enough to me—maybe if we fed it something, it would be back on its feet before we knew it.

"What would it eat, though?" Kreiz asked as he cocked his head.

Oh. That's a good question—what do foxes eat? I think they might be omnivores...?

Even if I was right about that, it would only apply to Earth foxes. Who could say if it was true of the ones in this world too? They could be carnivores, or even herbivores, for all I knew.

"Shall we head to the kitchens and ask for some ingredients, to start?" suggested Licia. "It may be willing to eat some of the food that we have stocked for ourselves."

"Considering we don't have any other clues about what it eats, I think that's our only choice. I'll go ask," I agreed. I was worried it would die if we left it in this state for too long, so I headed for the kitchen on the double.

"I'll help!" Licia said, following along after me. Wren and Kreiz wanted to come too, but I told them to stay behind and keep an eye on the fox instead.

We made our way to the kitchen, and the cooks working there gave us meat, some vegetables, milk, and eggs. We ended up with so many foods to test that I had to ask Licia to help carry it all.

We hurried back to the fox and laid all the food out in front of it. The milk caught its attention, in the end, and it started thirstily slurping it down.

"Oh, look! It's drinking!" said Kreiz.

"It must like milk!" Wren exclaimed. She and her brother seemed ecstatic to see the creature drink.

The fox drained the dish of milk that we'd brought for it. It seemed that Wren had been right—it might really have just been hungry. The moment it was finished drinking, it closed its eyes and drifted off to sleep.

"It's napping!" said Kreiz.

"I guess filling its stomach must've made it sleepy…" I muttered. "Well, I'd feel bad for leaving it in the hallway like this. Let's find a room to put it in."

"Okay!"

We did just that, carrying the slumbering fox into one of the castle's chambers. We also put together an impromptu bed for it with the help of the castle's maids, which we set the fox down into.

"I hope it feels better soon," Wren said as she watched the fox.

I, meanwhile, was busy wondering just how it had gotten into the castle in the first place. Was saving it really a good idea? The foxes on Earth hadn't been particularly dangerous animals, but that might not apply to the ones in this world. Maybe it hadn't tried anything because it was weak and feeble, and the moment it recovered its strength, it would go on a vicious rampage. It could even be venomous, for all I knew. It looked downright adorable when it was asleep, so I didn't think that would be true, but I still couldn't dismiss the possibility…

Considering how much of a bookworm Rosell was, I had a feeling that if anyone knew what sort of traits foxes in this world had, it would be him. I decided to go ask him, and then after thinking about it for a moment longer, decided that it'd be easier to show him the actual creature itself and see what he thought of it. And so, I asked one of the maids who'd helped with the fox's bedding to go find Rosell and bring him to us.

A few minutes later, Rosell arrived in the room.

"Wh-What's with that thing…?" Rosell stammered, trembling

slightly as he looked at the fox.

Oh, so he doesn't know about this world's foxes? Or maybe he does know what it is, and that it's dangerous?

"It's an animal that found its way into the castle, apparently," I explained.

"Oh, is that all! I thought you were about to tell me you were taking it in as a pet," Rosell said, letting out a sigh of relief.

"Would that be a bad idea, or something?" I asked. *Maybe this world's foxes really are dangerous?*

"Yeah, it would," said Rosell. "I can't stand animals!"

Oh. So it's just a personal problem, then. Kind of surprising that a hunter's son like him would have that much of a problem with wild animals.

"Ah! I know that look... You're thinking that it's weird that a hunter's son would hate animals, aren't you?!"

Talk about perceptive! Was it really that obvious?

"Look, being a hunter's son is how I learned that animals aren't just cute. You can never be totally sure about what they're thinking, and there's always a chance that they'll do something you could never possibly predict at any given moment... And, well, I just don't like them, okay? I've gotten used to dealing with horses, but I'd rather not be around any other sorts of animals," Rosell said, rattling off his explanation at a rapid clip. I could tell that he felt pretty strongly about this.

"So then, you just don't like animals, right? This fox isn't a particularly dangerous species, or anything?" I asked.

"Well, yeah," said Rosell. "Foxes are pretty rare in these parts, but they're not considered all that dangerous. They might bite you if you give them a chance, I guess, but that's about the worst of it. They're not much different from dogs or cats in that respect."

I WILL USE MY APPRAISAL SKILL TO RISE IN THE WORLD

Judging by his description, this world's foxes really weren't all that different from the ones I knew. Apparently, I'd been overthinking the whole matter.

"It's pretty rare for them to have blue fur like that one, though... Hm? Come to think of it, I have a feeling I've read about blue foxes somewhere before..." Rosell muttered before sinking into thought. It seemed something had rang a bell for him, and a moment later, he looked up with a start. "That's it! That fox is a king blue!"

"A 'king blue'?" I repeated.

"It's a species of fox that're supposed to be as big as horses when they're fully grown! This one's probably still immature. They're supposed to be incredibly smart, for animals, and can run as fast as a horse, too."

"A-As big as a horse? Are you serious?" I asked. I'd gotten way more out of that answer than I'd bargained for, and it had left me a little bewildered.

And, wait, it's still immature? It already looks as big as the adult foxes where I came from!

"What's immature mean?" asked Kreiz.

"It means it's still a baby," Wren replied.

"Oh, a baby, huh? That explains why it likes milk so much!" Kreiz said with a nod.

"If they grow that large, then do you suppose it might be dangerous eventually?" asked Licia.

"King blue foxes are omnivores. They eat meat, yeah, but they tend to be pretty gentle as far as animals go, and don't attack humans very often. That doesn't mean never, though, and they'd definitely be dangerous if one decided to go after a human," Rosell replied. "Oh, and there are exceptions, but apparently they don't tend to take to humans very well."

"Aww, so we can't keep it?" Wren pouted.

"Right. Not that I'd want you to, even if they could be domesticated," Rosell said with a nod.

Wren and Kreiz looked a little disappointed by the news. As expected, it seemed they'd been hoping to keep the fox as a pet. I wasn't opposed to the idea, if it could get used to people, but if not, we wouldn't be left with much of a choice. We'd have to let it loose, once it recovered enough to get by on its own.

"They're very rare animals, though. They're not supposed to exist in Missian at all. Why would there be one in the castle?" Rosell muttered, cocking his head in confusion.

"Where are they supposed to live, out of curiosity?" I asked.

"In the north—they turn up in Rofeille and Canshiep, for instance. There's no clear reason why they couldn't live in the south, though, and nobody has a good explanation for why they're never seen down here. Maybe they have a natural predator in the area?"

It sounded to me like the foxes tended to live in cold regions, as a rule, which made me feel a little apprehensive about letting it loose, since it wouldn't adapt to the local climate. Plus, the fact that an animal that wasn't supposed to exist in Missian had shown up felt like a sign that something a little more complicated might be going on here.

"I think we need to figure out how and why this fox ended up here," I said.

"Fair enough," said Rosell. "But, wait…y-you're not saying you want to keep it in the castle until you have an answer, are you?"

"Well, if we're looking into its origins, then keeping it around would just make sense, right?"

"I guess… Y-Yeah, you're right. We'll just have to get a cage to keep it chained up in so it can't go on a rampage and maul someone."

I WILL USE MY APPRAISAL SKILL TO RISE IN THE WORLD

"I don't think we need to be that cautious about a baby fox, do we...?"

Just how much does Rosell hate animals, really?

Rosell's phobia aside, if foxes like it didn't tend to domesticate well, there was a high chance it would try to escape. I decided to keep it somewhere it wouldn't be able to get away from easily, just in case.

"Well, I'm leaving, then! I'll let you know when I've figured out how it ended up in the castle," Rosell said, then departed from the room without wasting a moment.

○

The next day, I told Rietz about the fox that had been found inside the castle.

"A king blue...? Really, now...? I believe I've read about them in a book, as well...but how would one end up in Missian?" Rietz asked when I'd finished my story.

"We're not sure yet," I replied. "Would you be willing to help investigate the matter?"

"Certainly. I'd like to take a look at the animal myself, to begin. Where may I find it?"

"It was sleeping in a bed we put together for it, last I saw. I was actually just about to go check up on it myself, so you can feel free to follow me."

Rietz nodded in agreement, and the two of us headed over to the room where I'd set up the fox's bed. I cracked the door open and peeked inside.

"Huh?" I gasped in surprise as I glanced into the room.

The fox, it turned out, wasn't alone—Wren and Kreiz were there with it. The fox was sitting quietly on Wren's lap, and Kreiz was petting its head. The fox looked like it was enjoying itself, and it was a really charming scene all around, but I couldn't help thinking that it was nothing like what Rosell had led me to expect the day before. Weren't king blues supposed to not take well to humans?

"Ah, Ars! Rietz!" Wren exclaimed as she noticed us. "Look! It just jumped up on my lap, all on its own! Isn't it adorable?" she asked, her eyes sparkling with excitement.

"It certainly seems to have taken a liking to you," I replied. "Was it friendly starting from the moment it woke up?"

"It was! We came over to check in on it, and it walked right up to us the second we stepped into the room! I think it must remember that we saved it!"

"Remember how Rosell said it wouldn't like us? I guess he was wrong about that!" Kreiz added happily as he kept petting the fox's head.

"We thought of a name for it, too! We're calling it Rio!" Wren added with a beaming smile.

"O-Oh, did you? Rio's a wonderful name," I replied.

"Isn't it?!" said Kreiz.

By the time I got here, they'd already given it a name...? Those two are head over heels for this fox, no question about it. I guess I can't deny that it's cute, to be fair.

"It's hard to believe that an animal that's normally not friendly with humans would end up being this attached to them," I muttered to myself.

"I've heard that animals tend to take more kindly to people when raised from birth by humans," noted Rietz. "Also—and I should stress that this is nothing more than a rumor I heard a long time ago—there are claims that somewhere in Summerforth lives a

I WILL USE MY APPRAISAL SKILL TO RISE IN THE WORLD

group of warriors who ride massive blue foxes into battle. I'd always dismissed those stories as baseless since I'd never seen anything of the sort, but perhaps there really are people out there who fight atop king blues?"

That's the first I've heard of that rumor... Though I suppose if they grow as big as horses, it really might be possible to ride them into combat.

Just then, the fox—now known as Rio—hopped off of Wren's lap, walked over to me, and started rubbing up against my legs.

"Ah, look! It walked right up to you! It must want you to pet it!" said Wren.

I gave it a try. Petting Rio felt like plunging my hand into a bag of fluff, and Rio closed its eyes as I stroked it, clearly enjoying the experience.

O-Okay, yeah. It really is adorable.

I had a newfound appreciation for why Wren and Kreiz had fallen in love with the critter so quickly.

The fox approached Rietz next. It had met with me, Wren, and Kreiz yesterday, but this was its first time encountering Rietz in any capacity. The fact that it was willing to walk right up to him proved that it really was friendly, and made me wonder just what in the world Rosell had been talking about when he'd said it wouldn't take well to people.

Finally, Rio went back to Wren and hopped up onto her lap again.

"So, umm... I think there's a decent chance we're going to end up keeping it," I said to Rietz. "It'd be hard to say no, considering how well it's getting along with those two. We'll have to keep it, yeah. For their sake, of course."

"Y-Yes, of course," Rietz said, seeming to hold back a chuckle. "And while I see no reason to object to keeping it in and of itself, I should point out that king blues grow to the size of a horse in the long term, meaning that keeping it indoors will prove challenging. We may have to raise some sort of small structure for Rio to live in."

We'll need a building all for Rio...? I guess keeping a pet isn't all fun and games. A fox of that size probably eats a ton, too. No turning back now, though.

"Oh? I see I've arrived late to the party," Licia said as she stepped into the room. It seemed she'd been curious about how Rio was doing as well. "My! It seems the three of you are the best of friends, aren't you?"

"Ah, Sister!" said Wren. "We gave it a name, too! It's called Rio now!"

"Oh, I see! Well, may I also pet Rio?"

"Yeah!"

Licia stepped over and gave Rio a pat on the head. "It really is a little darling, isn't it?" she said as she stroked the fox's fur. I'd known that she was a gardener, but it seemed that wasn't her only nature-related interest—she was apparently fond of animals as well.

"I came as soon as I heard the news!" a voice rang out as the door swung open. Charlotte strode into the room, followed shortly by Musia, who gave us a polite nod as she stepped inside.

"What is it, Charlotte?" I asked.

"I heard that you're keeping some sorta rare animal in here, so I came to take a look! I can't believe you didn't tell me about this first thing!" Charlotte grumbled.

Is she an animal lover too? That's news to me.

"Oh, and that must be it! What a cutie!" Charlotte said as she

I WILL USE MY APPRAISAL SKILL TO RISE IN THE WORLD

drew closer to Rio.

Rio, however, backed away from her just as quickly.

"Huh?"

Charlotte froze, standing stock still for several seconds. Apparently, she hadn't seen that reaction coming. She eventually tried to creep up on Rio once again, only to get the exact same reaction.

"So, uh... Did I do something wrong, or what?" Charlotte asked.

"I...really couldn't tell you, honestly," I replied. I couldn't think of anything she'd done that would've offended the fox. Some people seemed to naturally drive animals away—was Charlotte one of them, maybe?

Musia tried to approach Rio next, and the fox dodged away from her. It was like Charlotte all over again.

"Huh? I-It ran away from me," Musia said, sounding a little heartbroken.

Considering what those two have in common...it must have something to do with them being mages.

"Perhaps something about wielding magic on a daily basis gives people a quality that animals find unpleasant?" Rietz theorized.

Charlotte and Musia both looked taken aback.

"What? You have to be kidding me..." Musia groaned.

"That's it... I'm quitting the mage corps," Charlotte declared, to the shock and horror of everyone present.

"Y-You're what?! Don't be ridiculous!" I yelped.

"If being a mage means I can't play with the cute little fox, then it's not worth it! I quit!" Charlotte screamed. Her despair was driving her to a wild extreme.

"C-Calm down! That's a terrible reason to quit your job!" I said.

"H-He's right!" said Musia. "We wouldn't be able to get by without you, Charlotte!"

"M-Maybe it's just sensitive since it's still a newborn! It might let you touch it when it's grown a little more! The horses have never had a problem with you, have they?!" said Rietz.

Thankfully, our frantic appeals seemed to get through to her. "Hmph... Well, fine. I guess I won't quit just yet," Charlotte said. Her resignation was off the table, for now.

That was way too close... I'd never live it down if House Louvent lost Charlotte over something this stupid. Just think about how terrible a blow that would be to our army!

"So, umm, I think that we'll just scare it by being here, so we'll be on our way now," said Musia. "Come on, Charlotte, let's go."

"Fiiine," Charlotte droned.

The two mages left the room, still obviously let down by their failure to befriend Rio.

"I passed by Charlotte and Musia on the way here, and they both looked really depressed! What happened?" Rosell asked as he stepped inside, just moments after the two of them left.

No sooner had Rosell set foot in the room than Rio shot to its feet and leapt toward him.

"Huh?" Rosell grunted. It had happened so quickly, he didn't even have the time to properly react before Rio had jumped onto him, landing on his chest. "G-Gaaaaaah!"

Rosell lost his balance and toppled over onto his backside, where Rio landed atop him and started licking his face. From what I could tell, the fox was trying to play with him. It was the opposite of how things had gone down with Charlotte and Musia—for some reason, Rio was apparently drawn to Rosell.

I WILL USE MY APPRAISAL SKILL TO RISE IN THE WORLD

"Augh! H-Help... Somebody help me!" Rosell shrieked. He clearly hadn't gotten over his dislike of animals overnight, and Rio's affection was less than welcome.

Fortunately, Rietz stepped in to give Rosell the help he was begging for, lifting Rio right up off of him. The moment he was freed, Rosell shot to his feet and dashed for the exit.

"I-I-It attacked me! You all saw it! That thing's a vicious maneater! We've gotta throw it in a cage, before it's too late!" Rosell shouted.

"C-Come on, you're exaggerating! It was just playing around," I called over to him.

Rosell was terrified beyond all reason. I'd known he didn't like animals, but I hadn't realized he disliked them quite this much.

"P-Playing around?! That's a king blue! There's no way one of those would ever... Wait, huh?" Rosell said, confused. Rietz had set Rio down partway through Rosell's sentence, and the fox had hopped back onto Wren's lap. Rosell's eyes widened with shock. "Hold on a minute. It's getting along with her just fine! Is it attached to her, or something?"

"That's right," I confirmed.

"But my book said that king blues don't take well to humans at all! Was that a bunch of lies? I guess this goes to show that you can't always trust everything you read," Rosell said. Seeing Rio's behavior seemed to have given him a fresh perspective on the situation. "So, umm," he added, turning to me, "don't tell me you're planning on keeping it?"

"Well, I mean, it's so attached to Wren and Kreiz," I said. "And if king blues aren't native to Canarre we can't exactly let it loose into the wild, so..."

"Seriously?! Th-This is a terrible idea! Do you have any idea how hard it is to keep an animal like that as a pet?! And that's not even taking into account the few people who know how to raise a king blue!"

"You're not wrong about that... But just look at Wren and Kreiz, Rosell! Could *you* tell those two that they're not allowed to keep it?"

"Ugh..." Rosell grunted as he looked over at the twins, who were still happily playing with Rio. He didn't seem to have a response to that. "W-Well, okay, so maybe you have a good reason to keep it around...but shouldn't you be looking into how it ended up in Canarre in the first place before you make any final decisions?"

"Oh. R-Right, yeah, good point," I admitted. I'd been thinking about looking into how Rio had ended up in the castle while I was on my way to the room we were keeping the fox in, but somewhere along the way, it had completely slipped my mind.

"W-Well, anyway, I'll be leaving now. I'll just try to avoid this part of the castle from now on," Rosell muttered to himself as he departed.

He'd made a very good point: I couldn't decide to keep Rio as a pet until we'd figured out how the fox ended up here to begin with. If it was someone else's pet that had escaped and snuck its way in, for instance, we couldn't exactly keep it for ourselves. Rio seemed very used to being around people, so there was a very real chance that it had never been a wild animal at all.

"All right, Rietz—can you look into where Rio came from?" I asked.

"Certainly," Rietz replied before excusing himself to do just that.

○

I WILL USE MY APPRAISAL SKILL TO RISE IN THE WORLD

Rietz began his investigation into Rio's origins immediately. A few days came and went, and unsurprisingly, he hadn't turned up anything conclusive yet.

In the meantime, Rio had grown more and more attached to Wren and Kreiz. Many of the people who worked in the castle had taken a liking to the fox as well. Rio really did take to humans quickly, and within just a few days, the fox was the talk of the castle.

At that point, I was thoroughly convinced that we'd be keeping Rio around. I was curious about where it had come from, sure, but not knowing the answer to that mystery wasn't causing any problems for the time being. Little did I know, however, that we would run into a lead regarding Rio's origins far sooner than anyone expected.

One day, my retainers and I had gathered in Castle Canarre for one of our regular meetings. My retainers took turns reporting in on their recent activities, and we soon arrived at Braham's turn to speak.

Currently, the elite unit of troops that Braham led was helping maintain law and order in the city of Canarre. That was the town guard's job, in theory, but at that particular moment they didn't have the manpower to handle the task on their own, and I'd assigned Braham and his troops to support them as a stopgap measure. We would need to bolster the guard in proportion with the city's population in the long term, according to Rietz, at which point we'd be able to reassign Braham to a different responsibility.

"So, umm, we took down a group of criminals that's been causing trouble in the city. They were disguising themselves as merchants and selling off stolen goods along with genuine merchandise, I guess. Pretty tricky bunch. We took them into custody, so that's all wrapped up, but there's still a bit of a problem left over," Braham reported in a somewhat awkward, faltering tone. He'd been much more consistently successful in his work lately, but he still hadn't quite gotten used to speaking at meetings yet. "Thing is, we confiscated all their stolen goods, and some of them turned out to be animals... And, uh, a few of those animals might've run away..."

"Animals?" Rietz repeated. "Are any of the ones that escaped dangerous?"

Buying and selling animals wasn't illegal in Canarre in and of itself. It was perfectly normal in our culture for people to keep pets, after all. Bringing vicious or venomous animals that could pose a risk to human life into the county, however, was prohibited by law. Creatures like that weren't allowed as pets or as merchandise.

"Nah, it doesn't sound like it," said Braham. "They weren't the sort of animals that're banned outright. The problem's that they were stealing people's pets to resell."

"Well, it could be worse, I suppose," said Rietz. "Still, if they're pets, we'll need to find them at once."

"Y-Yeah, of course. Tracking them down'll be hopeless if they get out of the city, so we need to find them soon. We should've been more careful with the stolen goods in the first place, honestly..." Braham admitted, thoroughly chagrined.

"What's done is done. Regretting it accomplishes nothing," Rietz said in a comforting tone. "What do we know about the animals that escaped?"

"Oh, uhh, we wrote that all down! Here, I'll pass the descriptions out."

Braham passed each of us a small stack of papers. They had drawings of the missing animals on them, and similar drawings had apparently been posted all throughout town, along with a request for information from anyone who might have seen one of the missing animals.

I WILL USE MY APPRAISAL SKILL TO RISE IN THE WORLD

I took a look at the papers. There were three in total, which I took to mean that three animals had escaped. The first seemed to be some sort of snake, and the second was cat-like, but I'd never seen animals that looked quite like either of them before. Considering they'd been stolen, I imagined they were rare and valuable.

The animal on the third sheet, however, was a different story.

"W-Wait a minute," I muttered.

The animal depicted in the drawing had a big, fluffy tail, and a very familiar form overall. It was drawn in black and white, but had a detailed description written out in text beside it that confirmed that its fur was blue as well.

"Lord Ars, isn't this animal...?" said Rietz, who was sitting beside me and seemed to have put the pieces together. Licia, Musia, and Rosell were all present, and all seemed a little shaken as well.

"Y-Yes... This description matches Rio almost perfectly..."

My voice trembled as I replied. Nothing was set in stone yet, but the resemblance was so uncanny that it was incredibly hard not to jump to conclusions. Rio was a king blue—a species that had no business being found anywhere in Missian—and it being a stolen pet that had wandered into the castle would explain everything about its sudden appearance.

If Rio *had* been stolen, then we would have no choice but to return it to its owner. To be honest, a part of me hoped that it would somehow turn out that there were two king blues running around Canarre, and Rio was unrelated to the missing pet. I'd grown rather attached to the fox, and more importantly, I had no idea how I would explain that we had to let Rio go to Wren and Kreiz, who were more fond of it than anyone.

I guess there's just no way around these things, sometimes...

"Huh?" Braham said. "Wait, have you seen an animal like this around here, or something?"

"Actually...there's a decent chance that we're currently keeping the animal depicted in this picture in the castle," I explained.

"S-Seriously? L-Let me take a look at it!"

I didn't have any good reason to turn down Braham's request. "All right," I said. "I'll bring you to it as soon as this meeting's over."

"Great!"

○

The meeting ended without issue, and Braham, Rietz, Licia, and I made for the room we were keeping Rio in. We stepped inside to find that Wren and Kreiz were within, playing with the fox again.

"Ah! Elder Brother, Sister, and Rietz! Oh, and Hammy's here too!" said Wren.

"Ah, Ham! You've gotta train with me sometime soon, okay?!" added Kreiz.

"Oh, it's the little lord and lady... Look, my name is *Braham*, okay? Please cut it out with the weird nicknames," Braham awkwardly replied. He clearly didn't appreciate the terms of endearment those two had picked out for him.

"Ha ha ha, did you hear that? He called me a little lady! Your nicknames are just as weird as ours, Hammy!" Wren said, acting like Braham's name for her was the funniest thing in the world.

"I'm a lot tougher these days, y'know?! I bet I could even get a hit in on you!" Kreiz added as he drew closer to Braham.

My siblings, it seemed, more or less idolized Braham, which made a certain amount of sense to me. He'd matured a lot recently, yes, but I still couldn't describe his mental age as being high by any means, and that childlike side of his made it easy for actual children to take a liking to him.

"Ahh, sorry, but I'm on the clock right now," said Braham. "No time for fun and games! And also, you're a hundred years too early to be thinking about getting a hit in on me."

"O-Oh, come ooon!" Kreiz groaned indignantly.

"So, this is the critter you're keeping here in the castle, huh? Hmm..." Braham muttered as he compared Rio with the drawing on his pamphlet. "Yeah, that's pretty much an exact match... Same color, too... No doubt about it, this is the one! I thought we'd never find the thing—this is great!"

Braham was elated, but my feelings were a lot more mixed. Rietz and Licia's downcast expressions made me suspect that they were right there with me.

"We'd better bring it back to its owner right away!" said Braham.

"You mean right now?" I asked. "Do you already know who it was stolen from?"

"I sure do! The perps admitted everything, and we've already checked in with their victims as well, so there's no doubt about it!"

So we know exactly who Rio's actual owner is? That meant that I didn't have any good reason to stop Braham. The person Rio was stolen from was probably beside themself with worry, after all. It only made sense to bring the fox back to its true home as soon as possible.

"Are... Are you taking Rio away?" Wren asked. Always a sharp one, she must have guessed that we'd be giving Rio back to its true owner just by listening to our conversation.

"That's right. That fox is somebody's pet, so we have to give it back to... Wait, 'Rio'?" Braham said, cocking his head in confusion before putting the pieces together and leaning over to whisper to me. "Err... Were they planning on, y'know, keeping it? They gave it a name and all, so it kinda feels that way..."

"Yes... That was the plan," I replied.

"Oof... Got it... I mean, we could always just say that we didn't manage to find it, and—"

"Absolutely not," Rietz cut in.

"Yeah, figures..." Braham sighed.

Obviously, that wasn't an option. Now that we knew Rio had been stolen, and who it had been stolen from, we had an obligation to return the fox to its real home.

"*No!* We only just made friends with Rio! I don't wanna say goodbye!" Wren shouted. She was usually a very mature and well-behaved child, and it was rare for her to be this selfish, not to mention insistent. I could tell just how fond of Rio she was.

"I wanna play with Rio more too!" Kreiz added.

My siblings were putting up a united front, and both of them looked up at me with tears in their eyes. I was right there with them on an emotional level, but I knew I couldn't let that influence my decision making...and I also knew that getting mad and insisting that it was my way or the highway would definitely not help the situation.

As I fretted over how to bring my siblings around, Licia stepped up to them. She crouched down slightly, bringing her eye level to theirs, and began to speak.

"I understand how the two of you feel—I really do. It's hard to part with a friend you've only just made, isn't it?"

Wren and Kreiz nodded.

"But you know," Licia continued, "I'm sure that Rio's been wishing to go back home this whole time. You wouldn't want to be taken

I WILL USE MY APPRAISAL SKILL TO RISE IN THE WORLD

from your family and never get to see them again, would you?"

"No... I wouldn't," Wren admitted after a moment of hesitation.

"And that's not to mention Rio's real owner. I'm sure they must be just as sad as you are! Think about how lonely you'd feel if your pet disappeared without a trace one day! And so, Wren, Kreiz," Licia said, moving in toward her conclusion, "I think the two of you know what the best choice to make would be, for Rio's sake. Don't you?"

For a moment, Wren and Kreiz stood there in silence. Finally, they gave Licia a nod.

"And that's not all," Licia added. "I believe that Rio's home is located in the city of Canarre, is it not?"

"Ah, yes! Sure is," said Braham.

"Well in that case, I can't see any reason why they couldn't stop by to play with Rio every once in a while, assuming the owner is amicable to the idea. What sort of person are they?"

"Uhh... An elderly merchant, pretty sure. She seemed like a nice enough person, but I couldn't really say if she'd be willing to give permission for that."

"I see. Well, no need to worry," said Licia, turning back to the twins. "I happen to be an expert when it comes to persuasion. I promise that I'll convince her to let you visit Rio!"

"B-Big Sister..."

"Thank you, Sister!"

Wren and Kreiz gazed at Licia with looks of purest respect in their eyes. Their schedules were packed with studies and training, so they wouldn't have much free time in the first place, and even when they did we'd have to assign a guard to accompany them, since they certainly couldn't go out into town on their own. In other words, it was hard to imagine that they'd be going out to see Rio frequently, but every once in a while was still much better than never. The two of them, at least, seemed convinced.

Part of me thought that it should've been my responsibility to make my siblings see reason, and I was a little chagrined by the fact that I'd gone and relied on Licia again instead. It had all worked out in the end, though, so I decided to brush it off and move on.

We headed out right away to bring Rio back to its owner. Braham, Licia, and I ended up taking on the task. We'd need Licia to sweet talk the owner when we gave Rio back to her, and having me along would let Licia frame it as a personal request from the count himself, giving her words far more weight. I knew I shouldn't throw my authority around as a matter of habit, but this, at least, seemed like the right time to make use of it.

Rietz had volunteered to come along as well, but since Braham would be with us, I felt that we would be perfectly well-guarded even without him. Rietz was a busy man, and bringing a fox back to its owner was one task that I didn't feel like piling on his already excessive workload, so he ended up staying behind in the castle.

"We'll see you soon, Rio! Take care!" said Wren.

"We'll have so much fun together next time!" added Kreiz.

Rio let out a spirited yip as the twins said their goodbyes. With that, we set out into Canarre to bring the fox back to its owner.

Rio's owner's residence only took a few minutes to reach on foot. It turned out that she lived in a rather large house located just a short distance away from the castle. As a general rule, the closer one lived to the castle in Canarre, the wealthier that individual was. Braham had mentioned that Rio's owner came from a merchant family, and

I WILL USE MY APPRAISAL SKILL TO RISE IN THE WORLD

if this was where she lived, I assumed she had to be quite successful in her business—though then again, she wouldn't have been able to buy a rare animal like Rio in the first place if she was working with a commoner's salary. Her being wealthy felt like something of a given.

"'Scuse me! Are you in, Miss Arnold?" Braham shouted at the top of his lungs. There was a bell by the door, and I was quite certain the idea was that you could ring it if you had business with the house's owner, but Braham apparently hadn't noticed and just kept shouting until the door cracked open instead.

"Yes?" the house's owner—an elderly woman who was apparently called Arnold—said as she stepped outside. "Oh, my, if it isn't Braham! Good day to you!"

"Good day, Miss Arnold! We stopped by to—" Braham began, but before he could explain himself, Miss Arnold cut him off with a report of her own.

"As a matter of fact, I have wonderful news for you! I'm sure you remember how my darling little Pina ran away? Well, he found his way home last night, safe and sound!"

"Huh?" Braham gasped in bewilderment.

Just then, I heard a bark from down by Miss Arnold's feet. Looking down, I saw what looked like a fluffy, blue-haired chihuahua standing beside her. Dogs in this world all had wings, as a rule, but this one was wingless.

"Isn't he just such a good boy? He remembered where his home was!" Miss Arnold said as she stroked Pina's head.

"Err, s-so, the pet that was stolen from you was a dog? A dog without any wings?" asked Braham.

"Yes, indeed! He's a very rare, wingless breed. Isn't he precious?" said Miss Arnold. It seemed my impression hadn't been mistaken, and wingless dogs really were the exception in this world.

"Y-Yeah, he sure is," said Braham.

"Hmm? And who might that little cutie be?" Miss Arnold asked as Rio caught her eye. "Oh, it's just adorable! And it must be rare, too—I've never seen anything like it! Have you come to offer to sell it to me, perhaps?"

"Huh? Ah, no, that's not it! It's not for sale, actually! Glad to hear you found your pet!" Braham frantically babbled.

"Oh? That's a shame, but I suppose... Wait... Is that the *count* behind you?!" Miss Arnold exclaimed.

Apparently, she'd only just noticed me. I was indeed the count, technically, and as such my face was well known to Canarre's citizens. It wasn't surprising that she'd recognize me.

"Th-This is so sudden," said Miss Arnold. "Oh, dear—d-don't tell me my husband has done something wrong...?"

"What? Oh, no, I was just out for a walk with Braham, that's all! I'm glad to hear everything worked out for you!" I replied, then urged us away before the whole awkward exchange devolved into a terrible misunderstanding.

"Th-That's so weird," said Braham. "I-I guess we had it all wrong from the start, eh?"

"Her pet did look a little like the drawing, I suppose, but... Actually, how *did* you get that drawn in the first place?" I asked.

"Oh, uhh, we listened to the robbers' description, then had a member of my team who's a decent artist sketch it up for us," Braham replied.

In other words, they drew it having never actually seen the animal in question. I guess that's obvious, since it had already run away by that point. They must have listened to a description of that dog and just happened to draw a picture that looked exactly like Rio while trying to

I WILL USE MY APPRAISAL SKILL TO RISE IN THE WORLD

depict it."

"You *did* show the drawing to Miss Arnold, right?" I asked.

"We did!" said Braham. "I showed it to her myself, and she said that it looked just like her pet..."

Well, I guess Rio does look a little like that dog. They're the same size, and the blue fur's a point in common for sure. It wasn't too hard to imagine her looking at the picture and deciding that it was close enough to her pet to do the job. She'd probably thought that a few details being wrong wasn't worth fussing over.

"I suppose I needn't have accompanied you," Licia said with a slightly strained smile. "But if Rio wasn't her pet, then how do you suppose it ended up in the castle?"

"Good question... We know that king blues definitely aren't native to Missian... Do you think it and the burglars were totally unrelated?" I asked.

"Hmm... Hard to say," Braham stated with a shake of his head. "I'll ask them about it, just in case that solves any mysteries."

"Sounds good," I replied.

I'd thought that it would take a long time for us to find any further leads, but that couldn't have been farther from the truth. In the end, we learned Rio's origins in practically no time at all.

Braham went to question the burglars he'd captured, and immediately learned that Rio hadn't been stolen. Rather, the burglars had captured the fox themselves. It had gotten separated from its parents, and the burglars had figured they could make a pretty profit by nabbing it while they had the chance. Rio, however, had escaped their clutches the day before the burglars were captured.

Apparently, the burglars hadn't mentioned Rio because they'd only been questioned about *stolen* animals, which Rio technically was not. From a certain perspective, that meant that Rio was their legitimate property...but I wasn't about to give the fox back to a band of criminals. They'd be doing heavy labor for quite some time to make up for their crimes, and per Canarre law, the personal belongings of criminals were to be granted to whoever was responsible for arresting them. Since Braham—a retainer of House Louvent—had brought in the burglars, Rio's ownership naturally and legally fell to us.

As a general rule, any belongings of criminals that fell into our hands in that manner were liquidated. A portion of the resulting cash was used to reward any informants who'd led to the criminal's capture, and also given to whichever of my retainers had apprehended them. We had some spare funding in our coffers, but not an excess by any means, and some criminals, of course, didn't have much in the way of belongings to speak of, meaning there were times we had to pay out those rewards with our own funds.

All that being said, there wasn't a chance that I was going to sell Rio for funding. I could pay Braham and the others involved with the arrest their rewards using my own personal funds, and that would be the end of it. In other words: Rio had become the formal pet of House Louvent.

○

"Rio! You're back!"

"*Rio!*"

Wren and Kreiz were both over the moon to learn that we'd be keeping Rio for good. Rio seemed just as ecstatic, and yipped happily as it raced over to them. The three of them had only been together for a brief period, but it was obvious that Rio had already thoroughly bonded with the twins.

I WILL USE MY APPRAISAL SKILL TO RISE IN THE WORLD

"I'm pleased you were able to keep it, in the end. We'll have to get to work building a dwelling for it right away," said Rietz.

I had no clue what sort of pace king blues grew at, but I had a vague idea that most animals matured much quicker than humans. There was a chance that Rio could be fully grown within a year.

"A-A-A-Are you seriously keeping that…that *thing*?" asked Rosell, the one animal hater among my retainers. He was definitely not okay with that idea.

"Yes, but it'll be living in its own little hut in the long term," I explained. "You just have to steer clear of it, and you'll be fine."

"I-I mean, I guess, but… Agh! It's coming this way!"

I really had to wonder why Rio was so taken with Rosell. Was it something about his appearance? Rosell managed to escape this time, but I had a feeling that I'd be watching him flee from the fox every once in a while for the foreseeable future.

"Let's take Rio for a walk right away!" Wren excitedly suggested.

"Yeah! Let's go!" Kreiz agreed.

My schedule had been packed lately, but happily enough, today was one of the rare days where I didn't have anything on my plate. "Sure. Sounds good," I said. I wanted to get to know Rio a little better myself, and unlike Rosell, I was fond of animals.

I invited Licia to tag along, and the four of us set out on a walk together. Going out into the city would risk losing Rio in the crowds, so we stuck to the castle's garden. Castle Canarre's gardens were vast, so we could have a nice, lengthy stroll even without leaving the grounds.

"Yip, yip!" Rio barked excitedly. The fox seemed to be in a fabulous mood.

"Hee hee! Rio is certainly a spirited one. And it's such a lovely day out today, too! You could hardly ask for a more pleasant temperature," Licia said with a smile as she watched the fox frolic. It was fall, at the moment, which was one of the nicer seasons in Missian. I had to agree—it was hard to imagine better weather to take a walk in.

"Ah!"

I heard a gasp of surprise from somewhere behind us. I spun around to find Charlotte standing a short distance away, eyes wide as she looked at Rio.

Oh, right! Rio ran away from her when she tried to pet it. My best guess was that something about being a mage drove the fox away from her, but an explanation for why that would be still eluded me.

"It's staying here after all... A-And this time, I'll pet it for sure..." Charlotte muttered as she crept toward us...only for Rio to scamper into hiding behind Wren.

"Charlotte... You're scaring Rio," said Wren.

"Ugh," Charlotte grunted. You'd think the world was ending, judging by the look on her face. "Wh-What's it have against me, and why only me?!" she wailed in despair as she ran off into the distance.

"Why *do* you suppose Rio dislikes her so much?" asked Licia.

"No clue," I said. "Maybe she reeks of aqua magia, and it can't stand the smell?"

Aqua magia was odorless by human standards, but it seemed plausible that it could smell terrible to a fox's keen nose. And so, whenever possible, I avoided leading Rio to the training grounds where our mages practiced their spellcasting.

Our walk continued, and before long, we happened to run into Braham and Zaht.

"Oh, hey, it's the critter! What was its name... Oh, Rio, right? Looks like it's doing well," said Braham.

"A fox that's comfortable around humans...? That's pretty rare,"

I WILL USE MY APPRAISAL SKILL TO RISE IN THE WORLD

noted Zaht. Braham was already acquainted with Rio and didn't seem surprised at all, but Zaht looked rather shocked by the sight.

"It really is a cutie, huh? Reminds me of a pet I used to have," Braham said as he gave Rio a friendly pat. Rio didn't seem put off by the affection at all, and even let out a cute little whine of satisfaction.

"You used to have a pet, Hammy?" asked Wren.

"Yup! Had a pet bear, back in the day."

"I-I'm sorry, a *bear*?" I repeated. I was convinced that I must have misheard him.

Bears existed in this world, and were known to be fierce and dangerous creatures. In fact, they were actually bigger than the bears we'd had back on Earth, making them even more deadly than the ones I knew. I'd never seen one for myself, though, on account of them not living anywhere near the County of Canarre.

"Yeah, I kept it until it got big enough I started worrying it was gonna kill me. Had no choice but to let it go in the wild. I didn't know very much about bears, at the time... It really seemed to like me, too... Probably thought it was playing with me, but it was just so big, it never would've worked out..."

Braham sounded pretty sad about his old pet, but to me, the whole incident was just plain absurd. Clearly, he'd been pulling stupid stunts since long before I met him. On the other hand, Rio was supposed to grow to a massive size in the long term, too. How was that going to work out? I could only hope that a fox like it wouldn't be as prone to violence as a bear.

Braham and Zaht headed off to the training grounds, leaving the four of us to resume our walk. We strolled through the castle gardens, which were remarkably well-maintained. I could tell that our gardeners were doing great work, though I couldn't give them all the credit. I knew that the flowers—of which there were quite a lot—had been grown by Licia, who gardened as a hobby. She liked helping the gardeners out with the plants that they were growing as well.

"So, umm, why am I the one carrying all the baggage?" a voice rang out from nearby as we walked along. I recognized it immediately as Rikuya's, which was confusing. I'd been under the impression that he and his siblings were in Lamberg. What would he have come to Canarre for?

I looked over in the direction I'd heard the voice from, and not only did I see the Fujimiya siblings, I also caught sight of Mireille, who I'd tasked with managing Lamberg in my stead. She paid regular visits to Castle Canarre, and I assumed that this time, she'd brought the Fujimiyas along with her. Rikuya was carrying a large backpack, by the way, which he seemed to be struggling with.

"Well, we can't have Takao carrying it, can we?" said Mireille. "He's our guard, so he needs his hands free. And since Maika's too scrawny to lift all that, you're the only choice left."

"I understand that, but you could carry at least a little of the baggage yourself, couldn't you?" Rikuya protested.

"What, you mean you'd have a woman carry your bags for you? What sort of man are you?" said Mireille.

"That's rich, coming from you. You're brawnier than most men I've met."

"Say something?"

"Nothing whatsoever."

Rikuya, it seemed, was being used as Mireille's personal pack mule, and was none too pleased about it.

"Oh! Master! What a coincidence!" Maika called out when she noticed me. Mireille, Takao, and Rikuya quickly picked up on our presence as well.

"Hey there, kiddo! Out for a walk?" said Mireille.

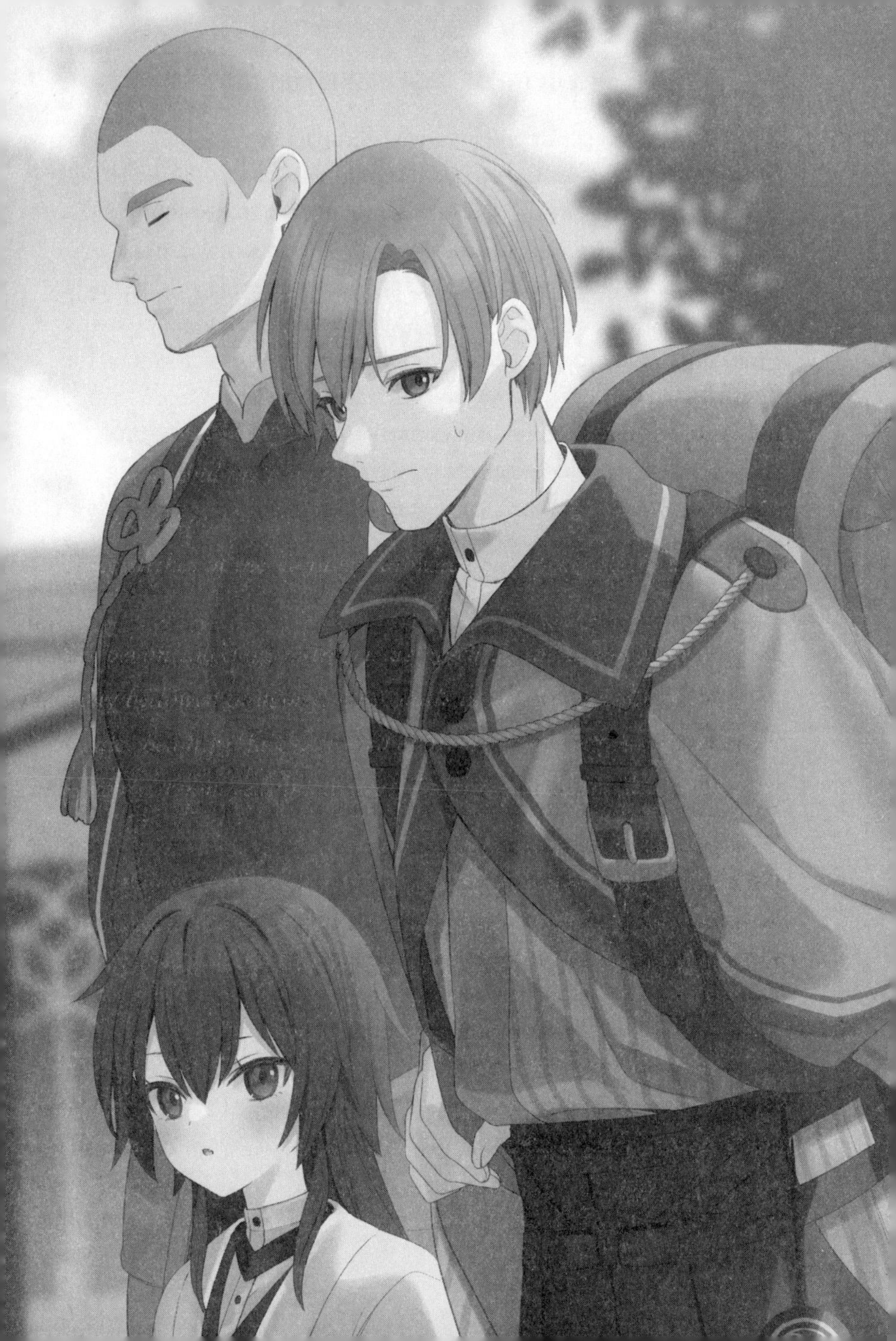

"We are, yes... But what are you doing here, Mireille?" I asked.

"Uhh, well, y'know, just checking in like usual," Mireille said after an awkward pause. I could tell by instinct alone that she was lying through her teeth.

"Hm? You told us that *he* called *you* here, did you not? I thought you had business with him," said Maika.

A look of panic shot across Mireille's face. It goes without saying that I had not, in fact, summoned her to the castle.

"I never said anything of the sort. What's this all about?" I asked.

"Well, y'know, everyone has a right to pop over to the big city and blow off some steam every once in a while, right? Especially considering I've been working my ass off lately!" Mireille said, pivoting on a dime to tell me the truth in as defiant a manner as she could manage.

To Mireille, coming to Castle Canarre meant being waited on hand and foot by the maids, not to mention treated to fine food and alcohol. She'd shown up out of nowhere for that purpose plenty of times in the past, and clearly, that was precisely her goal today as well. That being said, I'd given the castle staff explicit instructions not to serve her any alcohol under any circumstances, so I was hopeful that part of her plan, at least, had been quashed.

"So this whole trip was just you slacking off...?" Rikuya sighed with a roll of his eyes.

"Not so fast, Brother—clearly, this was Lady Mireille's way of showing us consideration! We've been exhausted by our unrelenting workload as of late, and she was trying to give us a chance to rest!" said Maika.

"Y-Yeah! That's exactly right!" shouted Mireille.

"Ah, I see. So having me lug all of your baggage here was your way of being considerate! I'm *so* very grateful!" Rikuya said, his

I WILL USE MY APPRAISAL SKILL TO RISE IN THE WORLD

words dripping with sarcasm.

"For the record," I said, "if you skip out on work too often, I won't hesitate to strip you of your position."

"Ugh... R-Right, I get it," Mireille said, ever so slightly flustered by my threat.

"Hm? Incidentally, that's a fox, is it not? Are you keeping it as a pet?" asked Maika, who was the first to take note of Rio.

"Yes! We just took it in recently," Licia explained.

"I see! How very nostalgic to see a fox again. All sorts of them lived in Yoh. Particularly rare were the nine-tailed foxes—nine-tails, as we rather bluntly called them. Our people believed them to be sacred animals," Maika reminisced, her thoughts drifting back to her homeland.

"A fox, huh...? Actually, wait a minute... Isn't that a king blue?" asked Mireille.

"Oh, you know about them?" I replied. "I've been told that it is, yes."

"Seriously? Now that's something."

"What is a 'king blue'?" asked Maika. I quickly explained the species' traits, and her eyes widened. "That large, truly? That's remarkable!"

"A fox the size of a horse really would be something. Even nine-tails were only about as big as a person, at most, right?" said Rikuya. By my standards, of course, being human-sized made the nine-tails impressive enough on their own.

"Y'know, king blues are pretty rare. It'd fetch a pretty penny if you—"

"We are *not* selling Rio!" Licia shouted indignantly, cutting Mireille's suggestion off before she could even finish making it.

"I-I was just kidding!" said Mireille. "Honestly, though, I've

67

never had much interest in animals. What's the point of taking care of a hairball like that thing? They can't even talk!"

I guess Mireille's not much of a pet person. Not everyone can be an animal lover, I suppose.

"So, uhh, anyway, have fun on your walk," Mireille said with a wave.

"And enjoy your *brief* stay," I replied.

"I-I get it, okay?!"

With that, Mireille and her escort headed into the castle. We, on the other hand, kept walking until around lunchtime, when Rio finally seemed satisfied and we decided to call it a day. It felt like I'd started to bond with the fox. I had my work to deal with, of course, so I wouldn't be able to walk it on a regular basis, but I decided to make time for it whenever I had another free day.

Then, a few days after we welcomed Rio into our home, a letter from Couran arrived at the castle.

Chapter 2: Proclamation of Independence

As soon as I read Couran's letter, I called an emergency meeting in Castle Canarre to discuss its contents. My retainers and I were already present in the castle, of course, but this time I also called in Mireille, who was managing Lamberg, and the Fujimiya siblings, who were working for her. In addition, I summoned Krall, the Baron of Coumeire, as well as Hammond, the Baron of Torbequista. With them in attendance, almost all of Canarre's most influential figures were gathered in a single chamber. The contents of Couran's message were just that significant.

"Let me ask one more time, to be absolutely certain: there's no doubt whatsoever that this information is legitimate?" Mireille asked Rietz.

"Correct. Lord Couran has informed us of his intent to secede from the Empire of Summerforth, at which point he will declare himself the King of Missian. He intends to make this proclamation in Arcantez, and has ordered all of Missian's counts to be present for the occasion, which will occur in two months' time," Rietz explained in a dispassionate tone.

Couran had made his intention to secede from the empire and re-establish the Kingdom of Missian clear to me long ago. That being said, he had also enlisted the aid of the emperor himself, as well as the Duchy of Paradille—a territory still fiercely loyal to the empire—in order to unite Missian under his rule. I had no doubt whatsoever that declaring independence now would cast Couran as a traitor on the political stage. In the worst case, it even seemed possible that the emperor would rally together a joint force to invade Missian and bring it back under his control.

On the other hand, I knew that the emperor had relatively little political influence in this day and age, compared to what he would have wielded at the empire's zenith. Not even Ansel, the seat of the emperor's power, seemed to be entirely under his control. Considering how capable the united armies of Missian were, it was hard to imagine that the empire would mount an immediate offensive.

The problem, however, was the persistent thorn in Missian's side that was Seitz. Was declaring independence really a good idea when we had such an active foe right across the border?

"He sure has come up with a real pain of a plan all over again," Mireille said with a fed-up frown. It seemed that she didn't look very highly upon Couran's decision.

"Why would he go out of his way to make a big proclamation about it, though? Do you think he's aiming for something?" asked Braham.

"It's possible that independence was simply his aspiration from the start...but if I had to assume a goal regarding the declaration itself, I would say that he seeks to strengthen the bonds between the only recently unified counties of Missian. Moreover, declaring Missian a kingdom will open the door to diplomatic relations with countries outside of the continent of Summerforth. Declaring war will become an easier prospect as well. The surrounding duchies have all been part of the same nation as us up until now, but once they're formally considered part of a separate country..."

Rietz mused. "The downsides would be that all the other duchies of Summerforth may choose to oppose us, and that any dedicated imperialist lords within Missian may oppose the secession altogether... Though of course, it's possible that flushing out any dedicated imperialist nobles is part of his goal from the start."

"W-Wait, what was that bit about all the other duchies opposing us? Wouldn't that be a huge problem?" asked Braham.

"It certainly would," said Rietz, "but I would also assume that Lord Couran has laid the necessary groundwork to ensure it doesn't come to that. If the emperor were to call upon the duchies to reclaim Missian, and they carried out his command, it would reaffirm his power over the empire. He may choose to take direct control over Missian under those circumstances as well, broadening his influence further. That would set the stage for the Summerforth Empire's revival in earnest, which is a state of affairs that a majority of duchies most likely do not wish to see come about. It's difficult to believe they would be eager to offer up the influence they've claimed for themselves to the emperor now."

That did make sense. It didn't seem likely at all that the emperor would be able to put together a joint force and storm into Missian immediately.

"All things considered," Rietz continued, "I do believe this move to be rather premature."

"I can't say I think it's a great idea either," Rosell agreed.

So the two of them are right there with Mireille.

"I thought it was strange as well...but a single count speaking out against the decision has no hope of overturning it. I'm sure Lord Couran wouldn't have sent this message if he didn't consider the matter to be set in stone," I said.

If Couran had had any interest in hearing my opinion on the

matter he would have asked for it before taking this drastic step, and he'd made no attempt to do so. I believed that I'd earned his trust, to some extent, but apparently not enough to prompt him to consult with me on matters of this magnitude.

"Well, one way or another, it'll all come down to how well Couran can navigate the politics of it all," said Mireille. "He's not quite stupid enough to declare himself a king without a plan in mind. The real question is what happens to Canarre from here on out."

"I believe we should make sure we're ready for battle," suggested Rosell. "Seitz might take this as their opportunity to go on the offensive again, after all."

Canarre sat on the border between Seitz and Missian. In other words, if Seitz chose to attack, ours would be the first county to be invaded. We'd been keeping a close eye on their movements already, and they'd been amassing a military force, but hadn't shown any sign of moving to invade so far.

"As far as Seitz is concerned, this will give them exactly the just cause that they need to invade. I'd think it will make recruitment easier too," said Rietz.

A just cause meant everything when it came to waging war. The last time Seitz had invaded, they'd done so under the pretense of freeing Missian from the control of Couran, who they claimed sought to seize control from the duke's true heir, his brother Vasmarque. Following Vasmarque's defeat Seitz had apparently formally acknowledged Couran as the duke and sent an offering in apology for their hostilities. So on paper, there was currently no bad blood between the two duchies. If Couran declared himself king, however, then Seitz would have the perfect excuse to brand him a traitor and raise an army to oust him.

"Maybe that's the goal?" I said. "Lord Couran might be hoping to lure Seitz into attacking us, turning the tables on them, and claiming their whole duchy in a counteroffensive. A lot of Missian's lords still don't seem very loyal to Couran, but if he can engineer a crisis, they'd be more likely to send troops to support him regardless."

"That...would put Canarre in a really nasty position," said Rosell. He wasn't wrong—if Seitz was going to invade, there was no question that we'd be their first target.

"Frankly, I don't understand what Lord Couran is thinking," said Rietz. "We're operating at a critical lack of information. We've gathered a degree of intelligence on the circumstances within Missian and Seitz, but we have no sources at all when it comes to matters in Paradille and Ansel. Perhaps Lord Couran is making decisions based on context we're simply not privy to?"

"That could be..." I muttered.

I might have to get more spies like the Shadows on my payroll and send them out all across Summerforth to gather information, in the future.

"In any case, it seems clear that there's a real chance of a large-scale conflict breaking out in the near future. We've been prioritizing Canarre's economy recently, but for the time being, we'll have to turn that focus to strengthening our military instead. We'll increase the amount of time our troops spend training, as well, and reinforce our castles and forts while we're at it. Is everyone in agreement?" I proposed, basing my call off all of my retainers' reports and opinions.

Times had been good lately, and the booming economy had led to a substantial tax yield. We had some money to spare, and this seemed like the right time to use it to strengthen our military.

In the end, no one objected to my plan of action and the meeting came to a close without incident.

○

At long last, the assassin that Boroths Heigand had been searching for had arrived at Fort Purledo in Seitz to speak with him.

Boroths was flanked by two knights, each of whom was a capable swordsman. Behind the trio stood a pair of retainers dressed as butlers, and behind them lay two large boxes.

"So... I'm to understand that you are Zetsu," Boroths said to the figure standing before him. The assassin wore a robe with its hood pulled up, and a mask concealing the remainder of their face. Boroths couldn't even tell what gender they were—the killer's short stature raised the possibility they were a woman, but it was by no means impossible for a man to have that sort of build either.

"That would be me, yes. Shall we get straight to business?" Zetsu said in a calm, polite tone. Their voice did little to solve the mystery of their gender—Zetsu's came out in a neutral, androgynous tone.

"Your target is Ars Louvent, the Count of Canarre," said Boroths.

"The Count of Canarre?" Zetsu repeated skeptically. "I had expected a man of your standing to aim higher. Perhaps Couran, the Duke of Missian, or maybe even the Duke of Seitz, if you were feeling ambitious."

"Couran would be one thing, but do you truly believe I would seek the life of my own lord? I have no time for this foolishness," Boroths replied with a scowl.

"I meant no offense," said Zetsu. "I must ask, however—why would you desire the death of a mere count such as Ars Louvent?"

"I must ask in turn: does an assassin need to know their employer's motives in order to carry out their task?" Boroths snapped back.

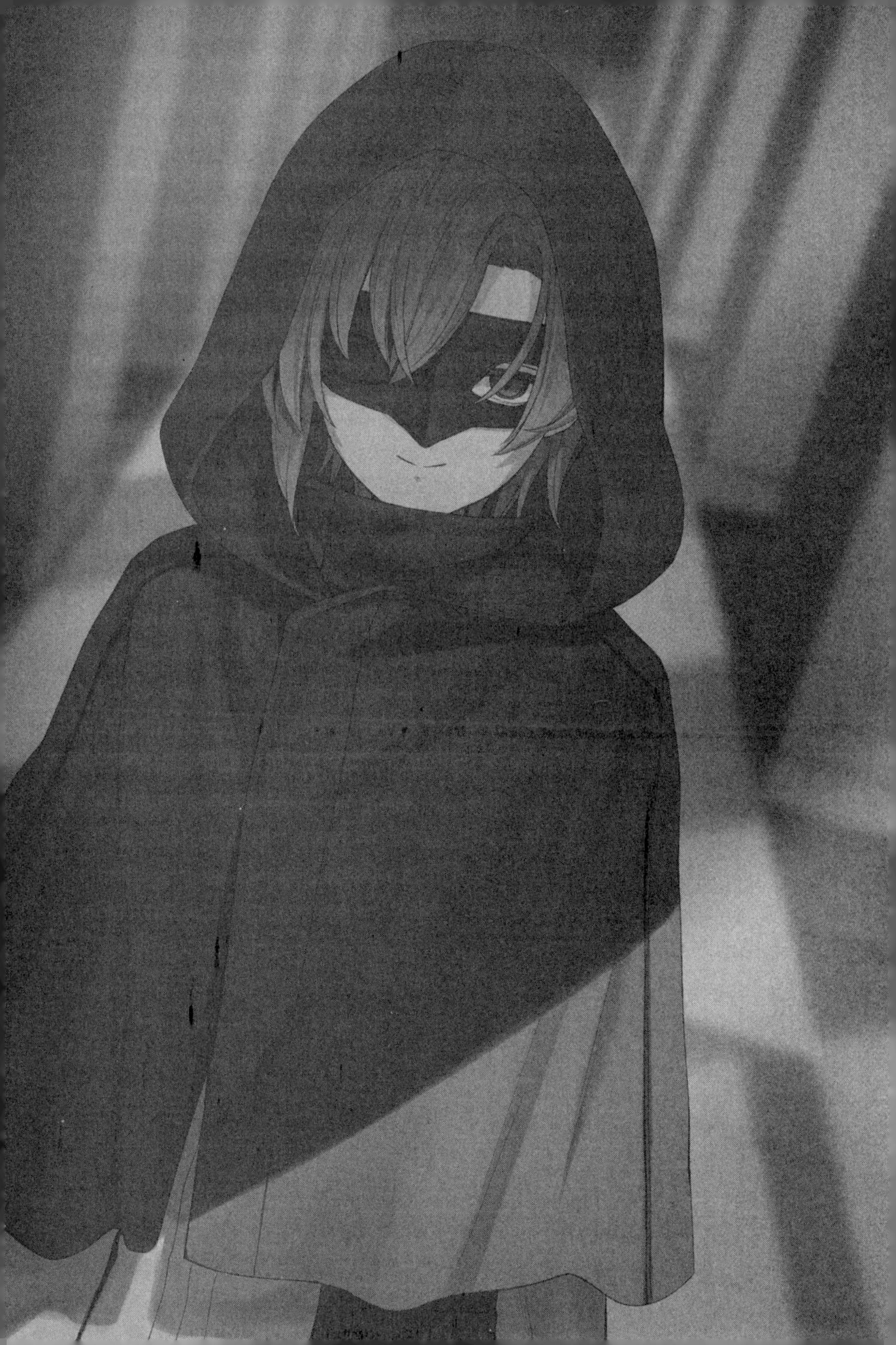

"No, not in the least. This is simply a matter of idle curiosity. Assuming you wish for me to succeed, however, it would behoove you to grant me as much information regarding Louvent as you can possibly provide. When all's said and done, I imagine you'll have to touch on your motives one way or another."

"I expected an assassin of your reputation to be a cold-blooded murderer. It's strange for you to take this much of an interest in others."

"What a terrible bias you find yourself afflicted with! I am but human, like everyone else, and I assure you I possess all the emotions you'd expect of your fellow man."

"Do you, now?" asked Boroths. "And do you find them a hindrance to your work? Perhaps you've inadvertently taken a liking to your target in the past?"

"Oh, no, never. I carry out my tasks to the letter, and nothing more. I'm not one to mix business and personal affairs," Zetsu casually replied. You'd think they were stating the obvious, judging from their attitude alone, and that indifference struck Boroths as terrifying in its own right.

"Very well, then," said Boroths. "You'll have all the information on Ars Louvent that I can provide."

Boroths proceeded to share everything he knew about Ars with Zetsu. He had already sought out information that would aid in an assassination attempt, and he disclosed every bit of it. Needless to say, that included the fact that there was a chance Ars had a special ability to judge the strengths of those he laid eyes on, as well as the fact that he had a great number of tremendously capable retainers in his employ.

"Oh? So he holds the Eye of Appraisal. Fascinating," said Zetsu.

"The Eye of Appraisal...?" Boroths repeated. "Do you know

something about this power of his?"

"It's spoken of in an old legend. Tradition holds that three individuals on the continent of Summerforth are blessed with unique powers of insight," Zetsu explained. "They're known as the holders of the Eye of Warfare, the Eye of Foresight…and the Eye of Appraisal. It's said that the bearers of those three powers once brought about upheaval in Summerforth, rising to the pinnacle of society before the empire's formation. A tale from a bygone age, if you will."

"Oh…? And why have I never heard any such stories before?" asked Boroths. He was a man with knowledge to spare who had read more than his fair share of texts of all varieties, and yet this was the first time he'd heard anything about the powers that Zetsu had described to him.

"That's only natural," said Zetsu. "The ancient tales I refer to are only passed down in a very particular region of Rofeille. Written accounts are few in number, and I wouldn't think that any would have made their way to Missian."

"Why, then, do you know the legends?"

"Because I hail from Rofeille, of course," said Zetsu.

Boroths knew that there was no way he could guarantee the assassin was telling the truth, but on the other hand, he also wasn't certain that their claim was a lie. He gave Zetsu a long, appraising stare, but no amount of observation would let him see through the mask and judge the individual beneath. Zetsu, for their part, displayed no signs of discomfort as a consequence of the inspection.

"So, then—Ars Louvent holds the Eye of Appraisal, and has been recruiting anyone with talent to be his retainer, regardless of their origins or social standing. In that case, this may be an easier job than I'd anticipated," said Zetsu.

Boroths raised an eyebrow. "Is that so? I'm told that the people he surrounds himself with are a cut above. However skilled of an assassin you may be, this will be no easy task."

"I have my ways! Trust me."

"Would you care to share what those ways might be?"

"I suppose, if you insist, but seeing is believing, as they say. Wouldn't results satisfy you more than an explanation?"

"Hmph... Fair enough," said Boroths. He'd heard enough about Zetsu's talent as a killer to have faith that the job would be done, and he could hardly order the assassin to change their methods if they weren't to his liking. There was no real point in pressing the question.

"More importantly, I'd like to discuss my payment now," said Zetsu.

"How much do you want?" Boroths asked after a brief pause. "I've prepared all the gold you could ask for," he added, gesturing toward the boxes behind him. Each of them was packed to the brim with gold coins—over a thousand per box, without question. Boroths was fully prepared to pay a small fortune to bring about Ars's demise.

"Some amount of gold will be necessary, yes, but not nearly that much," said Zetsu. "There's something else I want."

"And...what would that be?" asked Boroths, somewhat taken aback by the idea of an assassin wanting anything other than cold, hard cash. Generally speaking soldiers, spies, and killers alike all demanded payment in pure gold, and nothing else. Some rare cases asked to be taken into a lord's service in exchange for their work, but Zetsu didn't strike Boroths as the type for that.

"I want books," said Zetsu.

"You...what?" grunted Boroths, now thoroughly shaken by the assassin's unexpected demand. "Why books, of all things?"

I WILL USE MY APPRAISAL SKILL TO RISE IN THE WORLD

"Oh, my motives aren't especially complex," said Zetsu. "I just enjoy reading and expanding my breadth of knowledge, that's all. I'm sure a man of your standing has access to a number of texts that an ordinary individual could never hope to get their hands on, correct?"

Boroths was one of the most influential lords in all of Seitz. His territory was vast, and his collection of texts was large as well, including even a number of books that were genuinely one-of-a-kind. Furthermore, the tidbits from the prehistory of the Summerforth Empire that Zetsu had alluded to moments before weren't the sort of knowledge that the vast majority of people would have any awareness of. That lent credence to the idea that broadening their field of knowledge really was the assassin's primary motivation.

"Very well, then," said Boroths. "If you succeed in your mission, you can have whichever books you so please."

"Oh, I don't mean to *take* them from you! I'd be more than happy to simply read them. All that I ask is to be granted unrestricted access to your personal library for, say, a week. The knowledge contained within the texts is what I value—not the texts themselves."

Boroths hesitated for just a moment. "Have it your way," he finally said. "I have no objections."

Boroths saw no reason to turn the deal down. He wondered just how much Zetsu could possibly memorize within a single week, and whether the assassin would truly go to any lengths for the sake of knowledge, but ultimately he decided that there was no need to ask any of those questions out loud.

"Thank you kindly, Your Lordship," said Zetsu. "I trust you won't object to me taking a sum of coin as an advance on my payment?"

"Of course," Boroths replied. A brief period of negotiations regarding the advance later, the contract was sealed.

"I'll be on my way, then."

"And I will await news of your success."

With that, Zetsu took their leave without wasting a moment.

○

Preparations for my trip to Arcantez had begun. It was the twenty-first day of the fourth month, and Couran would be announcing Missian's secession in roughly one month's time. Fall would be over soon, and the days were growing chillier, though Missian was temperate enough on the whole that it wasn't unbearable yet. The real chill would set in during the fifth month, however, so we'd need to be ready to dress warmly while we were out and about.

My plan was to depart for Arcantez the very next day. That meant that if the trip went smoothly, I would arrive in the capital considerably earlier than I needed to. That being said, there was no telling what could go wrong on a journey of that length, and I had to be ready for delays. I wouldn't lose anything by arriving early, so it seemed best to depart as quickly as I possibly could. A vast swath of Missian's nobility would be attending Couran's ceremony, and I had no doubts that every count in the duchy would be there, so missing it on account of unforeseen circumstances was something I wanted to avoid at all costs.

Braham's unit and Pham would be traveling with me as my escort, and being my wife, Licia would be accompanying me as well. Rietz, Rosell, Mireille, and the rest of my retainers would be staying behind to manage Canarre in my absence. There was a mountain of work to get done back home, so bringing everyone with me simply wasn't an option. That being said, I *was* a count, which meant that there was every chance my life would be targeted while I was away. That's why I brought Braham's elites and Pham with me—between their combined areas of expertise, I was confident we could handle any attacker.

Rietz, of course, was as worried as ever to see me go, and had volunteered to travel with me. I needed him back in the castle making sure that everything ran smoothly while I was gone, though, so I declined. He was my most talented and capable subordinate, but his unfortunate tendency to lose his composure when it came to my safety may well be his one fatal flaw.

We finished our travel preparations without a hitch, and set out for Arcantez the very next day. Our journey proceeded much more smoothly than I'd anticipated. I'd expected the territories that had once been controlled by Vasmarque's faction to be in a state of unrest in the wake of the civil war, but I found them surprisingly well-governed instead, and we made it through without having to deal with a single bandit encounter. In the end, we arrived in Arcantez several days earlier than anticipated.

The fifth month had arrived, at that point, and the weather was as chilly as expected. I'd been to Arcantez just once before, and compared to then, the city felt notably more energetic and bustling. Missian's unification, I imagined, had drawn people to the capital from all corners of the duchy. The fact that Couran was a capable ruler had probably played a part as well, of course.

I wanted to speak with Couran in person before he made his declaration, so I made my way to Castle Arcantez and requested an audience. I was told that he was currently occupied, however, and wouldn't be able to meet with me immediately. That seemed fair enough—I could only imagine how busy he was preparing for the announcement he was about to make. It seemed I wasn't the only lord who had come to visit the castle, either. In the end, I managed to schedule a meeting with Couran a few days in the future. Specifically, I would see him the day before he made his declaration.

The same day I arrived in the capital I was led to Castle Arcantez's guest rooms, where I'd be staying over the course of the visit. As I entered the castle, by the way, I'd had a number of nobles who'd arrived before me strike up conversations. The attention they gave me made me realize just how much House Louvent had ended up in the public eye thanks to our accomplishments in the recent war.

This wasn't my first time dealing with other lords—I'd hosted visitors at Castle Canarre on a number of occasions—so I was well-versed in the proper etiquette and made it through the conversations without too much trouble. I was, however, tired from my journey, so I did my best to politely excuse myself the moment I had an opening and hurried to my chambers to drop off my luggage.

I was assigned two rooms for the duration of my stay. Licia and I would stay in one, and the retainers I'd brought with me in the other. That didn't give us enough space for all of my men, of course, so Braham and Zaht ended up staying in the castle while the rest of their troops found inns in town to lodge in. All of them, Braham and Zaht included, would be allowed to rest and recuperate as they saw fit for the duration of our stay in the castle. We'd need a guard when we went into town on occasion, but that would only take a few men for short periods, and everyone was thrilled when they learned they would have some time to take it easy.

Pham, by the way, was staying in the same room as Licia and I under the premise that he was our personal maid. I wanted to have a guard by our side at all times, just in case. It was easy to think that I'd be safe inside the castle, but I knew that I couldn't afford to be complacent. Other nobles were staying here as well, and some

I WILL USE MY APPRAISAL SKILL TO RISE IN THE WORLD

of them were surely less than pleased about my ascent to power. It wouldn't be impossible by any means for someone to send an assassin after me while I was here, and I figured there was no harm in being ready for that eventuality.

"Finally, a moment to relax," Licia, who seemed exhausted, said as we stepped into our room.

Traveling by carriage was never easy. We'd had a peaceful and uninterrupted trip this time, but that didn't change the fact that the act of traveling itself had been taxing. I'd been on plenty of journeys at that point, and yet I didn't feel even close to getting used to them.

"Right? How about we take it easy for the rest of the day?" I suggested.

"I would love that," said Licia. "I'm quite looking forward to taking a look around Arcantez, but that can wait until some other day."

And so we spent the rest of our first day in the capital relaxing and recovering from our journey.

○

I felt refreshed when I woke up the next day. My body was still young, thanks to my reincarnation, and that youth meant that a good night's sleep was all it took to recover from exhaustion. I knew that that wouldn't last as I got older, though, and I couldn't say I was very excited about going through the aging process all over again.

I'd only seen the capital in passing the last time I traveled to Arcantez, so this time, I decided to make a point of looking around more thoroughly. That would carry the fringe benefit of letting me search for new recruits as we toured around. There was always a chance I'd run into someone exceptional, after all. Arcantez was a big city with a large population, so the odds of meeting the right person felt considerable.

On the other hand, even if I did find someone with talent in Arcantez, it felt quite likely that they wouldn't be interested in any job I could offer them. Taking work from me would mean moving from the capital to Canarre, which was downright remote in comparison. Plus, although House Louvent's reputation had grown thanks to our role in the last war, we were still inexperienced upstarts compared to the more established noble families. I didn't think I'd be luring anyone to join me on the basis of my renown alone.

Then again, even if a talented individual I found wouldn't sign up with me, I could always recommend them as a potential hire to Couran. If someone I recommended accomplished great things as one of his retainers, it would raise my standing in his eyes by extension. It felt worth a shot, at the very least.

We left Castle Arcantez and wandered through the city streets. Licia, Braham, Zaht, and Pham—still in his maid outfit—accompanied me, making for a group of five in total. Zaht, Braham, and Pham were on guard duty. There was no telling what sort of people we'd bump into in town, so a little caution seemed prudent, since Arcantez had all the crime you'd expect from a city of its size and population.

"This place has changed a lot lately," Pham observed as he glanced around at the city. You'd never know he wasn't a girl, judging by both his looks and his tone of voice. He was also quite talkative when in disguise—apparently, talking a fair amount actually made people less likely to be suspicious of you.

I'd sent Pham to Arcantez to gather information in the past, and apparently it was vastly different now. I had no idea what it had been like back then, of course, so I couldn't even begin to guess what was so different about it.

"Is there anywhere in particular you were hoping to see in the city, Licia?" I asked. I could appraise all the people I liked no matter where we went, as long as there were people for me to look at, and Arcantez was so crowded I didn't think there was any danger of me running out of new targets regardless of location. That meant that our destination didn't particularly matter to me, so I figured I'd let Licia choose a direction for us.

"Let me think…" said Licia. "Oh—I've heard that there's a large botanical garden somewhere in the capital that I'd like to see!"

I hadn't realized that there was a botanical garden in the capital. In fact, I hadn't realized that botanical gardens existed in this world, period. Considering how much Licia loved flowers, though, it sounded like a destination she would probably enjoy.

"All right, then. Let's go see it," I said.

"Wonderful! I can't wait," Licia happily replied.

○

"The gardens were just wonderful, weren't they?" Licia said as we strolled through the streets of Arcantez once more. We'd finished our trip to the botanical gardens, which had left her as excited as could be.

The gardens were located in the capital's northern district. They'd turned out to be an indoor affair, housed in a fairly large building, and judging by the crowds we'd found there it was quite a popular destination. It had also turned out to be called the Arcantez Botanical Garden, which struck me as a rather straightforward name.

I'd appraised the various visitors to the gardens that we'd passed by, but hadn't found anyone with particularly high abilities. It was never that easy to find someone talented, though, and I knew that all I could do was keep appraising as many people as I could. I knew very well that I might not find anyone who met my standards during our whole stay in Arcantez, so I tried to keep my expectations grounded as I kept appraising away.

When I first walked into the gardens I'd been preoccupied by the thought that it was odd they could keep a facility like that active, considering this world's level of technology...but as it turned out, the whole building's climate was regulated through magical means. They had tons of plants growing there that you'd normally never see in Missian.

"Seeing the holy flower was the highlight for me! I had no idea flowers that large even existed," said Licia.

The holy flower was the garden's stand-out attraction. It belonged to a species of flower like none I'd ever seen before, with blossoms the size of trees, each petal of which bloomed in a different color. The iridescent powder that it had emitted made it more impressive still—it was such a fantastical sight, it was hard to believe it was real.

Technically speaking, holy flowers were apparently mushrooms rather than actual flowers. The shimmering powder was their spores, and they didn't grow that large unless they were kept in absolutely ideal conditions. The nature of those conditions, however, was sort of brushed past in the explanation we'd read.

"It was pretty, yeah... But it was a little shocking to learn that they're actually mushrooms," I said.

"J-Just let me forget about that, please!" Licia moaned. The fungal truth of the holy flowers had most definitely not been to her liking.

"Huh?! That thing was a mushroom?!" Braham exclaimed, clear-

I WILL USE MY APPRAISAL SKILL TO RISE IN THE WORLD

ly shocked.

"Captain..." Zaht sighed. "Did you not read the plaque at all...?"

"Well, y'know, I was just so focused on the flower! Wait, though—if they're really mushrooms, does that mean we can eat 'em?"

"They're poisonous, so no. And for that matter, I think anyone could tell you they're not edible from a single look at them," said Zaht.

True enough. I sure wouldn't try eating one of those things.

"Where shall we go next? I was thinking it'd be nice to visit somewhere you want to see, Ars," Licia suggested.

"Hmm. Let me think..."

I hadn't come to the capital to sightsee, so I hadn't taken the time to think of particular places that I wanted to visit. I also wasn't very well-versed in what there was to see in Arcantez in the first place—I didn't even know what the famous local landmarks were. You'd think the capital would feature all sorts of establishments that were worth seeing, but I had no clue where to start, and was having some trouble thinking anything up.

"Why don't we visit the market, for now?" I finally suggested. I knew that Arcantez's marketplace wasn't quite as big or bustling as that of Semplar, Missian's most thriving trade city, but it was still the capital, and would still have a wide variety of goods for sale. Plus, it would mean having plenty of people around to appraise.

"All right, then. Let's make our way to the market!" Licia agreed.

We left the botanical gardens behind, heading in the direction of the marketplace. It wasn't located in the very center of Arcantez—that real estate was occupied by the castle—but it was nearby.

When we arrived, we found a huge number of stalls lined up along the street. The marketplace was full of people, and the energy in the air almost felt like that of a festival.

Is it always like this? Or are there more people around than usual because Couran's declaration is so close at hand? Notice about Couran's intent to announce Missian's formal secession had been given a few days in advance, so the citizens of Arcantez were already aware of what was about to transpire.

I appraised various passersby as we strolled around the market. I'd already checked about fifty people that day, but as expected, finding someone exceptional really wasn't that easy. I didn't expect to find anyone at all on the first day, but that was no excuse to stop, and so I kept at it.

Suddenly, I happened to glance at a corner of the marketplace. Most of the area was thriving, but there was one stall in that corner with no customers at all. It was selling paintings, from what I could tell, though I had no clear idea if they'd been painted by the proprietor, or by someone else.

Either way, the stall was manned by a boy of somewhere around my age, if I had to hazard a guess. He had the sort of well-featured face that told you he would likely be quite handsome when he was a little older, and if he'd been the one who painted his merchandise, he was quite good. The paintings were easily of high enough quality to sell, but it seemed the customers just weren't coming.

Paintings are high-class goods, I guess. That's probably the sort of trade where you're lucky if you sell a single painting in a whole day. It'd probably be weird if there were a ton of people lined up at his stall.

I decided to give the boy at the painting stall an appraisal, just for good measure.

"*Huh?!*"

I WILL USE MY APPRAISAL SKILL TO RISE IN THE WORLD

> Keefe Venge
> Age: 13
> Male
> **Status:**
> LEA: 32/89
> VAL: 46/85
> INT: 55/98
> POL: 56/95
> Ambition: 33
> **Aptitudes:**
> Infantry: A
> Cavalry: C
> Archer: A
> Mage: C
> Fortification: C
> Weaponry: C
> Naval: A
> Aerial: A
> Strategy: A

Born on the twenty-first day of the twelfth month, 199 Imperial Era, in Arcantez City, Arcantez County, Missian Duchy, Summerforth Empire. Parents are both alive. Has four older brothers and two older sisters, all in good health. Marches to the beat of his own drum. Likes sweets; dislikes vegetables. A hobbyist painter. Likes kind women.

His current stats weren't breathtaking, but his maximum values were all exceptionally high. He was, without question, practically bursting with latent talent.

So his name's Keefe Venge, is it?

It had been a long time since I'd found anyone quite that talented. It just went to show that there really were people like that out there, if you took the time to look. It seemed he was an Arcantez native, and nothing about his background struck me as suspicious—the fact that he had a lot of siblings was the only aspect that seemed at all noteworthy. Considering all of them were alive, it seemed likely that he came from an affluent family. It was also notable that my skill hadn't said anything about his service to a lord, which implied he wasn't currently in anyone's employ.

"Ars... Have you found someone promising, perhaps?" Licia asked after I'd finished my appraisal. I didn't think I'd reacted in any noticeable way, but somehow, she'd picked up on my discovery anyway.

"I have, yes... But how did you know?" I asked.

"Your expression always stiffens up whenever you find someone worth recruiting—like this," Licia said as she demonstrated the face that I apparently made. "It's quite easy to pick out, if you know what to look for."

I never noticed at all!

When she put it that way, though, I could sort of tell that my expression had been a bit stiff. Her powers of observation were a force to be reckoned with...or rather, in this case, to be embarrassed by.

"So, would your promising new recruit happen to be that boy over there?" Licia asked.

I gave her a nod. "Would you mind if I took a moment to try talking with him?"

"Of course not! In fact, I'll accompany you!"

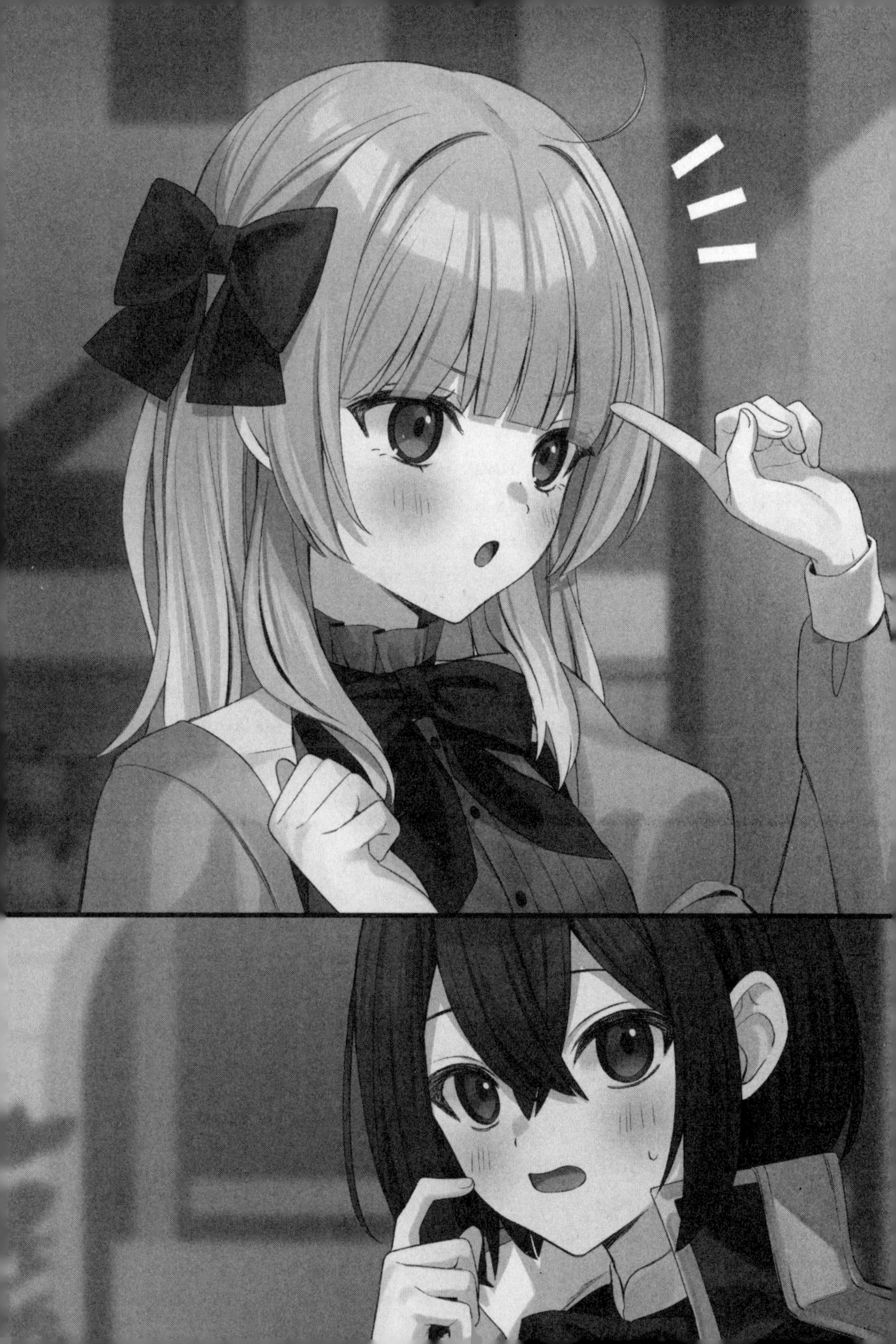

"That would be great, thanks."

The boy called Keefe had been born in Arcantez, and still lived there. It seemed very likely that he'd spent his entire life in the capital. That meant that the odds that the count of a land like Canarre would have any luck recruiting him were rather low. With Licia's powers of persuasion on my side, however, I felt like I had an actual chance. She was much better at bringing people around than I was, to be totally honest.

"That kid's amazing, huh…? W-Well, it's not like Lord Ars has been wrong about these things before," said Braham, who was clearly doubting my judgment a little.

Keefe was well-featured, but if I had to put my finger on it I would have described him as handsome in a more androgynous sense of the term. He didn't feel manly at all, and he was rather small-framed, meaning that you'd never think he'd be tough at a glance. He probably wasn't, in truth, considering his current stats weren't particularly high. Given his age, though, there was no mistaking the fact that his Intelligence and Politics scores were remarkable.

"Considering he picked out your talents, I think Lord Ars could see the worth in anyone," commented Zaht.

"Oh, is that…so…?" said Braham. "Wait, were you making fun of me just now?"

"Not at all. You're imagining things."

"Oh, okay. I… I guess…?" Braham said, still looking a little skeptical.

Licia and I approached Keefe.

"Ah… Welcome," Keefe said as we stepped up to his booth. It seemed he'd noticed us before we approached him, and he greeted us in a rather quiet tone.

"It's a pleasure to meet you. My name is Ars Louvent," I said.

I WILL USE MY APPRAISAL SKILL TO RISE IN THE WORLD

Making introductions was always the first step for recruitment, and Licia introduced herself as well when I was finished.

"O-Oh... Umm... My name's Keefe Venge," said Keefe. He seemed a little bewildered, but he still matched our introductions with one of his own. "Wait, Ars Louvent?" Keefe continued, studying my face more closely. "Does that mean you're *the* Ars Louvent? The Count of Canarre?" he asked, his eyes shooting wide open.

"Oh! You're familiar with me?" I asked.

"Of course! I heard all about how when Seitz invaded, you led your retainers into battle and won a glorious victory, repelling the invasion with ease!"

"G-Glorious, really...? I mean, we drove Seitz back, yes, but it was really my retainers who did most of the work..."

"And so humble, on top of it all! You really are the perfect superhuman, down to your personality! I can't believe we're the same age!" Keefe exclaimed, eyes sparkling with awe. He was very worked up, all of a sudden.

I'd known that my reputation had grown as of late, but I'd never imagined that an average citizen in Arcantez would have heard about me. I had no idea how to react, honestly, but the fact that Keefe was apparently a fan meant that I would hopefully have an easier time bringing him into the fold. This wasn't a bad sign, at the very least.

"The truth is, I've drawn a portrait of you, Lord Ars! Have a look, please!" Keefe said as he produced a framed portrait from somewhere beneath him.

"This is...me?" I asked.

"That's right!" Keefe replied.

The portrait he'd painted of me certainly had black hair, as well as clothing and a physique that matched mine...but my face had, shall we say, been given quite the glow-up. I was a little better looking now than I'd been in my last life, sure, but I knew for a fact that I wasn't *that* handsome.

"Oh, my! It looks just like you!" Licia exclaimed.

Does it...? Does it really? It definitely looks more than a little off, from my perspective! Oh, but then again, saying it looks wrong would lower Keefe's opinion of us. She must be acting like it's great just to bring him around!

"U-Umm... Y-Yeah, you captured his eyes pretty well, I guess," Braham awkwardly stammered. The look on his face told me he was wondering if he was even looking at the same painting as Licia. He knew something was wrong, clearly, but had picked up on the fact that saying so was a bad idea and was doing his best to bluff. I was impressed that he'd become at least a little capable of reading the room.

"Would you be willing to sell me that painting, perhaps?" asked Licia.

"Huh?" Keefe grunted. "Ah... I-I mean, I wasn't planning on putting it up for sale when I painted it, so..."

"Oh, truly? What a shame," said Licia. It almost sounded like she actually meant it, though surely she wouldn't want a painting that didn't even look like me.

She...is acting, right...?

"Well, in any case, we didn't approach you because we intended to buy one of your paintings," Licia continued.

"Huh? You didn't?" asked Keefe.

Licia shot me a glance. It seemed it was time for us to cut to the chase.

"I would like you, Keefe Venge, to become one of my retainers," I said, laying out my interest in no uncertain terms.

I WILL USE MY APPRAISAL SKILL TO RISE IN THE WORLD

For a moment, Keefe just stared blankly at me, slightly slack-jawed. Then, a few seconds later...

"You *whaaaaaaaaat*?!"

...he shouted at the top of his lungs.

"M-M-M-Me?! Your retainer?! Why?! Why *me*?!" Keefe babbled, shocked beyond all imagination. "Oh! Th-That's right—rumor has it that you have an incredible eye for talent... D-Does that mean that I have talent, too...?"

It seemed that as my reputation grew, rumors of my power had also started to spread. That saved me the time it would've taken to explain myself to him, thankfully.

"Does this mean that I have the potential to be an incredible painter?!" Keefe asked.

"Huh? A, uh, painter...?" I stammered. My power, unfortunately, didn't tell me anything about his talent for art. He was quite good for his age, as best as I could tell, and he certainly seemed talented to me, but I didn't want to blindly speculate. "I, umm, believe you're quite skilled...but I'm afraid that I don't have the ability to judge your talent for painting accurately. I can, however, say that you have the talent to excel as a warrior, a politician, a tactician, or in many other fields."

"H-Huh...? D-Do I, really? A twig like me, a warrior?" Keefe replied, bewildered by my answer.

"You may be weak now, but with proper training, I can assure you that you'll be very capable."

"Huuuh? R-Really? *Me?*"

He didn't believe me at all. It seemed that even knowing about my Appraisal skill, this was one thing he simply couldn't take my word for. The vast majority of people had absolute faith that they knew themselves better than anyone else ever could, which meant that it was never easy to accept it when someone told you something new and shocking about yourself.

"I know that there's a chance that you're right, considering who you are...but I want to make a living as a painter," Keefe said. He seemed totally baffled by the situation he'd found himself in.

I could certainly understand why it would be hard for someone who loves to paint to accept the idea that they should give it all up to become a warrior. I was at a loss, but as I racked my mind for a way to convince him...

"Oh? But there's no reason why you couldn't keep painting after becoming a retainer of House Louvent! As a matter of fact, I'd think that watching Ars and the others accomplish great things up close and personal would provide the most remarkable inspiration you could ask for, wouldn't you say?"

...Licia stepped in to throw me a lifeline. It was a pretty solid line of reasoning, too. It made sense that someone who wanted to be an artist would benefit from having all sorts of varied experiences.

"I-I see... That does make a certain amount of sense... I might never have the chance to get that sort of inspiration if I stay here in Arcantez..." Keefe muttered to himself. Licia's explanation seemed to have hit home, and he was very seriously mulling over his options. "G-Give me some time to think about it, please!"

It seemed we wouldn't be getting a clear response just yet. I couldn't blame him for that—even knowing who I was and what I'd accomplished, this wasn't the sort of offer I'd expect anyone to agree with at the drop of a hat. Rushing him was the last thing I wanted to do. I'd been planning on going home to Canarre the moment Couran had made his declaration, but I was open to the idea of waiting

I WILL USE MY APPRAISAL SKILL TO RISE IN THE WORLD

around until Keefe made his choice, if it came to that. Extending our stay here wouldn't be an enormous problem.

"All right, then," I said. "I'll come back in a few days to ask again."

"O-Okay!" said Keefe.

With that settled, we said our goodbyes to Keefe and went on our way.

○

A few days after I attempted to recruit Keefe, the time came for my meeting with Couran. It was the day before he would proclaim Missian's independence, and a rather frantic atmosphere pervaded Castle Arcantez. A celebratory banquet was scheduled to be held tomorrow alongside Couran's announcement, and while the preparations were all complete, the castle's staff were as busy as could be making their final checks to ensure that nothing would prove insufficient.

Couran's subordinates were hard at work ordering the castle's workers around. Couran himself was busy meeting with the nobles under his command, and had entrusted his people to handle all of the preparations in his stead. Licia and I, meanwhile, wove our way through the chaos as we made our way to Couran's meeting room.

"We thank you for your patience. His Lordship will see you now," a butler stationed in front of the room said as we arrived. He opened the door, and Licia and I stepped inside.

"Ars, Licia! It's been too long. Thank you for traveling all this way," Couran said as we entered the chamber, standing up and walking over to greet us with a smile. He seemed to be in a rather cheerful mood.

"Too long indeed, Lord Couran. We greatly appreciate your gracious invitation," I replied as I gave him a bow of greeting. Licia followed up with her own pleasantries in turn.

"I think that's well and enough stuffy formalities. Have a seat," said Couran.

Licia and I did just that, sitting down on a sofa in the chamber. It was a conspicuously luxurious article of furniture, and was as comfortable as a sofa could be. I immediately wanted one in Castle Canarre, though I knew it would probably come at a jaw-dropping price.

"Now, then," said Couran, "I can tell by the look on your face that you have something to say to me."

"Huh…? Oh, no, I mean, it's more that I have a question for you, actually," I replied. I'd been caught off guard by how quickly he'd jumped to the core of the matter, and found myself on my back foot as I replied in a fluster.

"You want to know why I chose to declare Missian's independence now, don't you?" asked Couran, guessing my question before I could even ask it. He was no fool, and figuring out that much had probably been the simplest of tasks for him.

"That's correct," I replied with a nod.

"Then before I answer, allow me to ask you a question in turn, Ars: What do you and your retainers think of my decision? Are you in favor? Opposed?"

"I…"

"Please, be honest with me. The matter is already decided, and your words will change nothing, whether you support my decision or oppose it. I'm simply asking for the sake of reference."

I hesitated, unsure of whether or not I should answer truthfully, but in the end I decided that the worst possible outcome would be for me to lie, and for him to realize it. I resolved to tell him the truth.

I WILL USE MY APPRAISAL SKILL TO RISE IN THE WORLD

"I...am opposed to this decision. My retainers are as well," I timidly admitted.

Couran's reaction wasn't dramatic. He didn't erupt in anger, instead simply nodding, as if he'd seen my answer coming—which, I imagined, he had.

"And your reasoning?" Couran asked.

"Most of us felt that the move was premature," I explained. "If, in the worst case, a combined army is dispatched to bring Missian in line, our current lack of resources means it would be difficult for us to emerge victorious... Declaring independence now dramatically raises the odds of a war breaking out."

"Hmm. Yes, I expected that objection to be raised," said Couran. "However, no such combined force will be formed. Who, after all, would form it? The Imperial House? They lack the influence to do so. The same is true of Seitz and Paradille. Rofeille possesses the strongest military force in Summerforth at the present moment, but they stand in opposition to the Imperial House themselves, and would never choose to cooperate. The power and legitimacy that the emperor would gain from defeating Missian would be nothing but a thorn in Rofeille's side."

Couran summed up the current state of affairs in Summerforth. His conclusion that a combined force being dispatched to Missian was unlikely lined up with that of my retainers.

"However...the fact that this decision will sow the seeds of war is, indeed, an unmistakable truth," Couran continued. He made no attempt to refute that point. "Do you loathe war, Ars?" he asked, shooting me a sharp, appraising glance.

"If I'm to be honest, Lord Couran...I am not at all fond of it," I replied, unable to bring myself to lie.

"You'd be hard pressed to find a man who was," Couran said

after a brief moment of hesitation. "Needless to say, I am not fond of it either. I freely acknowledge that in the short term, declaring Missian's independence will bring about strife and warfare. In the long term, however, if we do not seek independence, there will never be a hope of ridding our realm of war for good."

"For good...? What exactly do you mean by that?" I asked.

"Long ago, the continent of Summerforth was home to seven nations. There was the Kingdom of Missian, the Kingdom of Seitz, the Kingdom of Paradille, the Kingdom of Rofeille, the Kingdom of Ansel, the Kingdom of Canshiep, and the Kingdom of Scheutz. I'm sure you're well aware of this fact."

"I am," I replied. The old kingdoms were a matter of common knowledge. I remembered Rietz teaching me about their history when I was very young.

"One would think that the seven nations warred incessantly until the empire's founding—and one would be wrong. There were occasional conflicts, of course, but by and large treaties were forged and respected, bringing peace to the continent. That equilibrium lasted until Ansel's trade with a foreign nation from outside the continent led to an imbalance in power. Emboldened by their newfound might, Ansel brought about a war of a massive scale, ultimately resulting in the empire's birth. There was peace for a time after the kingdoms were unified, yes...but that peace, too, was only temporary. Now open warfare plagues the continent once again."

"Are you saying that the existence of the empire is the cause of those wars?" I asked.

"I am," said Couran. "Even if Summerforth were to be united once more, we would only go through the same process all over again. The seven duchies were all their own nations once, and we can never hope for perfect harmony between their peoples. If we are to bring about a lasting peace, then they must all be granted independence once more."

"So...do you think that Missian declaring independence will lead to the other duchies doing the same?"

"Some of them, I would think. Not immediately, perhaps, but I expect Rofeille, at least, to declare their own independence within the next few years at most. The other duchies will follow our example in time, one after another."

I couldn't say with confidence that Couran's prediction was mistaken. That being said, I also had doubts about his theory that the seven duchies regaining their status as independent nations would bring about a lasting peace. The odds of one of the nations trading with a foreign land, amassing power, and waging a war of expansion just like Ansel struck me as very high.

On the other hand, I certainly couldn't say that I had a method handy to bring about an actual, permanent peace. War would inevitably break out again eventually, no matter what we did. As such, I was more concerned about the prospect of whether or not a conflict would occur in Canarre in the immediate future.

"I understand your perspective, Lord Couran," I said. "However, the chances of a war breaking out once again in the near future are high, are they not? Ansel in particular seems to be a threat—given the historical precedent, it feels more likely than not that they'll attempt to obstruct Missian's bid for independence."

"I will not deny that," said Couran. "It's certainly true that allowing Missian its independence would further lessen the authority of the Imperial House. That said, the emperor is but a puppet of Ansel's ruling class, and his supposed vassals are locked in a power struggle of their own. The duchy lacks leadership, and while it would pose a dire threat if it could act as a unified front, in its current state, we have little to fear. Paradille, meanwhile, lacks the forces and provisions to threaten us. Even if they were to mount an assault, we would be more than capable of turning them back."

"What of Seitz, then?"

"Seitz...suffered a painful defeat at your hands only recently. They are not foolish enough to attempt another direct assault after incurring losses on that scale. If Missian were to become locked in a war with the other duchies and lacked the resources to mount a proper defense, they would likely go on the attack, but otherwise, I expect them to bide their time."

"It seems that they're bolstering their forces as we speak, though..."

"Which is further proof that they fear Missian—or, more accurately, that they fear *you*. Rest assured that should they attack again, you will have all the reinforcements you could possibly desire. Repelling an attack from Seitz alone would be the simplest of matters."

For a moment I hesitated, but in the end, I replied with a simple, "Understood." There was nothing more that I could say in the face of his argument. All I could do was accept it and back down.

"Will Missian not be declaring war on Seitz, then?" asked Licia. When she put it that way, it did seem like a necessary question to pose.

Now it was Couran's turn to hesitate. "I will not claim that it's out of the realm of possibility. If Seitz's movements prove sufficiently threatening, then there is a chance we will choose to launch a preemptive strike, yes," he said, once again making no attempt to deny the possibility. "Your realm, Canarre, lies on the border. I understand very well why this matter would be of great concern to you, but I swear that we will not allow Missian to wind up at a disadvantage. There are plans in the works, and you have no need to worry."

"Understood, Your Lordship," said Licia.

I WILL USE MY APPRAISAL SKILL TO RISE IN THE WORLD

I wasn't entirely convinced on a number of levels, but pressing the argument any further would run the risk of coming across as an attack on Couran's judgment. He would be Missian's king in the near future, and I couldn't afford to sour my relationship with him. As such, I feigned acceptance and refrained from voicing any more of my doubts.

"Understood," I said. "I will continue to do my utmost to support your endeavors, Your Majesty."

"Ha ha ha! Let's hold off on calling me that until tomorrow, shall we?"

With that, my business with Couran was concluded, and we excused ourselves from his chamber.

○

"What did you think about what Lord Couran told us, Ars?" Licia asked as we walked through the halls of Castle Arcantez after the meeting.

"That's...a very good question. Let me ask you the same: what did *you* think?" I asked, turning the question around on her rather than responding.

"Me? Hmm... To start, Lord Couran told us that the existence of the Summerforth Empire was a cause of war, but do you suppose that's really true? I thought that there was some logic to his argument, certainly, but I can't bring myself to believe that the empire's existence is the sole reason behind the recent conflicts."

"Agreed..." I said. "Wars start for all sorts of reasons, so I don't think there's any one thing that you can do to stop them permanently."

"That's very true," Licia replied. "And frankly, I have my doubts as to whether Lord Couran truly wants peace to begin with. Perhaps he merely spoke of peace to placate us, and won't be satisfied until he rules over the whole continent of Summerforth."

"That's certainly a possibility...but I would keep quiet about it, personally. You never know who might be listening to you."

"Yes, of course. I have no intention to blindly speculate about Lord Couran's true intentions in public. However, one thing I can say with certainty is that he has no intention of attempting to avoid war with Seitz."

"It really did come across that way, didn't it...?" I muttered. Couran had talked about Seitz being too scared of Canarre to invade, but he hadn't said a word about opening negotiations with the neighboring duchy to work toward reconciliation.

We had fought well in the last war and repelled Seitz's forces, but there was no guarantee it would go so smoothly next time. To make matters worse, if Couran chose to invade Seitz, I would have no choice but to offer up Canarre's armies to the cause. If such an invasion took place and was repelled, we would lose a massive chunk of our forces, and if Seitz were to invade when our troops were depleted, the odds of our loss would be very high.

Then again...I probably shouldn't be leaning this deeply into pessimism, should I? Couran's a capable man, and he wouldn't charge into a fight he had no chance of winning.

So long as Canarre was located on the border, the threat of war would always loom. All I could do was keep bolstering our forces, ensuring that we'd be able to fight our hardest in the event of an attack.

After our meeting with Couran concluded, we headed toward the market. Braham, Zaht, and Pham accompanied us.

I WILL USE MY APPRAISAL SKILL TO RISE IN THE WORLD

We were making our way to Keefe's stall. We'd been back to visit a number of times since our first encounter with him, but he had yet to reach a decision regarding whether or not he would become my retainer. Making that choice would mean leaving his hometown of Arcantez and moving to Canarre, so it was no surprise it wouldn't be an easy decision for him.

That said, he also had yet to clearly turn me down. He seemed to be deeply conflicted by the offer, which meant that there was still a chance he'd decide to take me up on it in the end. If I just kept meeting up with him and enthusiastically inviting him to join me, I knew my efforts could still bear fruit.

"Oh, Lord Ars!" Keefe said as I approached his stall. He seemed pleased as could be to see me. "Thank you so much for coming to visit me again!"

As I approached him, I noted that the stall was decorated with a different set of paintings than I'd seen the first time I visited. "Have you sold some paintings since last time?" I asked.

"No, no. Those just weren't selling at all, so I swapped them out," Keefe said with a slightly chagrined smile.

Clearly, paintings that would sell like hotcakes weren't so easy to create. I didn't know the first thing about painting, so most of this went over my head, but I'd gotten the impression that the art world was a tough one in a wide variety of ways.

I'd waffled over whether to buy one of his paintings myself, but had eventually decided against it, since buying one now would look like a transparent attempt to lure him into accepting my offer. Plus, I hadn't brought an incredible amount of money with me on this trip, and buying a painting would mean eating an uncomfortable amount into my travel expenses. Trouble could always crop up on the trip home, and that sort of issue usually took money to resolve, so I wanted to have as much on hand as I could manage.

"Of course, these ones aren't selling either!" Keefe added. "I'm starting to think I just might not be cut out to make it as a painter."

"That can't possibly be true," I said. "Your work speaks for itself—you clearly have the skill to be a professional. Maybe your shop just isn't set up in the right place?"

"I appreciate you saying that...though it's a little strange that you'd compliment my art, considering you want me to drop it all to become your retainer," Keefe said with a grin.

"I'm complimenting your art because I genuinely think it's good, that's all. I know that you'd be less likely to enter my service if you found success as an artist, but that's no excuse for me to lie about your skills, and I have no intention to do so," I said, speaking in total frankness.

"Yes, of course... You're not the sort of person who would do such a thing," muttered Keefe. "Umm, can I ask you a question, Lord Ars? Tell me—what do you think of my paintings? Do you have any desire for one?"

"Any desire...? Hmm... I'm not much of an art collector, to be honest..."

There were a number of paintings hung up in Castle Canarre, but I hadn't been the one who'd purchased any of them. I didn't have the aesthetic sense to tell a good painting from a bad one, and I knew it, so it was hard to give him a developed impression. All I could say was that they looked good to me.

"What about you, Licia? What do you think of Keefe's art?" I asked. She had a better understanding of art than me, at least, so I thought she'd be able to give him a more developed opinion.

"Let me see... This painting here is of the Arcantez cityscape, I take it?" Licia asked.

I WILL USE MY APPRAISAL SKILL TO RISE IN THE WORLD

"That's right!" said Keefe.

"You've drawn the buildings quite well, and your use of color is skillful enough...but—while I appreciate this isn't the nicest way to put it—it's rather boring to look at."

"Ugh," Keefe grunted. Licia hadn't minced words, and his ego seemed to have taken some damage as a result. I got the sense that he'd been aware of the issue himself, on some level.

"Ah, I-I'm sorry! I didn't mean to offend. It's just that I've seen so many paintings that were just like it," Licia frantically clarified as she realized how badly Keefe had taken her review.

"Y-Yes, you're right... It's painfully ordinary, isn't it...?" Keefe groaned.

"B-But the portrait of Ars that you drew was exceptional! I loved it!" Licia added.

Apparently, she really *had* meant it when she'd said she liked that one. I'd been convinced it was just flattery, but clearly I'd been wrong. Was that how she actually saw me?

"I let my imagination run away from me when I painted that portrait... It seems that I just can't imbue my paintings with a sense of energy unless I'm painting a subject that I have a passion for... They all turn out boring and commonplace otherwise... I love the Arcantez cityscape, to be sure, but I see it every single day, and it doesn't do anything to stroke my imagination anymore," Keeve muttered with a look of consternation on his face. "Lord Ars...I've made up my mind. If you'll have me, I would be glad to become your retainer!" he declared with no warning whatsoever.

"R-Really? You're sure?" I asked.

"I am! I see now that there's nothing left in this city that could take my paintings to the next level. I need to gain all sorts of experiences, and give my work the inspiration it needs to evolve!" Keefe explained, suddenly as enthusiastic as could be. His zeal for painting, clearly, was genuine.

"I see..." I said.

"But really, though—is it all right for me to become your retainer for the sake of improving my artwork? I'll do any work that you ask of me, of course, but still..."

"That's no issue at all. I'd love to see more of your paintings, myself."

Keefe took a deep breath. "Thank you so, so much!" he said, thanking me with a broad smile.

"Is it all right for you to make this decision so suddenly, though? You don't have to get permission from your parents?" I asked.

"Oh, I'm the fifth son of a local innkeeper," said Keefe. "It's a big business, and my parents have always been fussy about passing it down, but being the fifth son and all, that's got nothing to do with me. I'm sure they won't mind at all."

The son of an innkeeper, huh? And if it's a big one, then he must come from a wealthy family. Art supplies aren't cheap by any means, so if he didn't have some wealth backing him up he probably never would've been able to paint at all.

"Well, I'm glad to hear it. Allow me to ask you again: will you become my retainer, Keefe Venge?"

"Gladly!" Keefe replied with a spirited nod.

○

The next day, Couran's ceremony was carried out. It occurred in front of Castle Arcantez. There was a balcony built into the castle, intended to be used for public addresses, and Couran stood atop it to make his declaration. Said balcony was quite high up, and as

I WILL USE MY APPRAISAL SKILL TO RISE IN THE WORLD

a natural consequence, he ended up looking down on the crowd below him.

Below the balcony stood a crowd of nobles. The citizens of Arcantez weren't allowed to get too close when he gave his speech, but instead, sound magic would be used to broadcast his voice all throughout the city.

After a moment of waiting, Couran stepped out onto the balcony. He always made a point of wearing extravagant clothing, but his outfit that day was a step above even his usual garb, complete with a crown atop his head.

"Oooh," cooed a nearby noble.

"That's the crown from the legends—the one that was worn by countless generations of Missian kings!" said another.

"Its display was prohibited when the empire rose… To think I'd be able to see it with my own two eyes…"

The gathered lords seemed astonished to see Couran in his crown. I, however, hadn't heard the story that they all seemed to be familiar with.

I wonder if he'll be wearing that all the time from now on?

"His Majesty bids you to be silent! Listen, one and all, to his royal decree!" called out Robinson, who was standing by Couran's side.

A hush fell over the crowd of nobles. Once the silence was complete, Couran began to speak.

"It brings me great joy to see you all gathered here on this finest of days. Until last year, this city of Arcantez languished in the clutches of my younger brother. Now we have reclaimed it, and have come together today thanks to all of your efforts. I know well that all of you will continue to accomplish great things for your fair land," Couran began, speaking in a calm, mild tone. "Once, the Kingdom of Ansel swept across the land in an invasion as brutal as it was evil.

It brought the other nations of Summorforth to heel, and founded the empire, which has reigned for more than two centuries."

As Couran spoke on, his tone of voice began to shift, taking on a harsh, hostile edge. HIs intense animosity toward the Summerforth Empire was plain to hear.

"Two centuries ago, our legacy was stolen from us. Countless citizens of Missian were murdered and abducted. What money and food we had was pilfered. Even the seat of our monarch was stolen. When we were defeated in that terrible war, Missian suffered the greatest humiliation it will ever experience…but now, the age of the empire is over. The Imperial House's power wanes, and their right to rule has long since ceased to be. The time has come for our nation to reclaim the pride that was stolen from us!"

Could it be that all that's driving Couran to declare independence is a simple desire to redeem his ancestors?

He'd talked about seceding for the sake of peace the day before, but I was having a hard time believing that was really what drove him.

"Henceforth, Missian shall no longer bow to the Summerforth Empire! I hereby declare our independence—from this day onward, we shall be the Kingdom of Missian! And on this day, I shall ascend to its throne as Missian's king!"

Couran declared the beginning of his reign from on high, and the nobles below burst out in joyous cheers.

On that day—the twenty-first day of the fifth month, in the two hundred and thirteenth year of the Imperial Era—Couran Salemakhia ascended to Missian's throne. The Kingdom of Missian had been revived.

○

I WILL USE MY APPRAISAL SKILL TO RISE IN THE WORLD

The celebratory banquet that followed ended without any particular incident. Other nobles rushed to speak to me, and I had to take the time to deal with each of them in turn, but I'd gotten used to that sort of socializing and didn't even feel particularly exhausted by the time it was over.

The next day, good news arrived at my doorstep.

"They gave me permission!" Keefe said with an elated smile. He'd asked his parents if he could enter the service of a noble, and had gotten their consent without a hitch.

They must be pretty hands-off parents to sign off on something this major that easily... Actually, it almost feels like this goes past hands-off and enters the realm of straight-up neglect?

They had, at least, given him plenty of funds to carry him through his travels. It sort of felt like they had a policy of giving him all the money he could ever want, under the condition that he raised himself in their stead. That was problematic in its own right, but it was also the reason why he'd been able to pursue his dream of becoming a painter, so it had its upsides, from a certain perspective.

"All right, then! It sounds like you'll be coming to Canarre with us," I said.

"Gladly!" said Keefe.

We set out from Arcantez, making our way home with a new companion among our number.

○

Winter had set in by the time we began our trek back to Canarre.

The weather was quite chilly, but it hadn't snowed yet, so our journey was largely unobstructed.

"Ugggh... It's freezing," moaned Braham, who was shivering violently. He wasn't dressed for the cold at all—from what I could tell, he was still wearing his fall outfit. It was no wonder he wasn't taking the chill well.

"I told you to wear something warmer, didn't I...?" Zaht said with a fed-up shake of his head.

"I didn't know it would get this cold..." Braham grumbled back at him.

The fifth month in Missian wasn't always this chilly, but it also was by no means unprecedented for the cold of winter to set in this early. There really wasn't any good excuse for Braham's lack of preparedness.

"You'll catch a cold, at this rate," said Pham, still dressed as a maid and sounding rather concerned for Braham's health.

"Never caught one of those in my life," replied Braham. "This isn't the first time I've had to deal with a little cold, either."

People said that idiots don't catch colds back in Japan, but this is definitely the first time I've seen someone actually prove that superstition true. Then again, considering how much he's grown recently, he might have lost his immunity by now?

Anyway, frigid weather aside, our trip home continued without issue.

One evening, we'd stopped to make camp for the night. We'd planned out our trip back to Canarre to ensure we could stop in towns and cities as often as possible, but there were some nights when we simply had no choice but to camp out in the wilderness.

We set up tents, made a fire, and set about preparing the camp-

I WILL USE MY APPRAISAL SKILL TO RISE IN THE WORLD

ground for our night's stay. Winter nights were particularly frigid, and camping out in the cold was by no means a pleasant experience, but there was no way around it. Cars, trains, and planes weren't a thing in this world, after all.

Braham, Zaht, and Licia had already gone to sleep, while Keefe and I were sitting near the campfire together. Pham was patrolling the vicinity, making sure that no one could sneak up on us, so the two of us were alone.

"It sure is nice and warm, huh?" Keefe said as he gazed into the fire, looking perfectly relaxed.

At a glance, he looked like an ordinary boy—so much so that I almost had to question whether he really had the talent to be a capable warrior. That, I supposed, was what made my power so valuable: it let me identify talents in people who no one would ever suspect were capable deep down.

"So, what sort of place is Canarre City?" asked Keefe. "I've heard stories about it, but I've never been there myself."

"What sort of place is it? That's a good question... Up until just recently, I would've called it an ordinary border city with no real distinctive traits. Ever since the civil war ended, though, it's been developing like crazy. It's a pretty nice city, these days."

"Oh, is it?! And I'm sure you deserve most of the credit for that development, right?!"

"No, no—if anyone deserves the credit, it's my retainers. They did all the hard work. I'm not skilled enough to be of much use in that field."

"There you go, acting all humble again!" said Keefe. I'd just been telling the truth, but it seemed he'd interpreted that as me playing down my achievements. "I'll have to work hard to be someone who can contribute to your cause! I mean, if I end up being useless it'd make everyone think that your eye for talent misjudged me!"

"I have high hopes for you, trust me, but there's no need for you to feel rushed. You can take your time," I said.

Keefe's current stats weren't particularly high. I didn't expect him to be achieving great things right out of the gate—I'd take my time helping him develop his skills instead.

As I thought about Keefe's future, I decided to take another look at his stats on impulse.

>
> Natasha Valhan
> Age: 29
> Female
> **Status:**
> LEA: 5/12
> VAL: 99/99
> INT: 100/100
> POL: 21/25
> Ambition: 50
> **Aptitudes:**
> Infantry: S
> Cavalry: C
> Archer: S
> Mage: A
> Fortification: D
> Weaponry: A
> Naval: A
> Aerial: A
> Strategy: S

Born on the eleventh day of the eleventh month, 183 Imperial

I WILL USE MY APPRAISAL SKILL TO RISE IN THE WORLD

Era, in Rapin, Solecia City, nation of Partonne. Parents are both alive. A ruthless individual. Likes spicy food. Enjoys reading. Has little interest in the opposite sex.

"...Huh?"

I let out a gasp of bewilderment. The status box displayed before me was completely different from the one I'd seen before. Even his name had changed. Keefe was now called Natasha, was a woman, and was from a totally different nation. I thought that something must have gone wrong with my skill, so I appraised him again just to be sure, but was met with the same results.

What's going on? Is my skill glitching out? Nothing like this has ever happened before!

I wanted to test my skill out on someone else, but there wasn't anyone around for me to look at other than him, and no matter how many times I tried re-appraising him, I got the same results.

Okay—so what if these results are *correct?*

That, presumably, would mean that the error had occurred the first time I appraised Keefe, and everything had gone back to normal now. There was a hole in that theory, though: back when we'd first met, Keefe had clearly identified himself as Keefe Venge. It was hard to believe that appraisal had been flawed, since it had told me the same name that he had.

So then...could he have used some sort of method to fool my skill, maybe?

Perhaps he'd somehow falsified his appraisal's results, and the method he'd used to accomplish that effect had had a time limit? Maybe it had worn off, and I was seeing his actual, proper status box now.

Am I overthinking this...?

AS A REINCARNATED ARISTOCRAT

If he had, hypothetically, fooled my skill, that begged the question of *why*. To trick me into taking him in as my retainer? Would that mean that Keefe was a spy sent by one of my enemies?

Then there was another possibility: that the real Keefe had been killed sometime between our first meeting and our departure, and I was now speaking with an entirely different person who was disguised as him. That seemed hard to believe, though—if he'd really been disguised the whole time over the several days we'd been on the road together, then surely one of us would have noticed by now? Pham in particular was an expert on disguises, and it was very hard to believe he wouldn't have picked up on it.

In any case, I knew what I had to do for the time being: act like I hadn't re-appraised him at all, and wait until I had the chance to appraise someone else. If that gave me strange, clearly wrong results, then I could conclude that something was wrong with my skill. That would be bad in its own right, of course. I had no clue how to go about fixing my skill, and the thought that I could lose it altogether was terrifying.

If, however, the other members of our party gave me the same results as always…I'd be forced to make my suspicions that Keefe was a spy known. It would still be possible that my skill was having problems appraising him specifically, so I wouldn't be able to say with complete certainty he was up to no good, but I would certainly need to take a much deeper look into the matter to ascertain his guilt or innocence.

As I thought my options through, Keefe glanced over at me.

"Oh? Don't tell me it's worn off already?" Keefe spoke in the same tone as always, and as a result, it took me a moment to register what he'd actually just said.

"It's worn off"? What has? Don't tell me…

I WILL USE MY APPRAISAL SKILL TO RISE IN THE WORLD

"Shame. Time for a change of plans, then..."

He pulled something from the breast of his shirt. By the time I'd realized he was holding a knife, he'd already dashed toward me at an unbelievable speed and thrust it at my face.

"Wha—?!" I gasped, lurching backward and just barely dodging the stab. I hadn't evaded it completely, though. The knife had grazed my cheek, leaving a slight cut that burned with pain.

"Oh? So you *can* dodge! You have better reflexes than I thought you would," Keefe said, still in the exact same tone he'd spoken with for as long as I'd known him. I'd never had a knack for combat, but I *had* witnessed warriors like my father and Rietz train, so I was more used to picking out rapid movements than the average person. Dodging, at least, I had some confidence in.

"Keefe—or, no... Your real name's Natasha, isn't it? What have you done with the real Keefe?" I asked.

"I don't know why you'd think I'd answer that, but I suppose at the very least, I can tell you that he doesn't exist in this world," she said.

Does that mean that she killed him, or that Keefe never was a real person to begin with? She could've easily meant it either way.

"You know my real name, though? That eye of yours and its power are the real deal," she said with an air of curiosity.

It seemed that she'd learned about my power in advance, though from whom, I couldn't say. If she also knew how to fool it, as I suspected, then it seemed possible that she knew more about my Appraisal skill than even I did.

"It's a potent power, to be sure, but if I can offer a word of advice: you'd be better off not over-relying on it."

I didn't say a word.

"Not that there's much of a point to giving you that warning now, I suppose."

So she plans to kill me here and now, then.

Keefe—or rather, Natasha—raised her knife and charged at me once more. Before she could reach me, however, something burst out of the darkness and interposed itself in between the two of us at an unbelievable speed. It was Pham, who must have realized that something was wrong and intervened in the nick of time to save me.

"Whoops! Fighting you would certainly be a hassle," commented Keefe—no, Natasha.

Pham clicked his tongue in irritation, shooting her a glare as she stepped backward, distancing herself from him.

"Hiyaaah!"

Just then, Braham charged in from behind Natasha, bellowing as he swung his sword toward her. I'd been positive that he was fast asleep, but he must have heard the sounds of battle and come running.

I would've thought Braham's attack would catch Natasha by surprise, but she sidestepped his slash with ease. Her Valor stat had been incredibly high when I appraised her a moment beforehand—she was clearly a masterful fighter.

"Yes, this certainly puts me at a disadvantage," said Natasha. "But there's no particular need to deal the killing blow. I'll be on my way now."

"You think you can get away from us, huh?" roared Pham, his gaze still fixed on her.

"I do," Natasha replied with a nod.

Once again, she produced something from the breast of her shirt—not a knife, this time, but a small object that she flung to the ground, producing a billowing white smokescreen that engulfed the campsite in the blink of an eye. For a moment I couldn't see

I WILL USE MY APPRAISAL SKILL TO RISE IN THE WORLD

anything at all, and when the smoke finally cleared, Natasha was nowhere to be seen.

"H-He got away! We've gotta find him! Can't believe that guy was an enemy!" Braham shouted.

"Don't bother. You wouldn't catch him anyway," Pham snapped, his irritation clear in his tone of voice. "He's an expert, and worst case, it might turn out that running was a feint. We can't have him coming back for another try while we're gone. We have to raise our guards and be ready for anything. Acting like we wouldn't let him leave was a bluff—when all's said and done, letting him get away's our only option."

"Dammit," Braham muttered with a scowl. It seemed that he knew Pham was right. I had to agree as well—Natasha had made it sound like she was dedicated to running away when she raised the smokescreen, but that could easily have been a ploy to set up a second chance for her to take my life from up close.

"More importantly, she said something about not needing to deal the killing blow," Pham added.

"Huh? I mean, yeah, she did…but this is barely a scratch. It's not a big deal at all," I said. A little cut on my cheek wasn't enough to worry me.

Pham's expression, however, turned grave the moment he looked at my injury up close. He was usually a portrait of composure, but for once, he seemed seriously shaken.

"Damn it all… That knife might've been poisoned."

Pham delivered the news in a terribly serious tone.

"P-Poisoned…?" I repeated in horror. It made sense—of course an assassin would poison their knife. I didn't feel like anything was wrong with me now, but there was no telling how long that might last.

"I'll apply first aid," Pham said before setting to work, doing whatever he could to purge any potential poison from my body. He washed the cut with clean water, then applied pressure around it to squeeze out some blood and—hopefully—any poison that might have remained. After that, he produced some pure alcohol from a first aid kit to disinfect the wound and covered it up with gauze.

"Nothing feels wrong so far?" asked Pham.

"N-No, it doesn't," I replied.

"It could be a slow-acting poison, but… Hmm… What sort would it be…? I have antidotes for all the common ones on hand, so I could deal with any of those, but it's not looking like it…"

If Pham couldn't immediately identify the poison, I knew it had to be a rare one indeed. To make matters worse, the way Natasha had spoken about it implied that it had a very high rate of lethality.

"O-Okay, but maybe it wasn't poisoned, right? He's not showing any signs so far, so you never know!" said Braham, who must have realized how anxious I was feeling.

"I'd love to be that optimistic…but someone who put an incredible amount of time and effort into getting close to me just left without putting up a fight. You wouldn't do that unless you were positive that your target was as good as dead," I said. Frankly, I couldn't bring myself to see any positive side to the situation.

"I-I mean… I dunno about that! Maybe he just ran because he knew he was doomed if he stayed…? Anyway, I can't believe he was an enemy! Didn't seem the type at all," Braham said. I had a feeling that he hadn't been able to come up with anything reassuring to say, and had resorted to awkwardly changing the topic instead.

I guess it's not completely certain that the knife was poisoned. I'm

I WILL USE MY APPRAISAL SKILL TO RISE IN THE WORLD

not displaying any symptoms yet, and until I do, we won't be able to say for sure one way or the other.

"Sorry... I let my guard down," said Pham. It was very rare for him to be this openly in low spirits. He clearly thought that he was to blame for the attack.

"You have nothing to apologize for," I said. "I'm the one who overestimated my power and got myself in this position. I should've done way more looking into his background before I recruited him..."

"Except that's my responsibility. Every time you bring a new retainer in, I refuse to trust them until I've learned everything there is to know about them. It's part of the job...but I completely missed the fact that he was an assassin," Pham said, teeth gritted with regret. The fact that Natasha had managed to fool him proved above all else how skilled of an assassin she was.

"M-Me too... I was asleep the whole time... I'm sorry... I was supposed to be your guard, and I was useless," said Braham, following up with an apology of his own. "Wait, what am I getting all gloomy for?! This isn't the time, right?! What's done is done, so I'll just be more careful next time! And seeing as you've got a wound to recover from, Lord Ars, you should be getting to bed on the double!"

He's definitely forcing himself to act cheerful. I guess that must be his way of trying to put me at ease.

"Y-Yes, I'll do that," I said, then made good on my word by heading back to my tent.

I was sharing a particularly well-made tent with Licia, who hadn't noticed the commotion at all and was still fast asleep. Licia didn't have much in the way of stamina, and I suspected that the journey was particularly exhausting for her.

I tried to get some rest, but sleep wouldn't come no matter how hard I tried. My mind was racing with a muddled mess of thoughts. How would I tell Licia about what had happened? We didn't know that the knife had been poisoned, but surely she'd be beside herself with worry if it turned out that it had been. And, taking that logic a step further, what would happen to her if I died...? I didn't want to think about my own death at all, frankly.

Why had Natasha tried to kill me? Was the assassination self-motivated? That seemed very unlikely to me. Most likely, she was a hired assassin working on someone's orders—but whose? Another Missian noble? Or had one of Seitz's rulers decided to take me out in an act of retribution for the war they'd lost? Plenty of bandits had been brought in at my command, too, so it was possible that they'd decided to get back at me. Making your name as a lord inevitably meant earning grudges and envy as you climbed the social ladder, and there were, upon reflection, a surprising number of people with reasons to send an assassin after me.

On another note: how in the world had Natasha managed to fool my Appraisal skill? There were so many things about it that I didn't understand. I'd been born with the power, and I'd never met anyone else who possessed anything like it. I'd never met anyone who knew anything about it, either. Maybe it would be a good idea for me to take researching my own power a little more seriously.

Well...if I survive for long enough to do it, anyway.

I still didn't feel unwell in any particular way. I wasn't totally convinced I'd been poisoned at all, and hoped that when all was said and done, I'd end up kicking myself for being so paranoid. And, although sleep didn't come easily, as the hours dragged on my exhaustion took hold and I drifted off into slumber.

I WILL USE MY APPRAISAL SKILL TO RISE IN THE WORLD

I woke up the next morning feeling right as rain. That said, I knew I couldn't let my guard down. Some poisons took a long time to take effect, and it wasn't out of the realm of possibility that one could take more than a day to start revealing its symptoms.

"Good morning… Wha— Ars! What happened to you?!" Licia exclaimed the moment she saw my face. I still had a piece of gauze covering up the cut Natasha had left on my cheek, held there by a bandage. That bandage probably made it look like a much worse injury than it actually was.

"Oh, it's nothing! Just a scratch, really," I said.

"Is it, truly…?"

I hesitated, unsure of whether or not to tell Licia what had happened the night before. In the end, I resolved myself to fill her in. It would be far more of a shock to her if I collapsed out of nowhere, after all, so I explained everything that had transpired overnight.

"That can't be… Keefe was an assassin? And he poisoned you…?"

"Keefe was our enemy, yes. As for the poison, we don't know for sure yet. Nothing's wrong with me so far, and the cut itself isn't bad at all. If the knife wasn't poisoned, it'll heal in no time."

"I-I see…" Licia said. She didn't seem to be taking the news well. "I-In any case we should hurry back to Canarre! There are doctors you can see there, so even if worse comes to worst and you start showing poisoning symptoms, they might be able to cure you!"

"Yeah, good idea…"

Per our original schedule we were still three days out from Canarre City, but that was under the assumption that we traveled at a comfortable pace, with time built in for potential delays. If we rushed, we could make it home within a day and a half. I ended up taking Licia's suggestion and aiming for that timeline, speeding up in an effort to get back to Canarre as quickly as we could.

AS A REINCARNATED ARISTOCRAT

I'd hoped that I would make it through the trip without any poison symptoms rearing their head, but unfortunately, that proved too optimistic of me. A few hours after we set out I came down with a fever, followed by a sense of all-encompassing weariness. It was minor enough to pass for a common cold, at first, but the symptoms gradually began to escalate, and I was soon confident that I really had been poisoned. Pham brewed a medicine that was supposed to bolster my body's natural immunities, and drinking it made me feel a little better, but before I knew it the symptoms were back, and worse than ever.

A few hours later, I felt so sluggish and heavy that I could barely stand. It almost felt like I'd lost control of my body. I'd been sick a number of times since my reincarnation in this world, but I'd never felt this awful—possibly even including in my previous life.

"We're almost there, Ars! We'll be in Canarre before you know it, and you'll be better in no time!" said Licia, who was riding in the carriage that I was lying down in. She was keeping her tone bright and cheerful to raise my spirits, but I could tell by the look on her face that her optimism was a front.

"Y-Yeah..." I weakly replied. It took everything I had just to open my mouth, and even then, speaking wasn't easy. "Licia..."

"Wh-What is it? Do you need water?" Licia replied, putting on a transparently affected smile.

"If I die...take care of House Louvent. Kreiz will probably be my heir, but he's too young. He won't be able to lead everyone. You have to support the House in his stead... Please..."

I found myself preoccupied by thoughts of what would happen to House Louvent if I didn't make it, and asking her to take care of everyone was all I could do. Considering the state I was in, I had no

I WILL USE MY APPRAISAL SKILL TO RISE IN THE WORLD

choice but to anticipate my death, and she was the only person who could possibly bring all of my retainers together. Licia was strong-willed, smart, and decisive—she had everything that a leader could need.

"Wh-What are you saying?! You will *not* die in a place like this, and I refuse to make any such promise!" Licia snapped furiously. "Ah! I can see Canarre in the distance!" she added a moment later, now sounding overjoyed.

Oh. We're almost back?

"Ars…? Ars?!"

Perhaps thanks to the relief of knowing that we were almost home, I felt the tension drain from my body. My consciousness gradually began to fade.

"*Ars!*"

Licia's shout was the last thing I heard before the world was engulfed in darkness.

Chapter 3:
An Emergency for House Louvent

It was the sixth month of the two hundred and thirteenth year of the Imperial Era. Ars Louvent, afflicted with a terrible poison, made his return to Castle Canarre in a state of unconsciousness. He was rushed into treatment, and perhaps thanks to that rapid medical care, his symptoms began to wane and he even briefly regained consciousness.

Shortly thereafter, however, Ars's symptoms worsened once more and he drifted into a persistent slumber. The poison that had been used on him seemed to have been a particularly nasty one, and unless it was fully purged from his body, a full recovery was likely out of the question. That said, not even House Louvent's dedicated physician could identify precisely what sort of poison it was. Rosell, who had engaged in a degree of medical studies, attempted to analyze the poison and develop an antidote, but the task proved far more difficult than he had anticipated.

Ars's condition could not be cured, and as hour after hour passed by, he grew weaker and weaker. House Louvent found itself in a state of unprecedented emergency.

○

"Well? Let's hear your report," Boroths said to Zetsu, who had just returned from their mission. The Seitzan lord listened as his hired assassin explained how they had carried out their operation.

"You fooled his Eye of Appraisal? Is that even possible?" Boroths asked after Zetsu explained a particularly eyebrow-raising detail.

"It is," Zetsu replied.

"How?"

"That's confidential," said Zetsu, flatly shutting down Boroths's line of inquiry.

Boroths could tell he wasn't going to get that information easily, so for the time being, he moved on. "So, then? I understand how you infiltrated Ars Louvent's group, but was the assassination a success?"

"That is the question, yes...and I believe that I can honestly say that it was. Ars Louvent is alive, at the present moment, but he won't be for long."

"Explain yourself," Boroths said with a glare. The ambiguity of Zetsu's report was getting under his skin.

"I've poisoned him. The toxin I used is slow acting, however, so he won't be dead just yet."

"What? When *will* he die, then?"

"I wasn't able to deliver a full dose, so longer than I'd prefer, perhaps. I imagine he'll last a month, at the longest."

"A month...? What if he finds an antidote?"

"I don't believe that's a cause of concern for us, no matter how exceptional House Louvent's retainers may be...but you never know."

"'You never know'? Are you certain or not?"

"There's very little in this world that you can be completely certain about. All that's left is for us to wait and find out for ourselves,"

I WILL USE MY APPRAISAL SKILL TO RISE IN THE WORLD

Zetsu replied with a smirk.

Boroths's expression, in contrast, grew enraged. "Why didn't you use a poison that would be instantly fatal?!" he roared.

"That was a matter of necessity, not choice. My target had a number of highly capable guards with him, and the bulk of poisons can be detected by smell alone, if you know what to watch for. I simply picked a poison that could kill, and that was guaranteed to be indetectable. Of course, my initial plan was to kill him personally—the poison was just a contingency—but those bodyguards stopped me from following through. That, I'll concede, was my mistake."

Boroths took a deep breath. "If he survives, then you can consider your reward—and, for that matter, your *life*—forfeit."

"How terrifying! I certainly won't object to you rescinding my reward, but as for my life, I'm afraid I'll have to decline. It's not cheap enough for me to owe it to you over a single failure."

"'A single failure'…? Surely you understand how much weight 'a single failure' carries in your line of work? Have you never failed to kill your target before?"

"I'd love to say I haven't, but that would be dishonest of me. I am, at the end of the day, only human. I've failed missions, and had my former employer attempt to take my life in the past, even—which meant that I had no choice but to end them before they could finish me off."

Boroths's gaze could hardly have been more wrathful, but Zetsu simply brushed it off, their attitude never wavering for a moment. Boroths, for his part, had never truly intended to order Zetsu's death. He knew any such attempt would be hopeless unless he dispatched a small army to get the job done, and Zetsu's life just didn't have that sort of value to him.

AS A REINCARNATED ARISTOCRAT

"Allow me to give one piece of advice," said Zetsu. "All question of his death aside, my poison will most certainly make the immediate future very unpleasant for Ars Louvent, and in the meantime, House Louvent will likely be in a state of disorder. If ever there was a time to press the attack, it may well be now."

"You must have a very low opinion of me, to think that I would take strategic advice from a mere assassin," Boroths growled.

"Excuse my impertinence. Mulling over these sorts of scenarios happens to be a hobby of mine. Feel free to forget I ever said anything," said Zetsu, once again unmoved by Boroths's implicit threat.

Hmph. This assassin's a crafty one. Hiring them may have been a mistake, thought Boroths. Zetsu's attitude was beginning to make him second guess his choices.

"In any case, my report ends here. I'll be back as soon as Ars Louvent's death has been confirmed," said Zetsu.

"Let's hope you will," Boroths commented.

Zetsu made to leave the room, but then stopped in place. "Oh, of course! I almost forgot," they said, producing an unexpected object: a landscape painting of the Actantez cityscape, which they showed to Boroths.

"What is this painting supposed to be?" Boroths asked.

"Well, I painted it myself," said Zetsu. "What do you think?"

"What do I *think*?"

"You know—any impressions? Thoughts?"

"Why in the name of decency should I humor this drivel...?" Boroths grumbled. "Well, fine. If I had to evaluate it...I would say that it's a pedestrian work that was painted by a mildly skilled amateur."

Zetsu hung their head in shocked disappointment. "Y-You think so...? Painting's a hobby of mine, and one I engage in quite often, but my work's sold disappointingly poorly. I suppose I'll have to practice the fundamentals all over again."

Boroths was speechless.

"Well then, I'll be on my way now," said Zetsu. This time, the assassin really did depart from Boroths's chamber.

"Wh-What was *that*...?" Boroths muttered, a look of disbelief on his face. "They're deranged. I really may have hired the wrong killer for this job."

Th-Though of course, as they said, if Ars Louvent is in critical condition, then House Louvent must be in a state of chaos. This truly is the moment to press the attack. Much as it pains me to look like I'm taking that madman's advice...I can't let my emotions keep me from doing what needs to be done, Boroths thought. He knew, deep down, that the strategy Zetsu had proposed was sound. *But before anything else, I must confirm the situation. I'll determine what sort of state House Louvent is in, and if the situation is advantageous enough, I'll send my troops to storm Castle Canarre at once. If Canarre's leadership is in a state of disarray, they won't be equipped to respond to an attack and the castle will fall with ease.*

With that plan in mind, Boroths ordered his followers to determine the current state of House Louvent on the double.

○

"Ars..." Licia muttered to herself as she stood by Ars's bedside, looking down upon him. He looked so terribly feeble, it was almost painful to watch him. His cheeks were gaunt, and his breath came in pained gasps. He'd regained consciousness to a degree two days before, but for the past day his eyes had remained closed, and he didn't respond at all when prompted.

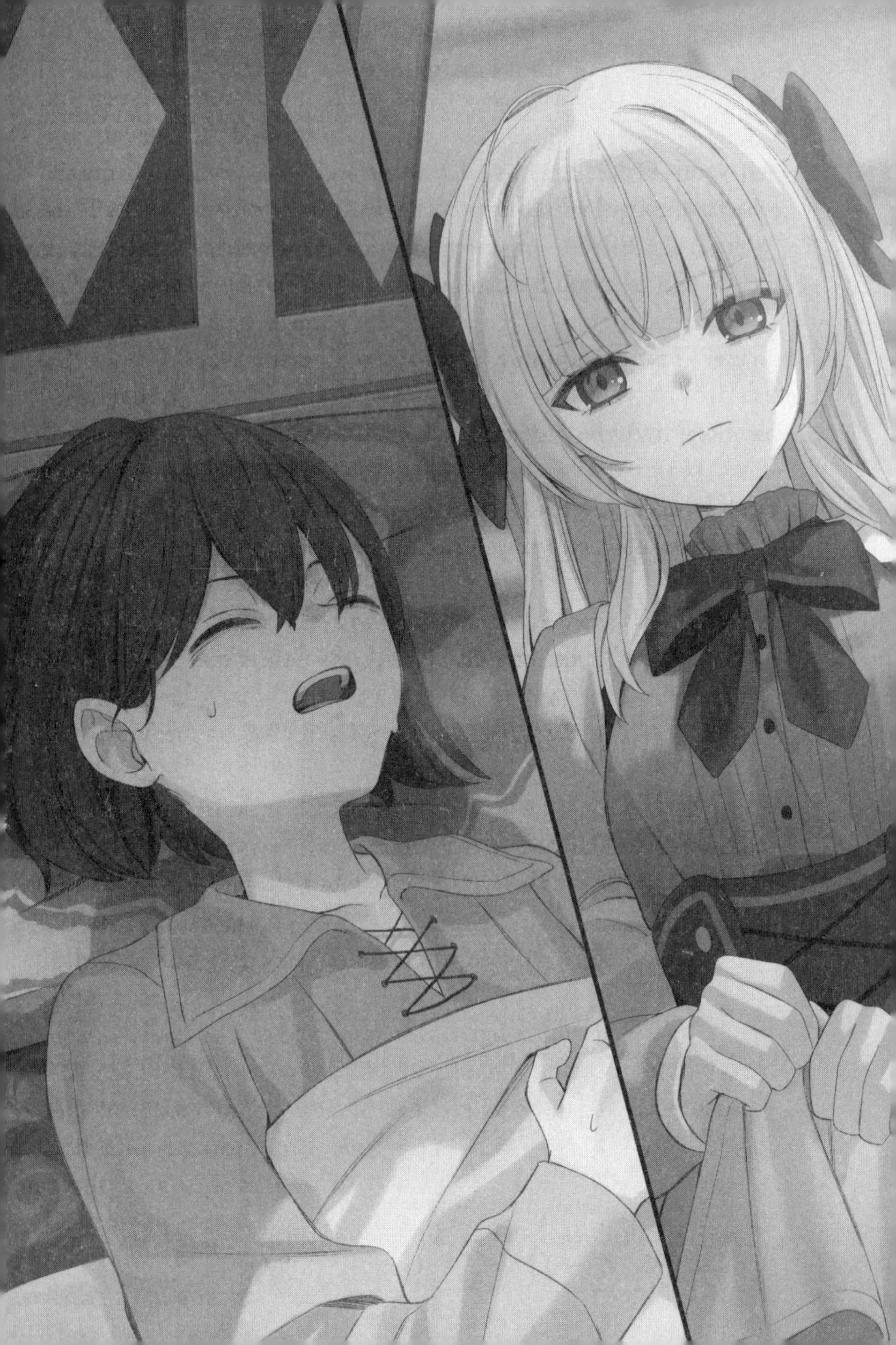

I WILL USE MY APPRAISAL SKILL TO RISE IN THE WORLD

Licia knew there was a chance that Ars didn't have long left. The physician had told her that in no uncertain terms. She'd been by Ars's side ever since they returned to Canarre, nursing him day and night. The castle's maids had told her that they could take care of him, and that she'd be better off getting some rest, but Licia had insisted on doing everything herself, paying their advice no heed.

She'd been nursing him for days now, with no time for rest, and her own exhaustion was plain to see. Her eyes were red and swollen from the countless times she'd broken down in tears, and dark bags hung beneath them thanks to her lack of sleep. Her hair was a disheveled mess, as well. It only took one look to know that she was nearing her limits, both physically and mentally.

"Lady Licia... It's high time you allowed yourself to rest. Your own health will suffer if you carry on like this," said Castle Canarre's court physician, Mike Mains. He was a slender, middle-aged man with a naturally gentle look in his eyes that matched his warm and caring personality well. It was very rare to see him angry.

"I'm afraid that isn't an option for me," said Licia. "Ars is suffering so terribly. How could I, his wife, rest at a time like this...?"

"Perhaps...but if you were to collapse, My Lady—"

"I'm perfectly all right, thank you," Licia said.

It was clear that she was putting on a front. The truth was that she *was* on the verge of collapse. Still, she couldn't bring herself to leave Ars's side while he was suffering. Mike knew all of this, and found himself unable to say another word.

"I'll tend to Ars," said Licia. "Please help Rosell with his work in the meantime."

"Understood, My Lady."

Rosell was still hard at work researching the poison Ars had been afflicted with. Mike left the room Ars was being kept in, and hurried to join the research effort. That left Licia and Ars alone in the chamber.

Licia took Ars's hand in hers. His body temperature had fallen, and his hand was terribly cold—especially so when she remembered how warm his hands had always felt before.

"You told me that you'd leave House Louvent in my hands, Ars...but I can't even bear to imagine living on in a world without you. I can't do it," Licia said as tears streamed down her cheeks. She'd wept so many times over the past several days, and yet her tears still showed no sign of running dry. "So, please—come back to me soon..." she whispered, barely managing to squeeze out her pained request.

Ars showed no reaction to her words at all. He just laid there, eyes closed, his breath as strained as ever.

○

Kreiz, Wren, and their pet Rio were walking through the castle's corridors together. Rio had grown considerably since joining the family, and now stood nearly as tall as Kreiz and Wren's chests. The fox was roughly the size of a particularly large dog now.

"Ars is still sick, huh? I hope he gets better soon! I wanna play again!" Kreiz grumbled with a slight pout.

Wren, who was walking beside him, seemed much more concerned. The look on her face was grim.

"You wanna play with our brother too, right, Rio?" said Kreiz.

Rio yipped happily, almost as if it was responding to his question.

"Kreiz, our brother..." Wren began, but her words caught in her throat. Unlike Kreiz, who was very much the boy he looked,

I WILL USE MY APPRAISAL SKILL TO RISE IN THE WORLD

Wren was a remarkably clever and emotionally mature young woman. She understood how dangerous of a state her elder brother was in, and knew there was a chance that she might never speak with him again. "...If something happened to our brother, you would be the next head of House Louvent," she finally said.

"Ha ha—what do you mean, 'if something happened'? He'll be better in no time, trust me!" Kreiz said with a smile. He seemed to think that Wren was just joking with him, and genuinely believed that Ars was sure to recover.

"Don't *laugh*!" Wren shouted. "Listen to me! If our brother dies, we won't have time to be sad! You'll have to be the head of House Louvent, and lead all of our brother's retainers! That, Kreiz, is why you need to be ready. You need to be prepared to act right away when the time comes. I know it's going to be hard for you, and I know you won't feel like you're ready for it, but I'll be there to help."

The look on Wren's face was mature beyond her years. You would never imagine that she was a little girl who hadn't even celebrated her tenth birthday.

"A-As if that would ever happen! You're worrying too much!" Kreiz shouted back.

"You're just being naive!"

"What's that even mean?! Do you *want* Ars to die, or something?!"

"I-I never said anything like that!"

The twins were now both red in the face as they openly screamed at each other. Both of them were on the verge of tears. As different as their personalities were, it was very rare for them to actually fight in any real sense of the word. This was the first time one of their disagreements had escalated this badly.

"I don't wanna be the stupid head of the house! I'm gonna become the strongest warrior ever and help Ars make House Louvent the best! He *can't* die now!" Kreiz roared as loudly as he possibly could.

Wren didn't so much as flinch in the face of her brother's outburst, staring him straight in the eye as she shouted back. "Listen to me, Kreiz! If Ars dies, then we can't be kids anymore! We'll have to come together as a family and support House Louvent ourselves!"

"I don't understand any of this stupid stuff, and Ars wouldn't die no matter what! Never, ever say that to me again!"

"Kreiz!" Wren shouted, but her brother ignored her, storming off in a rage.

Rio let out a sad little whimper. The fox could tell that something bad was happening.

"Kreiz, you stupid little... I don't want to think about him dying either, you know...?" Wren muttered as tears finally began to trickle down her cheeks.

Rio could tell how sad she was, and made another whimpering noise as it nuzzled up against her, then gently licked the tears from her cheeks.

"You're so nice, Rio..." Wren muttered. She pressed herself into Rio, shoulders trembling as the fox's fur muffled the sound of her sobs.

○

Rietz Muses sat in the study of Castle Canarre, brow furrowed as he looked over a stack of documents. Rietz was usually an affable man with a friendly smile, but now the look in his eyes was so sharp and intense, it would likely frighten anyone who happened to see it. The bags beneath his eyes made him look like he hadn't been sleeping enough recently, and in truth, he'd barely slept at all for days on end. He'd been consumed by his work, pressing on without so much as taking a break. To him, the idea of resting while his lord Ars laid on the verge of death was simply unthinkable.

"Sir Rietz? Mister Pham is here to see you," one of the castle's servants reported.

"Send him in," Rietz said without hesitation.

Moments later, Pham hurried into the chamber.

"Have you learned anything?" asked Reitz.

"Sure have…" said Pham. "Most likely, the assassin was acting under Seitz's orders. Seems Boroths Heigand's underlings have been searching for an assassin named Zetsu recently."

"I see. So it was Seitz… There was always a chance that another Missian noble had commissioned the deed, but Seitz did seem the most likely suspect," Rietz said. His tone sounded neutral at first, but listening closer would reveal the deep-seated rage that his words were laced with. "Zetsu, you said? I've heard that name. They're supposed to be a very skilled killer."

"In this business, having your name be known far and wide isn't exactly a sign you're great at your job…but it looks like Zetsu really is as good as they say," said Pham.

"Have you been able to take them into custody?"

"No. I searched all over Seitz, but didn't find any sign of them. My people have been searching other likely places, but they haven't turned up anything either. I just met up with them to go over our info and hash out a new plan for how we'll search from now on."

"You what…? This is no time to be laying careful plans and dragging our heels! Finding the assassin is our top priority!" Rietz shouted.

His obsession with catching the assassin was not rooted in a desire for revenge. Rather, Rietz believed that catching Zetsu was their best possible option for treating Ars's condition. Few people would carry a poison that they didn't have an antidote to. One needed an antidote to offer when using poison as a threat, after all. Assassins who were purely concerned with killing didn't have a strict need for such antidotes, of course, but the slightest mistake when applying poison could prove fatal without an antidote handy, meaning they were still useful even in those cases.

As such, Rietz believed that catching the assassin could be his ticket to an antidote for Ars. Even if Zetsu didn't have an antidote on hand, he could at least interrogate them and find out what sort of poison it was. That would make the process of manufacturing an antidote from scratch much less daunting.

"I know that, but we're dealing with a master assassin," said Pham. "This isn't someone who'll leave a trail we can follow that easily."

"What choice do we have...? It's either find them, or let Lord Ars perish!" Rietz snapped, venting all his fury on Pham before pausing to take a deep breath and collect himself. "I... My apologies. I lost my composure. I understand that the killer will not be easy to find, yes," he continued. He'd realized that he was only lashing out, and knew that he had to apologize.

"Don't worry about it," said Pham. "Ars wouldn't be in danger at all if I hadn't messed up. Blame me all you want."

"No...it wasn't your fault. I should have been there to protect him...and I should have realized how much I was relying on Lord Ars's ability to recruit the right people without error," said Rietz. He fully believed that Ars had only been hurt because he'd made the wrong call, and regretted it deeply.

"Anyway," said Pham, "no time to waste. I'm getting back to my

I WILL USE MY APPRAISAL SKILL TO RISE IN THE WORLD

search."

"Good... I'm counting on you," said Rietz.

With that, Pham left the room. Just a moment later, Rosell said "Excuse me," as he stepped inside.

"Just grabbing some resources from in here," Rosell explained. The study was full of texts of all varieties, some of which Rosell needed for his research into antidote creation.

"Understood. I'll come help with the antidote as soon as I've finished my business here," said Rietz. He wasn't as well-versed in medicine as Rosell was, but he did have a baseline of knowledge, and had been helping whenever he could spare a moment.

"No, no, you don't have to do that! You should get some rest, Mister Rietz!" Rosell protested.

"There's no time for me to—"

"Do you know how terrible you look right now?! I'm focused on making an antidote, sure, but you've been doing all of your usual work, ordering around Pham and his spies, *and* searching through all the resources on poison you can find! There's no way you've gotten any sleep lately! Leave the antidote to me, and rest while you can, please!"

"I can't. Resting is off the table for me..."

"If you collapse, then House Louvent will completely fall apart!" said Rosell. "I get it, okay? I want to work as hard as I can for Ars too..."

Rietz fell silent. From Rosell's perspective, he was very clearly pushing himself. Rietz always seemed to keep busy, but the truth is that he was quite careful about getting the rest he needed. That still meant that his workload was heavy enough to crush an average person, of course, but Rietz was far from average and had the sheer endurance to get it all done without trouble. Not even he, however, could handle the number of tasks that currently rested on his shoulders, and Rosell was afraid that if nothing changed, there were sure to be terrible consequences.

"What happens to me isn't important," said Rietz. "All that matters is saving Lord Ars…"

"Of course it's important! I don't want to have to say this out loud, but if Ars dies, or if he can't carry on as the head of House Louvent after he wakes up, you're going to have to lead in his place," said Rosell.

"Me? You think *I* would lead House Louvent if Lord Ars passed? That's outrageous. It would never happen. *Never*," Rietz said with absolute confidence. "I'm a Malkan. No matter how well-known my capabilities might be, there's no changing my origins. It was only because Lord Ars found me—because he was there to support me—that I was able to rise to a position of such importance in House Louvent. If he weren't around, I would inevitably be cast to the wayside."

"Th-That's not true! Everyone knows how incredible you are, and that includes me!" shouted Rosell.

"Maybe you do, but the bulk of Canarre's citizens don't. Without Lord Ars around, my existence loses all worth and meaning," Rietz said with a smile tinged with self-loathing.

Even after becoming a retainer of House Louvent—even from those whose recognition he'd earned—Rietz had been looked upon with contempt time and time again. Not everyone viewed him with that sort of disdain, of course, but Rietz had no confidence that he would be able to carry on within House Louvent if Ars's influence were to vanish.

"You're overthinking this! That's not true at all. Calm down and

I WILL USE MY APPRAISAL SKILL TO RISE IN THE WORLD

look at the situation rationally, please!"

Rosell knew how highly Rietz's compatriots valued him. He knew that Rietz's words were coming from a place of dejection and pessimism.

"That's not the only reason why I won't be able to lead House Louvent," said Rietz. "If Lord Ars dies...I intend to travel to Seitz and kill Boroths Heigand, the man who hired the assassin. I don't imagine I'll be able to return to Canarre after my work is done."

"Wh-What are you saying?!" said Rosell. "You're planning on taking revenge on him?!"

"Yes. I don't mean to involve our troops in the effort, of course. I wouldn't waste their lives in a hopeless battle. I'll infiltrate the duchy and kill him myself. No need to worry—I think you appreciate how capable in a battle I am. I won't let him escape."

"I'm not worried about whether or not you'll manage to kill him! There's no way Ars would want you to risk your life for a vengeance killing in his name!"

"And yet that's all that I could possibly do for him."

"Are you listening to yourself...?"

The look in Rietz's eyes was as serious as could be. He believed every word that came out of his mouth, and Rosell found himself unable to say anything else to bring him around.

"Of course," said Rietz, "Lord Ars will not die, one way or another. There's no particular need for us to discuss the circumstances following his passing in the first place."

"Y-Yeah. Yeah, you're right," said Rosell.

"All right! I'm finished with these papers, and ready to help with the antidote now," said Rietz, who hadn't stopped working at any point throughout his conversation with Rosell. His multitasking capabilities were a force to be reckoned with...but the moment he stood up, his field of vision suddenly distorted.

"Wha...?!"

Suddenly, Rietz's strength seemed to abandon him. His vision grew more and more blurred until he couldn't see anything at all. His legs were in just as poor of shape, and he collapsed to the ground on the spot.

"Mister Rietz!"

Rosell's frantic shout reverberated through the study.

○

"A clear case of overwork. It's no wonder he'd collapse after carrying on for that long without sleep," said Mike, the court physician.

The moment Reitz collapsed, Rosell had called out for the castle's servants and had them carry him to a nearby sickroom, after which he'd been brought to the castle clinic for a formal diagnosis. Rosell was relieved to learn that Rietz wasn't seriously ill, but it seemed clear that he'd overworked himself so severely he'd be in no condition to exert himself for some time.

Wh-What're we going to do without Mister Rietz?! thought Rosell. *Lady Licia's too busy taking care of Ars to get any work done, so...sh-should I be giving orders to everyone now?! I can't! I have to keep working on my antidote! What am I supposed to do?!*

Rosell clutched at his head as his panic overtook him. He'd always been a pessimist, but the crisis that he found himself faced with now was so dire that even a generally positive person would find themselves at a loss for upsides to point out.

"I, umm, believe that you should keep working on your antidote, Rosell," said Mike. "Rietz is only suffering from overwork,

I WILL USE MY APPRAISAL SKILL TO RISE IN THE WORLD

so he'll be right as rain before too long... Our domestic affairs will be held up for a few days, yes, but I don't imagine that any terrible issues will crop up in the meantime."

"Ugh... R-Right, yeah. That makes sense," said Rosell. Mike's advice had helped him calm down, at least a little.

I'll save Ars, no matter what. There's no way I'm letting him die!

Rosell clenched his fists as he swore to see his work through. Rietz and Licia—two people who he had believed had wills so strong they could never be shaken—had been thrown into a state of unrest thanks to Ars's peril. For the sake of House Louvent's future, Rosell knew he couldn't allow Ars to die, no matter what happened. And, above all else, Rosell wished from the bottom of his heart to save his friend, his benefactor, and the only lord he'd ever known.

"I'll make an antidote, no matter what it takes. Please look after Mister Rietz in the meantime!" said Rosell.

"Understood," replied Mike.

With that, Rosell left the sickroom.

Ars is the only one who could tell that I was talented. Now it's my turn to use that talent to make an antidote and save him!

Rosell set off to resume his research, his motivation as high as it had ever been.

○

Meanwhile, in Canarre's magical training ground, Charlotte and Musia were taking a break from their day's exercises.

"I can't stop worrying about Lord Ars," Musia muttered dejectedly. The news that Ars's condition was grave had been making the rounds among his retainers, and had made it to her recently.

"Huh? Oh, he'll be fine. Just give it a few days, and he'll be right back to normal again," said Charlotte.

Her whimsical attitude, at least, hadn't changed a bit. It was like she had absolute, unshakable faith that Ars would recover. The thought that he might not make it didn't seem to have crossed her mind in the slightest.

"A-Are you really sure...? I've heard that he's in a very risky state right now," said Musia.

"You're such a worrywart, y'know that?" Charlotte replied.

"W-Well, of course I'm worried! It's natural to worry when things are this bad! I want to know how *you* can act like nothing's wrong at all!"

"Hmm. Not much to it, really. I just think he'll get better, that's all. Lord Ars is a pretty big deal when all's said and done, right? He's not the sort of person who'd die like this," Charlotte bluntly replied.

Charlotte acted like she had absolute confidence in her logic, and she'd barely even had to think about it before giving her answer. Her claim was almost totally baseless, but strangely enough, Musia found herself believing that Charlotte might actually be right.

"If he does die, though... I'll go murder the person who attacked him and whoever hired 'em myself," Charlotte added with a look of purest fury on her face.

Musia gulped as she took in Charlotte's expression. She'd never seen Charlotte look truly enraged before—not even in the heat of battle—and a sense of dread came over her as she witnessed it now.

"I bet Rietz'll say he's gonna go kill them too, but I'm not letting him get them before I do. I'll burn them to ash, then burn the ashes

I WILL USE MY APPRAISAL SKILL TO RISE IN THE WORLD

till nothing's left at all," said Charlotte.

Musia knew that Charlotte wasn't kidding or exaggerating, and knew that nothing could be done to stop her. She couldn't utter a word in protest.

"'Course, Lord Ars isn't gonna die in the first place, so it's not like that really matters anyway," Charlotte declared, the rage vanishing from her expression in an instant. The tension that had overtaken the conversation drained away, replaced by a much more relaxed air. "Things might still be pretty bad right now, though. Seitz might attack now that Lord Ars is bedridden."

"Huh? How in the world do you know that?" Musia asked, shocked by what she'd just heard. She'd never seen Charlotte do anything even close to predicting an enemy's movements before.

"Well, they're the ones who sent an assassin after him, right?" said Charlotte.

"Huh? Were they? Who did you hear that from?"

"I didn't. Seemed pretty obvious, though. No way they wouldn't want payback after how we thrashed 'em last time. It's what I'd do, for sure."

"Oh... So you're just speculating...?" Musia said with a tired sigh. Charlotte's assertions really were baseless, so that made sense.

"Seems Rietz collapsed a while back, too, so if Seitz attacked now, we might not have anyone who could take command," Charlotte added offhandedly.

"What?! Doesn't that mean we're in incredibly deep trouble?!" Musia shrieked, the color draining from her face.

"Guess I'll just have to do something about it myself," said Charlotte.

"What do you mean, 'something'...? What exactly would you do?"

"Hmm... Probably blast 'em to bits with my magic, to start. The rest'll work itself out, I figure."

"R-Really...? That's barely a plan at all..." moaned Musia.

"For now, though, we'd better make sure all our mages are ready to fight at the drop of a hat," said Charlottte.

"Y-Yes, of course," Musia agreed.

Charlotte quickly gave the order for all of her subordinate mages to be prepared to move out at any moment.

○

Maika and Rikuya walked through the corridors of Castle Canarre. Mireille had been keeping the Fujimiya siblings busy in Lamberg recently, but the moment she'd heard that Ars had been poisoned, she'd hurried to the castle on the double with the trio in tow.

"Is Takao still in the training grounds?" Rikuya asked.

"So it would seem," said Maika. "Apparently, Sir Braham requested that he join in their training session once more."

"Again?" Rikuya sighed. "Well, I suppose Braham's a capable fighter in his own right. I'm sure this will make for good practice for Takao as well."

"Indeed it will, particularly considering that Sir Braham seemed more motivated than ever."

"Did he, now? I guess he was part of Ars's guard detail when the attack happened. He probably feels responsible."

The siblings' expressions were somewhat grim as they walked along.

"We've certainly landed ourselves in a troublesome situation this time, haven't we?" Maika muttered.

"I guess we have. One minute we've become a lord's retainers, and the next, that lord is at death's door," Rikuya replied.

The two siblings were both at a loss. It hadn't even been a year since Rikuya, Maika, and Takao had agreed to serve House Louvent. The idea that their new lord would be fatally poisoned so soon was something none of them had anticipated.

"We owe Lord Ars a great debt," said Rikuya. "Even if he passes away, we'll stay in House Louvent's service. The question is, what will become of House Louvent if that comes to pass?"

"A troublesome question indeed... My Master's presence within House Louvent is great indeed. His brother is still young—too young to lead the House without great difficulties. His bride, meanwhile...seems to have experienced a tremendous mental blow as a consequence of the present circumstances. Sir Rietz, the most reliable source of guidance, has collapsed. Though there's much we still have yet to understand, it seems clear that Sir Rietz is firmly devoted to my Master. Who can say what actions he would take should my Master pass on...?"

"Oh, right—Rietz did collapse, didn't he...? From the sound of it, he was pushing himself way beyond his limits. I wish we could've done something to help," Rikuya said with a regretful grimace. Having just joined House Louvent, he and his siblings had yet to be entrusted with any majorly significant work. They simply weren't ready to help Rietz in that way.

"Sir Rosell is a remarkably sharp young man, but he is young indeed. He hasn't the ability to lead House Louvent just yet. Lady Mireille...hmm... Her capabilities are beyond dispute, but I wouldn't think that others would be so inclined to follow her... Moreover, she is a woman who keeps her thoughts exceptionally well-guarded. She may well choose to abandon House Louvent and move along the moment Master passes. Charlotte, however, is a presence worth considering. Not only is she remarkably capable, she has the firm and unyielding heart of a warrior. Even if Seitz were to invade in our weakest moment, with her fighting on our side, they'll be hard pressed to claim the castle quickly."

"You're right about Charlotte's magic being incredible, but I don't think she has what it takes to bring House Louvent together," noted Rikuya.

"True," said Maika. "We could hardly expect her to help in that area."

"What should we be doing, though?"

"Hmm. Having only just entered the House's service, setting it back on the right path will be a difficult task for us. Still, we've no choice but to do what we can," Maika concluded with a troubled frown.

"Do you have any ideas about what sort of poison they might've used on Lord Ars?" asked Rikuya.

"What a strange question. If I did, would I not have mentioned it before anything else? Besides, I have little to no knowledge when it comes to poisons. Nor am I knowledgeable in the field of medicine, meaning there's nothing I can do to help Sir Rosell. The half-baked theories that I could contribute would do nothing but get in his way. It seems that focusing my studies so single-mindedly upon tactics was a poor decision," Maika sighed regretfully.

"Fair enough," said Rikuya. "Regardless, I have the strangest feeling that Lord Ars is going to survive. I have a feeling that when all of this is over, we'll be kicking ourselves for worrying for no good reason."

"How can you be so certain?"

"Instinct," said Rikuya. His expression was as earnest as could be.

I WILL USE MY APPRAISAL SKILL TO RISE IN THE WORLD

"Instinct...?" repeated Maika. "And *your* instincts, meaning... it's hardly guaranteed to prove true."

"Huh? Y-You think?"

"Indeed. Your instincts guide you true roughly half of the time. I couldn't describe them as good or bad."

"Y-You're saying that even my instincts are perfectly average?!"

"Actually, that's not what I said at all..." Maika sighed, shaking her head at her brother's overreaction. "In this case, however, I believe that your instincts will prove accurate."

"Why do you say that?"

"Instinct."

"Right. Instinct. Well, yours always seem to lead us in the right direction."

"But of course. I am all but infallible! Unlike you."

"...Did you really need to share that last part?" Rikuya said with a bitter smile as he watched his sister strike a confident pose.

○

Braham and Takao were engaged in a mock duel in Castle Canarre's training grounds. Braham wielded a large, two-handed wooden sword, while Takao held a smaller sword in one hand and a shield in the other, both also made of wood.

Takao carefully guarded himself with his shield, warding off Braham's ferocious offensive and slipping in a swift strike of his own whenever he had the opportunity. Both fighters displayed remarkable skill throughout the exchange of blows, but in the end, Takao was unable to withstand Braham's relentless strikes and was thrown off-balance.

"Gotcha now!" shouted Braham.

Takao took in a sharp breath as Braham swung for his neck, stopping at the last second before his sword made contact.

"That's a win for me!" Braham declared.

"It's my loss..." Takao said. He was a little frustrated, but still freely admitted his defeat.

"All right! Let's fight another round!" said Braham.

"I-I'm getting hungry, actually," Takao protested. His words were punctuated by his stomach picking that moment to growl loudly.

"Didn't you just finish eating something a minute ago?" asked Braham.

"That was a snack," said Takao. "I have to eat a real meal, or I won't be able to keep moving."

Takao certainly looked as listless as he claimed to be. Braham, however, could have sworn that the so-called snack his training partner had eaten shortly beforehand had been what most people would call a full meal. He found himself wondering if he'd been seeing things.

"O-Okay, then... I guess you can't fight on an empty stomach... All right! Let's get some bread in here!" shouted Braham, content to assume he'd misremembered and take Takao at his word. Braham sent out a few of the soldiers waiting in the wings to bring a meal.

"I want rice balls..." Takao groaned.

"Rice balls? What're those?" asked Braham. He'd never heard of a food with a name like that before.

"Oh, right...you don't have them here. I guess I have to make do with bread..." Takao sighed with visible disappointment.

"What do you mean, make do?! Bread's the best!" Braham snapped back. "Anyway, while I'm waiting for you to finish eating... Zaht! You're sparring me next!"

I WILL USE MY APPRAISAL SKILL TO RISE IN THE WORLD

"No," Zaht called out from the room he was resting in. "How many rounds are you planning on having me fight today? I'm not as young and sprightly as you, Captain—have some consideration for your elders."

"Quit acting like some sorta senior citizen and get your butt over here!"

"My body's like a senior citizen's compared to yours, anyway. Fighting another round with you right now would just get me hurt, so I'll decline, thank you very much. Maybe you could try taking a break too, or train on your own, if you just can't stomach the thought. Everyone else is as tired as I am."

All of the soldiers who were present in the training grounds nodded vigorously in agreement. They'd all been forced to play along with Braham's excess of training, and were as exhausted as you could be without literally passing out. Braham, however—the one man who'd been moving that whole time—showed no signs of fatigue at all. His endurance was superhuman.

"Grrr... Fine! I'll just practice on my own, then," Braham conceded. He knew that forcing his soldiers to train with him would risk losing their loyalty, so he decided to back down for the time being. He made good on his word, though—even if everyone else was resting, taking a break simply wasn't an option in his mind, so he set about training on his own.

"Ahh, I'm beat!"

Several hours later, even Braham's seemingly endless well of stamina was depleted and he collapsed in the center of the training grounds. He did, as it turned out, have limits.

"Took you long enough," called out Zaht.

"Oh! You're still here?" Braham replied, a little surprised. All the other soldiers had long since left, and Braham had assumed that Zaht had gone with them.

"I was getting in some extra training too, that's all—though unlike you, I interspersed my practice sessions with proper rest."

"You're taking this pretty seriously all of a sudden, huh?"

"I've always taken my training seriously."

"You sure about that...?" Braham asked, cocking his head.

"Anyway," said Zaht, "I have something to discuss with you, and since you just wouldn't stop training, I had to find some way to kill time while I waited."

"Something to discuss with me? What?"

"I can't believe you have to ask. The soldiers have been complaining about our training regimen lately. We've been putting all of our focus into raising our troops' personal combat skills, but we haven't done any exercises to improve our teamwork as a unit at all, and that's a problem. To make matters worse, those solo drills you've been running everyone through have been a brutal gauntlet. At this rate, our morale and combat capability as a unit will suffer."

"Ugh... But I have to get stronger!" Braham protested.

"Because you failed to protect Lord Ars?" asked Zaht.

Braham hesitated. "Right," he eventually said with a nod. "Lord Ars dragged me out of prison and gave me a job as his retainer. I owe him everything. I thought it was only natural he'd recruited me at first, considering how talented I am, but I've started to realize lately that that's not quite right. I mean, if he hadn't been there back then, I would've either been executed like all the other soldiers or driven out of the army for being useless. Probably would've ended up being a bandit or something. I owe Lord Ars—more than I could ever pay him back—but I couldn't even protect him when push came to shove. I need to get stronger...way, *way* stronger than I am now,"

I WILL USE MY APPRAISAL SKILL TO RISE IN THE WORLD

Braham said, his teeth gritted with frustration.

"I never thought the day would come when you'd think something through this seriously," Zaht commented.

"I-I'm always serious, dangit! And besides, you were part of our party too back then, so you should've been guarding him too! You've gotta understand how I feel, right?!"

"Unfortunately, no, I do not."

"What?" Braham asked as he turned a sharp glare upon Zaht.

"Regretting past mistakes never helps amend them," said Zaht. "Even if I trained like a madman and grew stronger, it wouldn't change the fact that we failed to protect Lord Ars."

"I-I know that! I'm training so that I'll be strong enough to protect him next time!"

"You don't get it, Captain. You're so consumed by your regrets, you've lost sight of what you should actually be doing right now. Is prioritizing your own training so much that our unit loses the ability to fight in coordination really the right thing to do for the sake of House Louvent? I'd like you to think that through one more time."

"Ugh..." Braham grunted. He was frustrated, and it wasn't hard to see it, but deep down, he knew that Zaht was right.

No matter the circumstances, he'd been entrusted with leadership over House Louvent's most elite soldiers, and that meant that he had to prioritize keeping their morale high and their skills polished above all else. Braham understood that...but still, he couldn't bring himself to look past the fact that he'd been too weak to protect his lord. He couldn't allow himself to remain that way.

"No need to panic, in any case," said Zaht. "You're still young, and Lord Ars knows how talented you are. Getting in a rush and overloading yourself with training drills isn't even necessary—you'll get stronger just by training like a normal person."

"Yeah...you're right. I'll switch back to our usual training sessions starting tomorrow," Braham conceded. He was finally, truly reflecting on his mistakes.

○

Well. I certainly didn't see this coming.

Thomas Grunzeon was alone in one of Castle Canarre's chambers, mulling over the current state of affairs at great length. He was not a formal retainer of House Louvent. Although he led Canarre's soldiers in training drills and taught lessons to the Louvent retainers, he had yet to cross the final line of pledging his own service.

Having seen firsthand how talented House Louvent's retainers were, however, he had to concede that Ars's power was genuine. On some level, he found himself thinking that being Ars's retainer himself would be a sound move. No sooner had that thought crossed his mind, however, than news of Ars's poisoning reached his ears.

Who would have sent the assassin...? Seitz seems the most likely culprit, but you'd think they would have targeted Rietz or Charlotte—the most direct and visible threats—rather than their lord. If Seitz truly was responsible, it stands to reason that they've done a very thorough investigation of the state of things in Canarre, Thomas thought to himself. He hadn't asked Rietz who had hired the assassin, but given how it had played out, it was easy enough for him to guess.

I hate to admit it, but Mireille has a talent for making the right calls. I was starting to think that she was right, and that the kid would take over all of Missian someday...but it seems she was off the mark this time.

Thomas freely acknowledged his sister's abilities. He despised

I WILL USE MY APPRAISAL SKILL TO RISE IN THE WORLD

her personality, and had no interest in forging a friendly relationship with her, but her skill, at least, he could accept.

All that talent he built up will still be here even if the kid dies...but I have a feeling it just won't work out without him around. That means I won't have any reason to stick around with House Louvent. It might be time to start searching for a lord in another duchy that I could serve...

Thomas's goal was to take revenge on Couran, the man who had slain the one lord Thomas felt truly loyal to, Vasmarque. He knew that without entering into a lord's service, that goal would remain forever out of reach. Whether or not he could find a lord who would take him in the first place was in question, but he couldn't afford to just give up.

I guess the kid's not dead just yet, anyway. I'll stick around and see how things play out for the time being.

Chapter 4:
An Unexpected Meeting

I, Ars Louvent, awakened to find myself floating somewhere in the vicinity of my chamber's ceiling. I acknowledge that that's a very confusing situation to wake up to, and one might wonder what in the world I was talking about, but there's really no other way to describe it. I had spent a lengthy span of time following my poisoning drifting in and out of sleep, unsure whether what I was seeing was a dream or reality, and the next thing I knew, I was staring at the ceiling from point-blank range.

My best, most unfortunate guess was that my spirit no longer occupied my body. Thankfully, being in that state meant that I no longer felt any pain at all, which was quite the relief...though on reflection, that probably wasn't something to be thankful for at all. If my spirit had departed from my body, I was, in the best case, on the verge of death.

That said, I didn't know for sure that I couldn't return to my body, so I wasn't quite prepared to declare myself dead as a doorknob just yet. From what I could tell, my court physician had yet to declare me legally deceased. My body was still functioning—there was just no telling when it might stop.

Looking down, I could see my own body. I was gaunt, and the skin of my face had a ghastly, blueish pallor to it. It was the face of an infirm young man who could easily pass away at any second. I looked like my spirit had departed me...which, well, it apparently literally had.

Licia had been watching over me up until just recently, but at the moment, she wasn't present. She'd nursed me for so long without rest that she'd taken ill herself, apparently. I felt terrible thinking that she'd put her own health at risk for my sake. The court physician, Mike, was currently taking care of me in her stead.

I quickly learned that I couldn't move very far from my body, even in my new ghostly form. I was stuck in the room, and couldn't move any lower than I was currently floating, either. All I could do was hover by the ceiling—the floor was totally out of reach.

I had to wonder: would I make it through this? If I was being completely honest, from an outside perspective, I couldn't give myself very high odds of survival. Would my body even last if I remained unconscious? I couldn't eat when I was passed out, and IV drips were way beyond this world's level of technology. I could see myself lasting a little while longer if there was some way to feed me, but if not, it wouldn't be surprising if I wasted away in no time.

The problem was that I had no clue how to go about returning to my body. Even if I could, and managed to wake up for long enough to eat, it wouldn't get rid of the poison coursing through my veins. It might just prolong my suffering, really, which seemed pretty pointless to me.

I'd already died once, but my first time was very abrupt, and I'd already been reincarnated by the time I'd realized what was even happening. The fact that I'd died had never really sunk in fully. Still, it was an undeniable fact that the version of me who had been born and raised in Japan had died. My life in this world had only begun after my first passing. With that in mind, it wasn't too terribly hard

I WILL USE MY APPRAISAL SKILL TO RISE IN THE WORLD

to accept another death.

My little brother Kreiz was still young, and I didn't think he'd have much luck leading House Louvent at the moment, but my retainers were capable enough that even without me, I had a feeling the House would carry on just fine. Leaving Licia behind was something that weighed heavily on me—she seemed devastated by what had happened to me—but I knew she had what it took to move on eventually. The thought that I'd never be able to speak with her again, however, made me so sad it actually brought me to tears. They flowed down my cheeks, dripping toward the floor before disintegrating into particles of light midair and vanishing.

Well, I guess this means ghosts can still cry.

"...Ars."

Suddenly, someone called my name from behind me. It rang out in the familiar voice of a man who I hadn't spoken to in a long, long time. I spun about...and gasped with shock.

A man stood before me. He had golden-blonde hair, a sharp look in his eyes, and a genuinely incredible physique. Just a glance was all it took to tell me that he was a powerful man. He was also my father, Raven Louvent.

"Father?!" I exclaimed. I think my shock was pretty understandable, considering. He looked a little bit younger than the father I remembered, but there was no mistaking him. He was, without a doubt, my father.

"Ars...? You can see me?!" my father asked. He seemed as surprised as I was. I gave him a nod. "I see... I've been by your side for so long, even after your soul left your body, and you never seemed to take notice of me at all...but now, things have changed."

"O-Oh, you were?" I asked.

He's been with me this whole time? I certainly never noticed him at

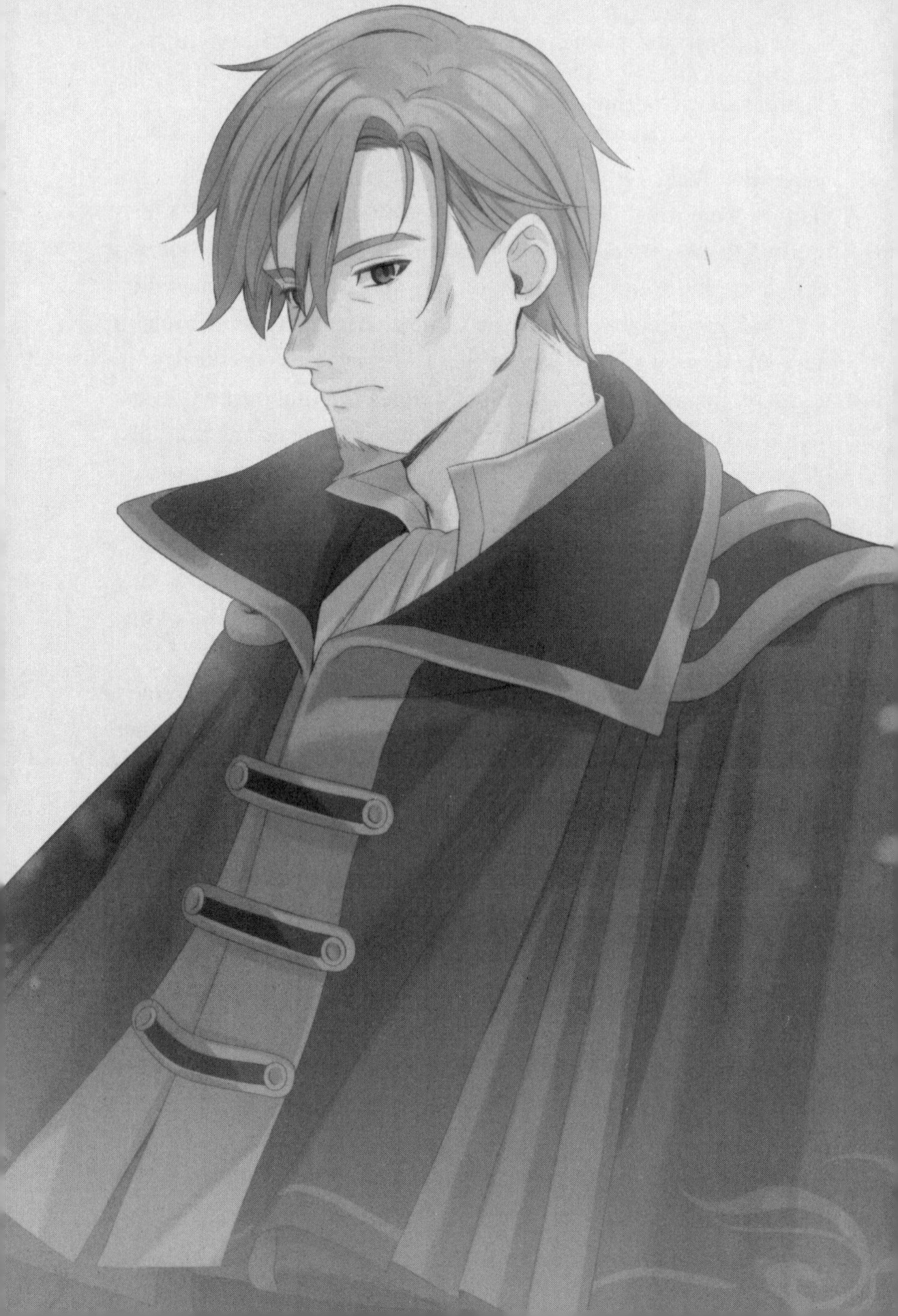

I WILL USE MY APPRAISAL SKILL TO RISE IN THE WORLD

all until now!

My father had died several years prior. It stood to reason that I was now talking with his ghost. Presumably, my own proximity to death was what had allowed me to finally catch sight of him.

"Ars...you've grown so much," my father said with a kind look in his eyes.

For a moment I was glad to see him again, but that thought didn't last long. I had sworn to my father that I would support House Louvent in his place, and at the rate things were going, it wasn't looking likely that I would make good on that oath.

"I'm sorry... I'm so sorry, Father," I said. Hanging my head and apologizing was the best I could do.

"What are you sorry for?" my father asked.

"What...? For meeting you like this, of course..."

"That's hardly an issue. Your soul may have left your body, but you're still alive, for now."

"B-But, I..."

"All the exceptional retainers you've found for yourself will work something out for the poison, I'm sure. To not believe in your followers' abilities is to fail in your duties as a lord."

It almost seemed like my father took my survival as a given. I, however, couldn't muster up that sort of positivity. Yes, Rosell and the others were working frantically to synthesize an antidote, but it didn't seem like the process was going well to me. They hadn't even managed to identify the poison, much less cure it. I believed in my retainers' abilities, but it was only natural that there would still be some things that were beyond them.

"Now then—it's been far too long since we've met, so let's have a talk, shall we? We'll be torn apart again in no time, so we should make the most of it while we can," my father suggested.

AS A REINCARNATED ARISTOCRAT

The idea that we'd be torn apart soon, I assumed, was founded on his insistent belief that I was not going to die. I had plenty of questions I wanted to ask him, though, so I was eager to take him up on his offer.

"All right," I said. "First, have you really been watching over me this whole time?"

"I have," said my father. "The moment I died I began to feel an incredible force attempting to pull me away. Where it wishes to take me, I cannot say, but by bringing all my willpower to bear I was able to brace myself and stay by your side."

"You *braced yourself*...?" I repeated in awe. I was fairly certain that normally, my father would have been whisked away to his next incarnation, just like I'd been reincarnated in this world. Instead, however, he had fought the forces of reincarnation through sheer willpower. Not even death had made the feats he accomplished any less absurd.

"No matter how incredible your power was, the fact remained that you were too young to reign over my territory," said my father. "I couldn't abide the thought of not watching over you—even if watching was all I could do. I was unable to intervene in the slightest."

"I'm sure you weren't...but just the thought that you were watching over me warms my heart."

After my father's death, I'd thought time after time that I wished he could see how House Louvent had grown and prospered under my leadership. I was glad to hear that he really had witnessed it all, even if only in spirit form.

"House Louvent has grown substantially thanks to you. To think—a Louvent, the Count of Canarre! By all rights, success like that should be unthinkable...but I always knew that my son had it

I WILL USE MY APPRAISAL SKILL TO RISE IN THE WORLD

in him to rise to untold heights."

My father wasn't being shy about doling out praise. He'd never complimented me that freely when he was alive, and I found myself feeling a little bashful as a result. At the same time, however, a murky gloom still lingered within me. I should have been happy to hear his praise, and yet part of me simply couldn't be.

"I trust that you'll continue to lead House Louvent into the future," said my father. "We both know that you can't afford to die now."

"Father... I've certainly found many talented followers, yes, but my ability to judge people is the only part about me that's grown at all. I've finally come to understand that I can't trust my power as completely as I have been up until now. I already have more than enough retainers who I can count on, as well. Maybe I don't need my power at all anymore."

I found myself speaking completely frankly to my father. The bulk of the so-called achievements that I had to my name had been my retainers' work, not my own. All I'd done was entrust them with the tasks I couldn't handle. To make matters worse, the knowledge that there was a way to obfuscate the results of my skill meant that I could no longer fully trust it. Perhaps, I thought, House Louvent no longer needed me at all.

"Kreiz is still young...but he'll be a more than worthy lord once he's grown up a little. As long as my retainers support him until that time comes, he'll get by just fine... So even if I die, I think everything will still work out..."

"Ars..." my father said. He raised a hand into the air...then brought it down on my head, hard.

"*Ow?!*" I yelped. I'd felt that impact very keenly. Apparently, ghosts still had a sense of pain. That was also, as a side note, the first time my father had ever hit me.

"Wh-What was that for...?" I whimpered. My father had been a stern man in many ways, but surprisingly, he'd never been the sort of man who'd raise a hand against his children to punish them.

"You know what it was for! Unbelievable," my father said with an exasperated shake of his head. "Here I was thinking you'd grown into a fine leader, but the truth is that you still haven't the foggiest idea what your followers are thinking."

I don't know what they're thinking? I mean, I'm sure that they'll be sad and confused when I'm gone, sure...but they're all more than capable enough to push through their mourning and move on.

This time, I didn't think my father was right at all. Just as that thought crossed my mind, the door to the chamber opened and someone stepped inside.

"Heya, kiddooo! Doin' okay? Hah, course y'aren't!"

It was Mireille, and she was holding a bottle, her face bright red. She was transparently three sheets to the wind.

"So that's Mireille..." said my father. "I'd heard plenty of rumors about her before the two of you met. I have to say, I was shocked when you took her in."

"Huh? You knew about Mireille already?" I asked.

"I did. Nothing detailed, mind you, but I knew that she racked up a remarkable number of scandals during her time as a baron, and was eventually banished from her territory. I only saw her once in person, and it was just a glance, but I still remember the look in her eyes. They were like the eyes of a blood-starved hound, ravenous for battle. Even I felt an instinctual urge to stay away from her."

"A-A blood-starved hound? Are we talking about the same Mireille?"

The Mireille I knew could be a little scary at times, sure, but

I WILL USE MY APPRAISAL SKILL TO RISE IN THE WORLD

she was quite cheerful for the most part. Maybe she'd softened up since she was young, and used to be much more intimidating? She would've had to have been, to make even my father hesitate...

"So, uhhh, think you could give us some privacy for a minute? I wanna talk to the kiddo one-on-one," Mireille asked Mike the court physician, who was in the room as well.

"Pardon?" Mike said, blinking with bewilderment. "I'm, uh, afraid that Lord Ars is currently unconscious."

"It's fine, don't worry 'bout it!"

"V-Very well, then."

Mike was practically chased out of the room by Mireille, who proceeded to sit down by my bed and take a long, gulping swing from her bottle. "Ahhh! Now *that's* the good stuff!" she said with a gasp.

"What do you suppose she's come here for?" asked my father.

"G-Good question," I replied.

Neither of us had the foggiest clue what Mireille was up to. She couldn't see us, and surely couldn't hear us either, so asking her was out of the question. We'd just have to watch and see where things went.

Mireille spent a moment staring at my face, slowly taking in my features.

"Hmm. Looks mosta the way dead already. Like his soul's already vacatin' the premises. This might be worse than I thought," said Mireille. That was a pretty shrewd insight on her part, considering my soul really had vacated my body. "'N if his soul's not in there, no point talkin' to his body, eh? His soul's gotta still be floatin' 'round somewhere, though."

Are her instincts just that sharp?

One way or another, Mireille was breaking down my current

situation with astonishing accuracy.

"And I bet the kiddo's soul...is right over there!"

Mireille pointed dramatically at a corner of the room. Specifically, the opposite corner from where me and my father were floating.

"Wrong! You have it backward!" I shouted. I knew she wouldn't hear me, but I just couldn't help myself.

"Is she capable, or not? She's a strangely hard woman to judge," my father said, sounding fed up with her already.

Mireille, meanwhile, had started talking to the empty corner of the ceiling she'd chosen.

"Gotta say, wasn't countin' on you gettin' messed up this bad, kiddo! Never know what the world's gonna throw at you next, eh?" Mireille said, pausing occasionally for another swig. She was speaking in the same tone she always did, but there was something oddly melancholic about her tone as well. "You die here, that's curtains for House Louvent. Considering' how lil' Licia's been lately, if you kick the bucket, she'll just keep worryin' until she collapses. Rietz'll prob'ly go berserk—guy's working himself to death already, too. Charlotte 'n Rosell don't have what it takes to bring the House together, and when everything's gone to hell, Seitz'll swoop in and clean up."

Mireille spoke about the fate of House Louvent following my demise as if it had nothing to do with her. The vision she had in mind was nothing like what I'd anticipated, either. There was always a chance that her speculation would prove wrong, but I knew that she was much smarter than I was, and most definitely had a broader, more developed perspective on the future than I ever could.

"As for me, well, you know what I'm like. Not the sorta person anyone winds up bein' loyal to. If I tried to pick up House Louvent, I'd bet only a fraction of your people'd follow me. My little brother

I WILL USE MY APPRAISAL SKILL TO RISE IN THE WORLD

Thomas'll pack up and leave the moment you're gone, too… And I can't see Couran lettin' House Louvent keep the seat of count without you around, so we'll be gettin' booted all the way back to Lamberg for sure. Yeah—we're pretty much toast. I might be sayin' my goodbyes to House Louvent sooner 'n I was planning on," Mireille said.

She looked disappointed by the thought, and I couldn't see any sign that she was either lying or kidding about anything she'd said. She'd meant every word of it. I wanted to tell her that she was wrong, and that things would turn out differently, but I couldn't even go check up on my other retainers, so how could I know that to begin with? My words would have had no basis even if they'd reached her.

"I bet you're thinkin' that we'll get by well enough without you, but you're dead wrong. Thing is, all those retainers you picked out? All that talent you unearthed? They were all a buncha nobodies. Look at me—if it hadn't been for you, I'd still be drinkin' one pub dry after another, wanderin' to who knows where. No other noble'd be mad enough to take in a woman with a reputation like mine. If you die, we'll all end up right back where we started: nowhere. Perfect place for nobodies like us," Mireille said, sounding disinterested in her own words. She paused to take a drink. "Ahh, what a bore this turned out to be. What'll I do next? Maybe I'll take this chance to say goodbye to Summerforth and see what else is out there."

She seemed to be thinking about what she'd do once I was dead now. It seemed that in her mind, my death meant the end of House Louvent was set in stone.

"It seems to me," my father said, "that Mireille has a far clearer perspective on the state of House Louvent than you do."

I didn't know what to say. I certainly couldn't disagree with him.

"Though I can't say I like the way she's assuming that you're sure to perish. No son of mine would die to a petty poison like this," my father added with an irritated scowl.

Is it just me, or has his time in the afterlife turned him into one of those parents who thinks their kids can do anything...?

"It looks like I can't let myself die after all, Father. I have to live, one way or another," I said.

The doubts that I'd felt just moments before had vanished. My death wouldn't only mean the decline of House Louvent—it had the potential to bring misfortune upon everyone who I'd recruited to serve me, as well. I had a responsibility to do right by them, and that meant that I couldn't let myself die.

Of course...I also had no idea what I could do to keep myself alive. I couldn't return to my body, so my only choice was to wait and hope that Rosell finished his antidote before that body perished. If I *could* find a way back to my physical form I might be able to buy a little time, but as things stood, I couldn't even approach it.

"Are you *still* hesitating?!" my father bellowed.

"Huh?! N-No, I'm not! I just don't know how to go back!" I frantically explained. Apparently, he'd taken my pausing to figure out how to get back to my body as a sign that I still had more doubts.

"You don't know how to get back? It's the simplest thing in the world: all you have to do is wish to live, then return to your body."

"I...huh?"

"I was gravely injured as well, once. I lost a tremendous quantity of blood, and my soul left my body, just as yours has. When that happened, I told myself over and over again that I would not die, prayed to live on, and forced my way back to my body. Then I lived. It's as simple as that."

It was one of the least practical explanations I'd ever heard. Then

I WILL USE MY APPRAISAL SKILL TO RISE IN THE WORLD

again, at the point where you're reduced to your disembodied soul, maybe putting some spirit into solving your problems was just about the only solution available to you? I was also, as a side note, shocked to learn that my father had gone through something that dramatic. I knew that he'd worked his way up from being a simple footsoldier to the bearer of a noble title, so on reflection, it seemed possible he'd had more than just one or two near-death experiences in his time.

"Of course, when I really did die in the end, nothing I did would let me come back. There's no way to resist when our time has come, I suppose," said my father.

His words brought me right back to the moment he'd died, and my heart ached as the memory overtook me. What was clear, anyway, was that if I didn't make it back to my body, I'd be dead for sure.

"Your time has not come yet, Ars. Now, go on. Return to your body."

"All right," I said. "I'll give it a try."

"Very good," said my father.

"I hope you'll keep watching over me, Father."

"That...is probably not possible, I'm afraid," my father said with an abashed shrug.

"Not possible...? But why?"

"As I told you before, I've resisted the pull of an immaterial force to remain by your side as a ghost. That pull is still present, and it won't be long before I lose the power to fight it. My remaining here is in defiance of the natural order, so really, things will just proceed the way they should have from the start."

I was speechless. That meant that my father would likely pass on and be reincarnated as someone entirely different. Who knew whether he would even keep his memories?

"Staring death in the eye is the sort of experience that makes a man grow, Ars. It did for me, and it will for you too. If you survive this experience, you'll be a man full grown in the truest sense of the phrase. You won't need me watching over you anymore."

"Father…"

My father looked me in the eye as he spoke. That ever-present sharpness of his gaze was still there, but now, it overflowed with kindness as well.

"Go on then, Ars," urged my father.

"I will," I said with a nod. "Goodbye, Father."

I will live.

I will survive, no matter what.

I poured my whole heart and soul into my wish, trying desperately to return to my body. I didn't seem to be moving, at first, but gradually, I began to draw closer and closer to my physical form.

"Graaahhhhhh!"

As I closed in on my body, an escalating and intense pain began to grow within me. Like my father's smack had taught me earlier, it was very possible to feel pain in spirit form.

I don't want to get any closer than this.

I just want the pain to end.

Negativity began to bloom within me. I pushed those feelings back

I WILL USE MY APPRAISAL SKILL TO RISE IN THE WORLD

down, though, shoving them away as hard as I could. The faces of my retainers, of Kreiz and Wren, and of my wife Licia floated through my mind's eye, one by one. How could I have been so stupid as to think that my dying wouldn't cause them any problems?

I can't die like this. I can't afford to die.

I'll survive. Whatever it takes, I'll survive!

I focused solely on survival, purging my mind of all other thoughts. The pain intensified, but I steeled my nerves and desperately endured it. Slowly but surely, I was growing closer and closer to my body.

Live. Live. Live. Live. Live!

I wished so intently to live on, I didn't have a moment to think about anything else. And then, finally, my hand reached my body. The moment my spiritual form touched my flesh, a blinding white light blotted out my field of vision. The agonizing pain that I'd felt just moments before vanished as well.

Then, a moment later, I could feel myself being dragged back into my body. My soul was returning to where it was meant to be. I didn't resist, needless to say.

I could almost feel my soul flowing back into my form, filling me up starting with my toes. It spread up to my waist, then my stomach, my chest, and finally, my head. I had successfully made it back into my body.

I clenched my fists, then opened my eyes, making sure I could move. I tried sitting up, but the fact that my soul had returned to me hadn't neutralized the poison. Frankly, I felt like garbage. I remembered now that my soul had fled from my body precisely to escape from the pain I was now feeling. The agony I'd felt when I returned to my body, however, had been even more intense than the pain I was feeling now, so I no longer felt the urge to escape from it.

Thank you, Father. I made it back safe and sound.

I looked over at the corner of the ceiling as I spoke those words in my inner voice. Then I dropped my gaze down to Mireille, who was staring at me with her mouth hanging wide open. Apparently, I'd really caught her off guard. It wasn't every day that I got to see her make a face like that, so it was nice, in a sense.

"Good morning," I said.

"M-Morning," Mireille awkwardly replied.

"I'd like to set the record straight on one thing."

"Wh-What's that?"

"I'm not going to die."

"Don't tell me you heard me monologuing?" Mireille asked, looking shocked all over again. I just nodded. "Wellll, c'mon! You really looked like you were mostly dead just a minute ago! Not now, though. There's a power in your eyes—I can see it. Your face still looks like death, by the way," she added with a smirk. "You really are one interesting guy, kiddo."

○

I didn't feel hungry after coming back to consciousness, but I still forced myself to choke down a meal, then took the medicine that

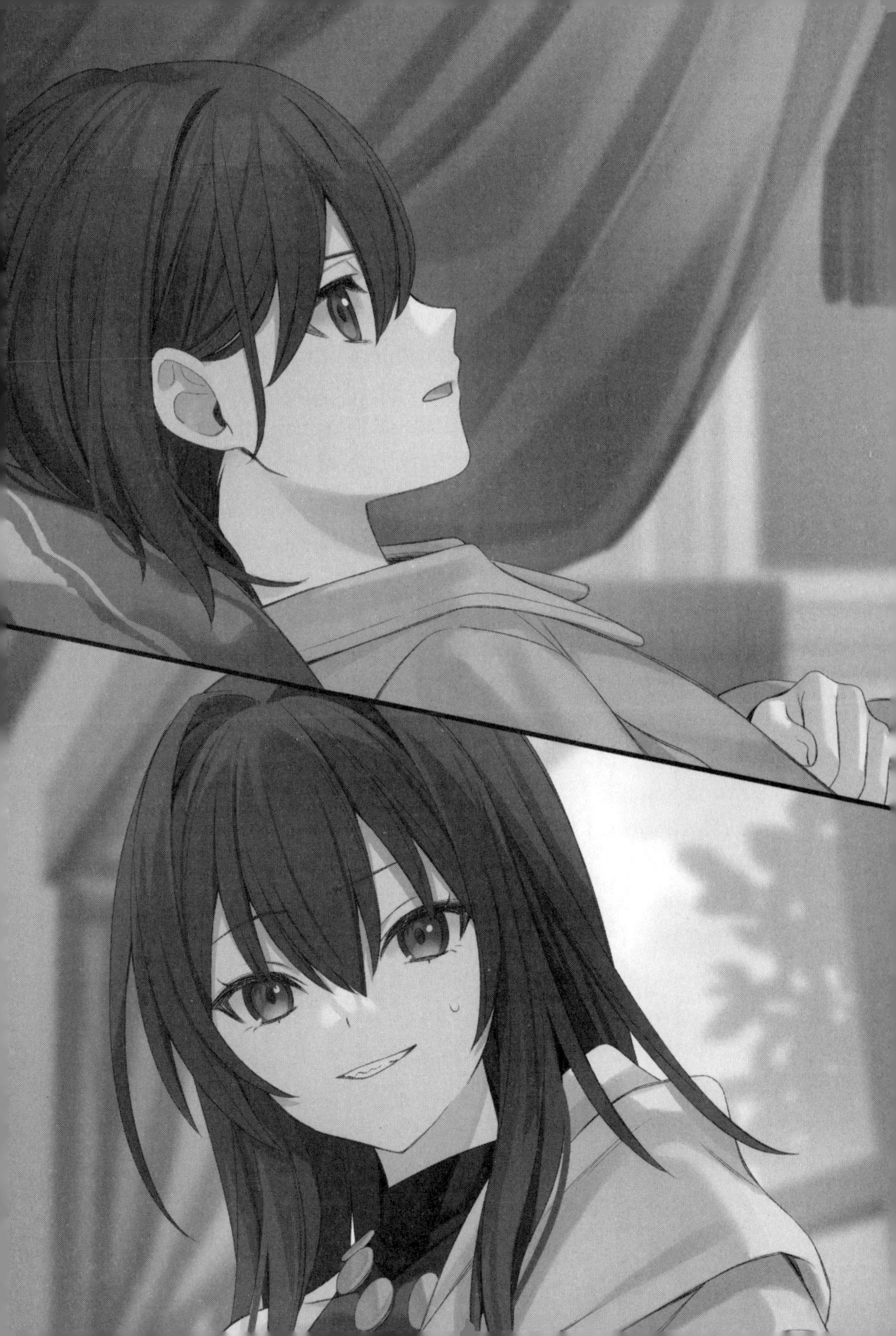

my physician had made for me, which helped a little with the pain. I'd come perilously close to giving up the ghost the day before, but I'd somehow managed to cling to life…for now. Needless to say, if no antidote was found, my newfound lease on life wouldn't last long.

The poison kept me from moving around in any real capacity, so all I could do was believe in my retainers' ability to figure something out. That wasn't too hard, though. I had faith—or something close to it, anyway—that they would all pull through and save me.

"Ars!"

Licia burst into the room and threw her arms around me, hugging me so tightly it actually hurt. I could feel her trembling, and tears flowed freely down her cheeks.

"Ars… Don't die… Please don't die… Don't leave me behind," Licia muttered, her voice wavering with every word. She'd been more worried about me than I'd ever realized. I thought of her as a tough, mentally strong girl, but the fact remained that she was still in her teens. Some part of her was still as frail as her age would lead you to believe.

"It's all right. I won't die," I said.

"Really…?"

"Really. I mean, I can't do much to help myself, but I'm sure my retainers will. They're all exceptional."

Licia didn't reply for a moment, but her trembling gradually slowed. "Yes, you're right," she finally said. "Your power led you to them, so they'd never fail to come to your aid. We have to believe in them."

She still sounded concerned, but it seemed I'd brought her at least a little peace of mind. Her shivering had totally stopped before I knew it.

I WILL USE MY APPRAISAL SKILL TO RISE IN THE WORLD

"Well, look at you two, all over each other again," Mirelle—who'd still been in the room the whole time—muttered. A mischievous smirk had spread across her face.

"M-Mireille?! What are you doing here?!" yelped Licia.

"Nursing your favorite patient, obviously. What else?"

"D-Don't lie to me! I know for a fact that you're not the sort of person who'd nurse anyone."

"What kind of crook do you think I am, little lady? I'm not lying a bit. Isn't that right, kiddo?"

"It is, actually," I agreed. She really was telling the truth, this time.

After I woke up, Mireille had stuck around to take care of me for quite some time, much to my shock. I had no idea whether it was just another of her whims, or if she was a kinder person than I'd given her credit for.

"I mean, just think about how doomed I'd be if the kiddo kicked the bucket! A little nursing's a small price to pay to keep that from happening. I don't know the first thing about medicine, so it's not like I'd be more helpful working on the antidote, or anything."

Oh—so it was just her being as mercenary as ever. In a way, knowing that this was classic Mireille behavior was actually reassuring. If a woman like her started suddenly acting nice for no clear reason, I'd end up paranoid for days as I waited for her to make some sort of demand from me.

"I see," said Licia. "And I trust that you didn't intend to do anything untoward while you were here?"

"Come on, what do you mean, 'untoward'? Try having some faith in me for once!" Mireille protested.

"I'm afraid you don't make it easy!" Licia jabbed back in an unusually harsh tone. She always seemed to be a little on edge around

Mireille.

"Good day to you all!" a spirited voice rang out as yet another person stepped into the room. This time Virge had come to visit, carrying a large bag with him. He'd brought something, apparently. "Ah, Lady Mireille and Lady Licia! The two of you are looking as lovely as ever. As for you, Lord Ars, do my eyes deceive me, or do you look a little healthier today? Why, I'd say you're well on your way to shaking off that nasty poison!"

Virge was as loquacious as ever. He could take that tendency to an obnoxious extreme every once in a while, but this time, I found the distraction from the emotional discomfort of my sickness quite welcome.

"Right, right. So, what're you here for?" asked Mireille, brushing off Virge's flattery.

"Oh, of course! I'd just finished a task that Sir Rietz had entrusted to me, and found myself at a bit of a loss as to whom I should report to, considering Sir Rietz's untimely fainting spell. That's when I heard that Lady Mireille had gone over to visit Lord Ars, and I decided to pop on over to fill you in!" Virge quickly explained.

"So, you're here to report to me?" asked Mireille.

"Quite! With Sir Rietz confined to his chambers and Lord Ars bedridden, I don't think there's any doubt that you, Lady Mireille, are the most reliable among us. I do apologize for bringing such a ruckus into your chamber, Lord Ars, but I felt it necessary to report what I've learned as quickly as possible. Do forgive my rudeness."

"Oh...? Seems you're a man who knows how to judge his superiors," Mireille commented. The look on her face told me that she was rather pleased by Virge's evaluation of her. She'd dismissed his open compliments just moments before, but if complimenting her reliability was all it took to get to her, she might have been easier to

I WILL USE MY APPRAISAL SKILL TO RISE IN THE WORLD

flatter than I'd thought. That, or Virge just had such a silver tongue he could flatter anyone.

"So, what exactly did Rietz assign you to do? Have something fun to share in that bag of yours?" asked Mireille.

I'd been curious about that as well. I couldn't imagine he would've brought a bag that big with him for no reason.

"Well, you see, Sir Rietz ordered me to gather up as much information and documentation regarding poisons and antidotes as I possibly could. I brought all the books on the subject I could find, as well as all the medicines that seemed likely to have an effect," Virge explained. He started rummaging through his bag. "This is a legendary curative that's supposedly effective against all forms of poison... This concoction is supposed to boost the body's natural resistances to toxins... This, umm... What *was* this...? Oh, yes—it's a medicine purported to entirely relieve the agony brought about by poisoning!"

Virge pulled one medicine after another out of his bag. Each sounded more dubious than the last to me, and I quickly started to suspect he'd been taken in by a snake oil salesman.

That last one doesn't even sound like an antidote, does it? Medicine that relieves the pain brought on by poison sounds like it wouldn't help with the actual poison itself at all. I really hope it's not intended for euthanasia use, or something like that!

"We've already tried all the reputable medicines we could get our hands on. I'm not giving any of those high odds," Mireille commented as she gave the medicines a skeptical glance.

"I agree... Testing them could very well just make the situation worse," noted Licia, who seemed opposed as well.

"Ugh!" grunted Virge. "Y-Yes, well, fair enough... I suppose we'd have to have someone test them and ensure the cures aren't more lethal than the poison itself... Oh, but of course! I almost forgot—this cost a pretty penny, but I had a feeling it might be of use and brought it along, just in case!"

This time, Virge pulled out a very small container filled with some sort of luminescent purple liquid. It definitely didn't look like medicine—in fact, it looked an awful lot like how I pictured poison.

"What *is* that? Medicine?" I asked.

"Not quite—this is poison-aspected aqua magia!" said Virge. "It allows you to use poison magic, naturally. The thought struck me that you may have been afflicted with poison created by a spell, so I bought it to find out! Poison-aspected magistones can only be found in Canshiep, it seems, and they're very rare and valuable in Missian as a result, but every once in a while aqua magia made from them turns up on the open market. I was just barely able to luck my way into purchasing a small quantity of it!"

Poison magic, huh?

Natasha had had a Mage Aptitude of C the first time I appraised her, but that was when her status was falsified. After her disguise wore off, she'd had an A-ranked Aptitude instead. A-ranked mages were very few and far between—a rank of B meant that you were capable enough to work as a mage, and a rank of A meant that you had an incredible talent. I'd never seen anyone with an S-ranked Mage Aptitude other than Charlotte, so far, and it seemed likely that there were so few mages with that sort of skill out there, you could count the number that lived in the Summerforth Empire on your fingers.

Anyway, the point is that a Mage Aptitude of A meant that Natasha was very likely to be a skilled spellcaster. It seemed natural to conclude that using poison magic would be well within her capabilities.

I WILL USE MY APPRAISAL SKILL TO RISE IN THE WORLD

"Looks like you need to brush up on how poison magic works, Virge," Mirelle commented in a chiding tone. "Yes, you can use it to synthesize poisons, but nothing powerful enough to use in an assassination. The stuff you can make with poison magic is only good for paralyzing people, sickening them, or reducing their abilities, and even those effects only last for a brief period of time. They're handy for hindering your enemy in a fight, and they've been used in war from time to time, but I don't think assassins would go for them much at all."

I'd had no idea—which only made sense, since I'd never done any deep research into poison magic. It almost never got used in battles in Missian, so I hadn't seen a need. If I was understanding Mireille correctly, it sounded more like a sort of debuff magic than anything else. That had its uses, even if it couldn't kill someone directly, but its lack of lethality did seem like it would limit its practicality in open warfare.

I see," said Virge. "B-But Mister Rietz told me to purchase any that I found, so…"

"Rietz said that…? That's strange. I thought he knew his stuff when it comes to magic," Mireille muttered before sinking into thought.

"Umm… I'm by no means an expert when it comes to magic, but is it possible that there's a poison magic spell capable of killing that simply isn't well-known to the general public? Perhaps the assassin used something like that," suggested Licia.

For a moment, Mireille didn't reply. "I know a lot more than the average person about magic," she finally said, "but that doesn't mean I know everything, and it'd be no surprise if there were spells out there that most people aren't aware of. A spell like that would need a specialized catalyzer to cast, though—the ordinary ones we use wouldn't cut it. They're made to cast all the conventional forms of magic, but nothing else."

"Interesting," said Virge. "In other words, my theory isn't completely out of the question?"

"The one thing is, there just isn't that much poison aqua magia out there, and it would be incredibly hard to develop a new spell. Spell development's tough even when you have a surplus of aqua magia, after all. It seems very unlikely to me, all around...but maybe Rietz decided that if there's even the slightest chance, it's worth looking into?"

If I was understanding Mireille's logic correctly, the odds that I'd been afflicted with a poison magic spell were low, but not non-existent. Natasha's Weaponry aptitude was A, which meant that it was entirely possible that she could have created her own specialized catalyzer. Considering that Pham—an expert when it came to poisons—had no clue what sort of toxin she'd used, the idea that she'd hit me with a poison magic spell that nobody knew anything about was surprisingly easy to believe.

"If this really was the work of poison magic, then how would we cure it?" I asked.

"Detoxification magic is a subset of poison magic," Mireille explained. "To be clear, it can't detoxify in a broad sense—it only works on toxins that were also created by magical means. Mundane poison would be completely unaffected. To make matters worse, even if we assume that you were poisoned magically, that doesn't guarantee that magic will be able to cure you. We might even have to make our own specialized catalyzer just for detoxification if we really want this to work."

That was a roadblock, to be sure. Creating a specialized catalyzer like that wasn't on the table—there was just no way I'd be able to

I WILL USE MY APPRAISAL SKILL TO RISE IN THE WORLD

last that long.

"For the time being, why don't we try casting a detoxification spell using an ordinary catalyzer? It might even work, for all we know!" Licia suggested. I had to agree. It seemed worth a shot, anyway.

"Well, guess we won't know till we try. Detox magic's supposed to be more potent in the hands of a skilled spellcaster...so I'd say we should call in Charlotte for this," said Mireille.

"I'll go get her now!" Virge shouted before charging out of the room to fetch our most capable mage.

A short while later, Charlotte arrived at my room.

"Poison magic? Never used it before. Dunno the incantations either," were the first words out of her mouth. She'd been in the middle of training with her unit, and had arrived quickly as a result, but the fact that she knew nothing about poison magic at all left me at a bit of a loss.

"I think we had some spellbooks in the castle's library... Oh! Rosell will probably have read all of those. Maybe you could ask him?" I suggested.

"I'll summon him at once!" Virge shouted, once again bolting out of my room at top speed. He was a real go-getter, in his own sort of way.

"Huh? Wait—you're awake, Lord Ars?" Charlotte belatedly noted. "Morning!"

"G-Good morning," I replied. Her reaction was rather casual, considering the circumstances. She didn't seem the slightest bit moved to see me conscious again.

"Everyone was talking about how you were gonna die, but I knew you'd pull through," Charlotte added.

That explained it: she had just never doubted my survival in the first place. She'd thought it was only natural that I'd wake up again, so it didn't seem like a big deal at all.

Virge returned in due time with Rosell in tow.

"Ars!" Rosell said as he walked inside. "You really are awake! I'm so sorry, I'm worthless! The antidote just isn't working out!" he continued, practically in tears.

"You don't have to apologize, Rosell. You've been doing your best, haven't you?" I replied.

"I... I..." Rosell began, but started bawling in the end instead. He must have felt responsible for not being able to save me himself.

"Oh, for the— This is no time to be sobbing your eyes out, Rosell! You've got an antivenom incantation memorized, right? Hurry up and teach it to Charlotte!" snapped Mireille. She could be quite strict when it came to Rosell, sometimes. I imagined that was a sign of how high her expectations for his growth were.

"I-I'm sorry, Master," said Rosell. "You managed to find poison aqua magia, then...? I thought it just might be the key to saving Ars, so I asked Mister Rietz to try to get ahold of some..."

"Oh, so you're the one who realized it could've been poison magic first?" asked Mireille.

"Yes, that's right. And if it was magical poison, then mundane medicine could never cure it... I really didn't think we'd manage to find any poison aqua magia, and even if we did the odds of it working seemed pretty low, but I thought I should try anyway, just in case..." Rosell said. Not even he seemed to think that the poison magic theory was all that likely. "Anyway, the antivenom incantation is really short: it's just 'Be cleansed of impurity.' Oh, and you should also know that the spell should affect anyone within a thirty-foot radius! How far away you are from them doesn't matter, so that's not an issue, and getting detoxification magic cast on us when we're not poisoned won't do anything at all, so it doesn't really matter if we're close by either. There's also no guarantee that the spell will actually cure even magical poisons—when less capable mages use this sort of magic, it often ends up lessening the symptoms of the poison without getting rid of it entirely."

"Hmm. So, you're saying that if I'm the one casting it, it'll get rid of the poison for sure," Charlotte said with a confident grin.

"Not for sure!" Rosell replied, shaking his head. "We still don't know that the poison the assassin used on Ars was magical, and even if it was, there's no telling how the special catalyzer that would've probably been used to cast it would factor into the equation. It's totally possible that this won't work at all."

"Hmm. So, basically, sometimes stuff just doesn't work out," Charlotte replied. I had a feeling she hadn't actually understood Rosell's explanation at all. "Might as well just try it, to start! I brought a small catalyzer with me, so let's get that aqua magia right in here."

Charlotte began preparing for the spell, pouring the poison aqua magia into the small catalyzer she'd been carrying. Once her preparations were complete, she recited the incantation.

"Be cleansed of impurity!"

The moment Charlotte finished her incantation. white particles of light began to fall like rain around her. They landed on all of us, me included, and I assumed that whoever was touched by the light would receive the spell's detoxifying effects.

Somehow, as the light continued to rain down, I started feeling slightly better, little by little. It carried on for several seconds, then came to a stop.

"All right, done! How'd it work? Feeling better?" asked Charlotte.

"I am, yes... I really do feel better now. I'm sure of it," I replied.

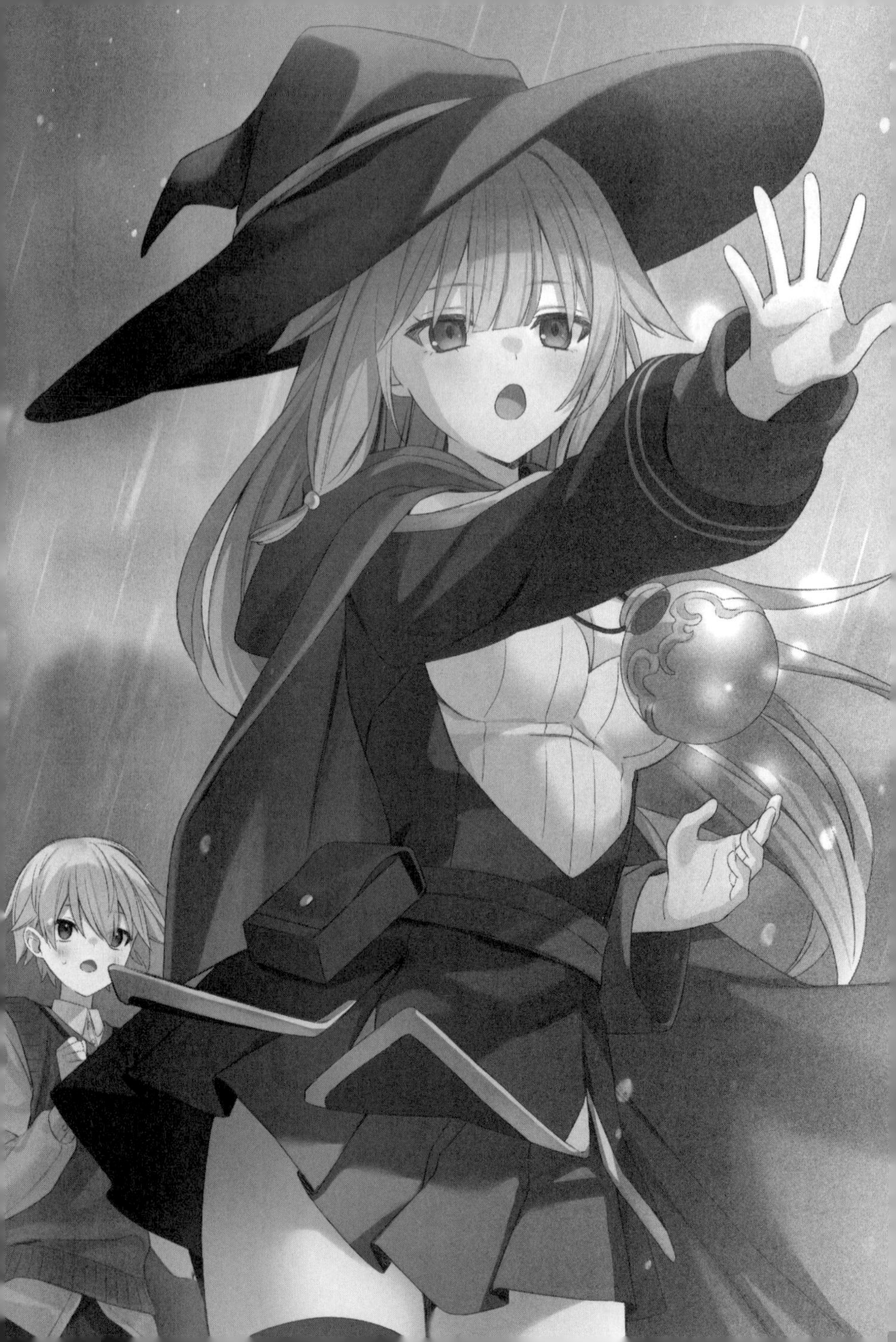

I WILL USE MY APPRAISAL SKILL TO RISE IN THE WORLD

I was being completely honest—it didn't feel like I'd made a complete, instant recovery, but my symptoms were most certainly less intense than they'd been just moments before.

"I-It really worked…" Rosell gasped. He seemed as shocked as he was overjoyed.

"Nice! In that case, you just need to rest up and you'll be all better in no time. All's well that ends well!" Charlotte commented flippantly. She really hadn't so much as considered the possibility that I wouldn't make it.

"Th-Thank goodness… Ars," said Licia. Her voice was full of emotion, and tears were pooling in her eyes.

I felt bad for raining on her parade, but it seemed a little too early to be moved just yet.

"W-Wait," said Rosell, who must have been thinking along the same lines. "You said you feel *better* now? So, not completely back to normal? That means that the poison's not totally gone, doesn't it?"

"Right," I confirmed.

"I see… To be honest, if we can't completely purge the poison from your system, I don't think we can relax just yet. It could get worse again, if we just wait around and let it."

I'd been worried about the same possibility. A magically-made poison seemed like it would be particularly hard for one's immune system to fight off naturally. If there was even a little poison left in me, then my condition could always deteriorate all over again. If this was like other magical poisons and had a natural time limit attached then I might get better if I just waited it out, but I knew that being that optimistic would be a terrible idea. I definitely didn't think that an assassin of Natasha's caliber would use that gentle of a poison.

"This poison's a real pain, all right, but for now, I think we can just take a moment to keep a close eye on you and see how things develop," said Mireille. She didn't seem to think the poison had been fully purged either.

"We've still got some aqua magia left. Why not use it to blast the rest of the poison away right now?" suggested Charlotte.

The bottle of aqua magia that Virge had bought was large enough to fill roughly three small catalyzers. In other words, we could still cast the detoxification spell two more times. Maybe that would be all it took to clear the rest of the poison out.

"I guess that is an option, if we have enough left. Go ahead and try it two more times," said Rosell.

Charlotte didn't waste time carrying out her plan. She cast the same spell twice in a row, and as its effects set in, I suddenly felt much, *much* better. In fact, I felt like I could get right out of bed and go for a run if I wanted to. It really did seem like Charlotte might have just done away with all the poison that remained.

"I-I think...I'm cured? I barely feel any symptoms at all anymore," I said.

"Well, to start, we'll watch you for a few days and see if that lasts. There's still a chance there's a little poison left in you," Rosell concluded.

A few days came and went. I'd been eager to jump to the conclusion that I'd been fully cured, but unfortunately, it didn't turn out to be that easy. Little by little, the poison's symptoms began creeping back in, proving that I wasn't out of the woods just yet. I did still feel much better, but if we didn't do something to address the problem, it was sure to escalate all over again.

The silver lining was that we now knew that detoxification spells could alleviate my symptoms. It wouldn't have been surprising if the spell hadn't worked at all, and the fact that it had was a major step forward in our understanding of the poison.

Rosell soon reached the conclusion that if we wanted to fully cure me, our best bet was to gather a massive quantity of poison-aspected aqua magia and use a large catalyzer to cast the same detoxification spell. It wasn't guaranteed to work, but it was certainly a more realistic option than inventing a whole new type of catalyzer specialized for curing magical poisoning.

Poison-aspected aqua magia was rare, but it was still sold on occasion, even within Missian. The magistones it was refined from could only be mined in Canshiep, but since poison magic wasn't exceptionally powerful, the duchy had never regarded it as important and didn't regulate its trade or export. Stocking up would be possible, if we put the effort in.

Buying that much poison aqua magia would be expensive, considering its rarity, but we didn't have any other options. The recent economic boom in Canarre meant our tax income had been bolstered, and we had more money to spend than usual, so while it'd be a painful expense, it wasn't unaffordable.

We decided to have the aqua magia brought in by sea. My representative would travel to Semplar, where they would negotiate for and purchase what we needed. I entrusted that task to Virge, in the end.

With our plan settled, all that was left for me to do was wait… or so I thought, before a whole new problem arrived.

One day, out of the blue, we received word that Seitz's armies had begun to march upon Canarre.

○

AS A REINCARNATED ARISTOCRAT

The retainers of House Louvent were gathered up in Castle Canarre's conference chamber for an emergency meeting. Ars was not present. The poison had yet to be completely cleansed from his system, and so he had stayed in his room to rest and recover as well as he could.

Licia was attending in Ars's stead, and served as the discussion's leader. She'd been terribly dispirited after Ars collapsed, but now that he had regained consciousness and his prognosis was much more hopeful, she'd bounced back immediately.

Rietz, who had overworked himself until he literally collapsed, was awake and about again, but still looked rather sickly. He didn't seem to have fully recovered yet, and Rosell had tried to convince him to keep resting until he was all better, but he'd argued that he couldn't afford to rest in a situation this dire and had more or less forced his way into the meeting.

"By the way—is the kid all right?" asked Thomas. His presence at the meetings in Castle Canarre was never a given, but today, he had chosen to make an appearance.

"He's doing just fine for now, but he's still a little under the weather. That poison just doesn't know when to quit," replied Mireille, Thomas's older sister.

"But once Virge gets his hand on a stockpile of poison aqua magia, we'll be able to fully cure him!" noted Rosell. "He's arrived in Semplar and conducted his negotiations, apparently, so the deal's been struck already."

Virge had been taking every opportunity he could to send updates on his work back to Canarre. So far, he'd been making swift progress.

"Let us move along to the topic at hand, shall we?" said Licia, formally kicking off the meeting. "The armies of the Duchy of Seitz have begun to march on Canarre. Let us discuss how we will go about responding to this threat."

"Let me fill everyone in on the details of the situation," said Rosell. "Seitz's armies have set out from Fort Purledo. They number less than ten thousand, this time, but they're well equipped and have a large number of mages in their midst. It's not the most impressively sized force, but that doesn't change the fact that it's a powerful one. They're advancing quickly, too, and will likely arrive at Fort Coumeire in just two weeks' time."

"Have we dispatched a request for reinforcements?" asked Licia.

"We have, yeah," Rosell confirmed. "We've sent a message asking for reinforcements to King Couran, but whatever forces he sends definitely won't make it here before we have to take on the enemy's first wave of troops. If we can fend off that first wave, though, his reinforcements should reach us and let us fight off the rest of the invasion without much trouble."

"So then, they seek to claim Fort Coumeire while Ars is bedridden? I suppose we can take this as confirmation that Seitz was indeed responsible for the attempted assassination," said Licia.

"Yes...that we can," Rietz practically growled.

"But we won't let their plans play out the way they think they will," said Licia. "We must band together, fend them off, then deliver Ars the good news."

Licia's words lifted the spirits of everyone present.

"I will take command of our defenses," declared Rietz.

"W-Wait a minute! You're still not in any shape to go out into battle, Mister Rietz," Rosell protested, clearly concerned.

"But I must. I know how much trouble I caused by collapsing, and now I have to make up for lost time," Rietz said with a look of frustrated impatience. He really did look terrible, to such an extent that everyone present at the meeting felt an urge to stop him. It was obvious that he would have a hard time going into battle in his current condition, but his overactive sense of responsibility drove him to spit in the face of reason and do it anyway.

"Rietz," Licia said. The look on her face was rather stern. "If you continue to push yourself, you'll only collapse all over again—and if an army's commander collapses on the battlefield, the battle might as well be lost."

"P-Perhaps, but—"

"As your lord's acting proxy, I order you to remain behind in the castle."

"...Understood," Rietz weakly replied. Licia was right, plain and simple. There was nothing he could say in protest.

"Charlotte and I will take to the field," said Mireille. "Don't let it get to you, Rietz. No way we'll lose if we just fight like we always do."

"Right? We'll blast 'em to hell and back, just like last time," said Charlotte. The two women were as confident as could be.

"Ah, right! You come too, Thomas," Mireille added. "A man like you should have his uses on the battlefield."

"Excuse me? I'd sooner die than fight by your side," Thomas spat. He looked positively revolted by the mere thought of going into battle with his sister.

"Oh, grow up already! Most kids would've been out of their rebellious phase a decade ago, you know? Just shut up and follow me, or I'll let everyone know how you used to—"

"N-No you don't! What are you trying to tell them?!"

"Who knows? You'll never have to find out if you just play along for once."

Thomas clicked his tongue with irritation. "Fine! I'll go, then. Have it your way," he said. Mireille had far too much blackmail

I WILL USE MY APPRAISAL SKILL TO RISE IN THE WORLD

material on him—he couldn't afford to refuse.

"I'm sorry...and thank you," Rietz said with a deep bow.

"I, umm, hope that the three of you don't let your guards down!" said Rosell. "We may have won last time, but they're sure to have countermeasures for all of our old tactics this time around. And they might have fewer troops than last time, but it's still a bigger force than Canarre's whole army."

"It'll be fine, trust me! Taking a fort's never easy, so we won't have any trouble holding them off. Sure, Fort Coumeire's a little on the old and rickety side, but it'll probably hold out," said Mireile. Her reckless optimism always cut a sharp contrast with Rosell's negativity.

"Urgent news," said a messenger—Ben, a member of the Shadows—who burst into the chamber at just that moment. He hadn't even knocked, and everyone present seemed a little shocked by the interruption.

"Umm... If memory serves, you were...?" Licia muttered as she searched for a name and turned up nothing.

"Ben, of the Shadows."

"Ah, Ben! Of course! I'm certain we've met before. My apologies for my forgetfulness."

"Don't worry about it. It happens all the time," said Ben.

It was incredible just how plain Ben looked—his face was almost perfectly nondescript. That lack of distinguishing traits was incredibly useful for the sake of intelligence work and subterfuge, but when it came to his daily life, it had the unfortunate side effect of causing people to forget who he was on a regular basis.

"It seems that a rumor that Lord Ars has died after a poisoning has been spread within Canarre City. A large number of the people already believe the rumors, and unrest is beginning to build," Ben explained, sounding rather blasé about the trouble he was reporting.

"It... *Huuuh*?!" Rosell yelped. He, at least, was shaken by the news.

"I see... This must be part of Seitz's strategy," Mireille said, calmly analyzing the situation. "The fact that it's not completely baseless makes it seem a lot more credible. The kiddo really did get poisoned, so it's not like he's made any public appearances lately."

"Y-Yeah, you're right... Ars usually walks around town to search for new retainers all the time, so him not being out and about would be easy to notice..." said Rosell. "This is a pretty big issue, huh? If rumors that the count's dead keep spreading, it's only a matter of time before the unrest reaches our soldiers and morale starts to plummet."

Rosell looked worried, and for good reason: most of the soldiers in Canarre's army lived among the perfectly ordinary citizens when they weren't training or away on campaigns. If the common folk were talking, the soldiers would hear it too, and rumors like that were very likely to have a disastrous effect on their morale. Morale, meanwhile, played a key component in deciding a battle's victor. This was, in short, grave news indeed.

"Why were the Shadows unable to stop these rumors before they spread this far?" asked Licia.

"Our Boss has been focused on tracking down the assassin. I'm the only Shadow operating in Canarre City right now, actually—we just don't have the manpower to keep that sort of talk in check. We're not living up to our name right now, and I apologize for that," said Ben. Even when apologizing, the blank look on his face barely shifted at all.

"No going back now, but in retrospect, it might not've been the best idea to put absolutely all of our resources into the assassin hunt," noted Rosell.

"Which was my order. This is my fault..." Rietz muttered regretfully.

"N-No, it wasn't a mistake on your part at all, Mister Rietz! We thought that finding the assassin was the only way for us to figure out how to cure the poison, so it was your only choice at the time!" Rosell chimed in.

"Even so, I should have amended my orders the moment it became clear that detoxification magic would be effective."

"Y-You were bedridden! How were you supposed to give orders?" Rosell protested. Rietz was sinking into a depression, but Rosell did what he could to lift his spirits.

"What's done is done. For the time being, we should consider our options moving forward. Assigning blame won't do us any good," Licia said, trying to steer the conversation back on track. "Does anyone have a suggestion?"

"That's a tough one," said Rosell. "Hmm... It doesn't feel like anything other than having Ars walk around in the open to prove that he's fine to the people will do the job... We can claim that he's alive all we want, but people might not believe it until they see him in the flesh. If anything, making a claim like that while keeping him shut away would seem more suspicious than anything. We could also always use a body double, I guess...but it wouldn't be easy to find someone who looks just like him quickly enough."

"It does seem like having him make a public appearance would be the most effective option. The question's whether the kiddo has the stamina to pull that off," added Mireille.

"There's no mistaking the fact that Ars's health is deteriorating again, for now...but I believe he's still capable of walking," said Licia. "His symptoms aren't worsening especially quickly, so I believe he'll be able to manage that much. I do, however, believe that it will place an undue burden upon him."

"Hate to say it, but that's a burden we'll have to ask him to shoulder. We're out of other options. Let's see what he thinks, at the very least," said Mireille.

"I suppose we should," Licia agreed with an apprehensive nod. She was deeply concerned that Ars would wind up pushing himself too hard and collapsing again.

"Plus, showing him off alive and well won't just alleviate the people's worries—it'll also prove to Seitz that the assassination was a failure. Best case, we might even head off the invasion before it starts," Mireille noted.

"Y-You're right!" exclaimed Rosell, who had instantly picked up on her train of thought. "If Seitz spread those rumors, then they must have spies operating in Canarre. That means that they'll learn that Ars is alive right away, and since they clearly don't think they can pull off an invasion without having him killed first, the assassination failing could make them decide to withdraw their troops for the time being! If this can prevent battle from breaking out, it's definitely worth a try!"

"One way or another, it will all have to come down to Ars. Let us ask him if he feels well enough," said Licia.

"Yeah...you're right," Rosell agreed.

"If he can't manage it, then we'll be fresh out of options and we'll just have to send the men into battle, low morale or not. I'll start getting them ready to move at once," said Mireille.

"Please do," said Licia.

"I'll help!" Charlotte exclaimed. She and Mireille set out to prepare for battle at once.

With that, a plan had been laid and the meeting was called to

I WILL USE MY APPRAISAL SKILL TO RISE IN THE WORLD

a close.

○

The moment we received word of Seitz's impending invasion, an emergency war council was organized. I'd wanted to take part in it myself, but my retainers told me to focus on recovering, and I spent the meeting resting in bed instead. It was frustrating not being able to help, honestly, but I knew how capable my retainers were, and I was certain that they'd come up with an optimal strategy to get us through this crisis.

Some time later, Licia, Rietz, and Rosell visited me in my room.

"The council just finished, Ars," Licia said as she stepped inside.

"Oh? Thank you all for handling that," I said. "I'm sorry that I wasn't able to participate. I should have been there."

"It's perfectly fine! No need to worry yourself," Licia replied.

"So, what's the situation? How many troops are they sending?"

"Well, about that…" Rosell replied in Licia's stead. He spent a moment explaining the circumstances to me.

It seemed that Seitz's goal was to send out an advance force of elite troops, which would attempt to claim Fort Coumeire as quickly as possible. They'd also already spread rumors in Canarre City about my having perished, with the intent to cause unrest among the populace. That latter plan, at least, had borne fruit: there were already a large number of citizens who believed that I was dead.

Clever. Of course the people would be distressed and the soldiers demoralized if they thought the lord who ruled over them had been killed.

Just denying the rumors was unlikely to wipe away all of the people's doubts. It wasn't that easy to make someone abandon belief in a rumor they've taken seriously. The best way to shut down the rumors, I figured, would be for me to make a public appearance and outright disprove them.

"How are you feeling, though? Do you think you'd be able to walk around outside? If not, then please, stay here and rest. Your safety is more important than anything, Ars," said Licia.

"Hmm..."

I mulled the question over. It didn't seem impossible...probably, anyway. I wasn't doing great, to say the least, but compared to when the poison's symptoms were at their most potent, I felt remarkably decent. The problem was that I'd barely been walking at all lately, and had no idea how moving around for an extended period of time would turn out. Collapsing partway through my stroll would just add fuel to the fire—I'd prove the rumors partially true instead of dispelling them.

"Please, Ars. You mustn't push yourself," Licia said, concern written all over her face.

"If need be, I'll wipe out our foes to a man. I'll stake my life on it, Lord Ars, so there's no need for you to endanger yours," Rietz added. Knowing him, he really wouldn't hesitate to sacrifice himself to ward off the invasion.

Still, the idea of spending day after day in bed when I had duties to attend to made me feel more than a little guilty. I'd only been poisoned in the first place because I'd been overly reliant on my Appraisal skill—was I really going to let that failure drag us into war and cause the deaths of countless soldiers? Would that not render me a failure of a lord on its own?

"I'll be fine. Let's head into the city," I concluded.

I quickly prepared myself for an outing, then set forth into the city. The longer we put the excursion off, the more the rumors would

I WILL USE MY APPRAISAL SKILL TO RISE IN THE WORLD

spread, and the more the poison would take hold of my body. There would be no benefit whatsoever to doing it at a later date, so the moment we settled on the plan, I set about going through with it.

Licia was walking by my side. To anyone not in the know, it probably looked like I was out on a pleasant date with my wife. Well, my wife and an escort of armed guards, of course. Braham, Zaht, Rikuya, and Takao—all capable warriors in their own right—had come along with us. Ben was also blending in with the crowd nearby, in theory, though I couldn't pick him out among the common citizens for the life of me. There was a chance that Seitzan assassins could be lurking around the city, so this was no time to go light on the guards.

To be honest, my body wasn't holding up all that well. The poison was part of the problem, but the bigger factor was my having been bedridden for a very long time. I'd lost a lot of strength over the course of my sickness. Nevertheless, I did my best to act as if nothing was wrong, hoping that the people wouldn't pick up on any signs of weakness.

The people, for their part, started excitedly chattering the moment they noticed us.

"Huh? That's Lord Ars!"

"I thought he was supposed to be dead?"

"So it really was just a stupid rumor!"

Some of the passersby were surprised, while others were infuriated about having been taken in by a false rumor. I saw all kinds of reactions as we walked along.

By the time we reached the city's plaza, it was bustling with people. It seemed that word about my being out and about had gotten around. I hadn't been planning on making any kind of statement, but this seemed like the perfect opportunity to reassure the populace, so I mustered up the relatively little stamina I had left and shouted out to them.

"I'm to understand that people are saying I've been killed, but as you can see, those rumors are nothing more than lies! The truth is that an injury to my leg left me unable to walk properly for some time, preventing me from coming into town. It was not, I assure you, the sort of wound anyone would ever die on account of!"

Delivering that message left me exhausted, but by doing so, I'd provided an explanation for why I hadn't been seen in public lately. Once that story spread throughout the city, all talk of me being dead would surely dry up before we knew it.

We didn't go straight home after the plaza. Instead, I spent a while longer walking through town and showing myself off, finally returning roughly two hours later. The instant I was safe and sound within the castle, however, my energy reserves ran dry and I very nearly fell flat on my face, just barely managing to keep myself upright.

"A-Ars! Are you all right?" Licia asked as she rushed to support me.

"I'm fine," I said. "Well…maybe not, actually… Honestly, I can't take much more of this. That should put those rumors to rest, though."

"It should. Thank you, Ars—you've done a wonderful thing today. Let's get you back in bed right away."

With Licia's help, I managed to haul myself back to my room and collapse into bed for a lengthy rest.

○

One of Boroths's subordinates arrived at Fort Purledo, bearing news regarding the state of affairs in Canarre.

"Ars Louvent has been sighted walking through the city streets, and the rumors of his death have dropped out of circulation. It would seem that not only has he survived, he's also succeeded in curing the poison he was afflicted with."

"Are we certain it was truly Louvent himself?" asked Boroths.

"His voice sounded the same as before... And his wife, Licia, and a number of his more prominent retainers were with him as well. I believe there's little doubt it was the genuine count."

"Damn you and your so-called incurable poison, Zetsu... Was it all a lie from the start?" Boroths muttered. His voice was calm, but his expression spoke of a fury so deep, it overwhelmed the subordinate who'd delivered the news.

"House Louvent has also dispatched a letter to you," the subordinate nervously added.

"A letter?"

"Yes, Your Lordship. Here."

Boroths scanned the missive. It began by stating that Ars Louvent remained in good health, then went on to claim that open warfare would not be to the benefit of Seitz or Missian and proposed an armistice. The note concluded by stating that if Boroths withdrew his troops, they would not be pursued or attacked during their retreat.

Them sending a letter like this means it's all but certain they know that I'm the one who hired Zetsu, and that they've figured out my strategy for the invasion as well. Is it true that they have no interest in fighting or pursuing my men, though? Should I order a retreat...?

Boroths considered his options. Pulling his army back carried relatively few downsides, if he did it now. It would mean that his plan had ended in failure, but since following through with the battle would risk suffering heavy losses, accepting the offer of an armistice seemed like a comparatively benign sort of failure. He'd already failed in Ars's assassination, and could certainly do without another major setback added on top of that one.

But, wait... Is it too early to write the assassination off as a failure? Perhaps they've only managed to temporarily treat the symptoms, and the poison's still doing its job. Zetsu would never have acted that confidently if it was the sort of poison you could cure without going to great trouble.

As Boroths's rage gradually faded, he began processing the situation in a calm, collected manner.

"I will write a letter in reply. Deliver it to House Louvent as soon as I'm finished," said Boroths.

"Understood, Your Lordship."

Boroths found a piece of parchment and began writing his letter to Ars at once.

○

A few days after I took my walk through Canarre City, my health had indeed taken a turn for the worse. Tiring myself out had not helped my condition in the slightest. I could only hope that Virge would arrive home with the poison aqua magia he was trying to purchase and I'd be fully cured soon.

In the meantime, it seemed my retainers had chosen to send an armistice proposal to Seitz. So far, however, their army had remained on the march. Had they realized that I wasn't as cured as I claimed to be?

I didn't want it to come to battle, if at all possible. As things stood I believed we'd be able to fend off a Seitzan assault, but even a

I WILL USE MY APPRAISAL SKILL TO RISE IN THE WORLD

winning battle would mean plenty of casualties on our side, not to mention all the resources we'd have to expend. If there was a path we could take to avoid the conflict, I wanted to pursue it.

"Ars? Is now a good time?" Licia's voice rang out from beyond my door. She seemed to have something to discuss.

"It's fine, yes," I replied.

"Pardon me," Licia said as she stepped inside. It turned out that Rietz and Rosell were both with her. "Are you feeling all right?"

"Not really, if I'm being honest, but it's still not nearly as bad as it was at its worst," I said.

"I see..." Licia replied. She looked a little worried about me.

"So, what is it? You had something to talk about, right?" I asked. She wouldn't have brought Rietz and Rosell with her for a simple checkup.

"We did," said Licia. "We've received a reply from Seitz. I thought it would be best for you to read it yourself, so I've brought it with me. Of course, there's no need for you to bother if you're not feeling well enough. What would you prefer?"

Licia held a rolled-up piece of parchment out to me. As bad as the poison was making me feel, I certainly wanted to read Seitz's message myself.

"That's no issue. I'll read it," I replied as I took the letter. I unfurled it and began to read.

To the honorable Ars Louvent,

I have received and read your recent missive, and am pleased beyond measure to hear that you are in good health. Regarding the recent movements of our soldiers, they were dispatched to the vicinity of the border between our duchies on account of rumored bandit activity in the area.

AS A REINCARNATED ARISTOCRAT

The bandits in question are former mercenaries with ample combat experience, and we deemed it best to use all means available to us to ensure their extermination. We do not, under any circumstances, intend to invade Canarre.

That being said, I appreciate how our actions could be perceived as an act of aggression from your position. Failing to inform you of our true intentions in advance was a significant oversight on our part, and if possible, I would like to personally apologize for this error. I hope that you will find such a meeting permissible, and will await your word on the subject.

Yours truly,
Boroths Heigand

He wants to apologize in person...? That must be a pretense, right? I bet he just wants to directly confirm that I'm not still poisoned.

The story about bandits was a transparent lie. No one would ever send ten thousand soldiers to mop up a bandit camp, no matter how skilled the brigands were. I assumed that using the bandit story as an excuse was his way of feigning an apology while still keeping his troops on the move.

Moreover, the fact that he'd sent a letter like this told me that Boroths Heigand likely believed we were unaware of who had sent the assassin after me. If he did think we knew it was his doing, he would presumably be too scared of retaliation to meet with me in person. I wouldn't actually do that, of course—assassinating Boroths during a meeting would do nothing to end the war. Perhaps he knew that was my primary objective, and was exploiting that fact to his advantage?

"I'm pretty sure you don't need me to tell you this, but all that

I WILL USE MY APPRAISAL SKILL TO RISE IN THE WORLD

stuff about wanting to apologize is definitely just him trying to make sure that you're actually still alive," said Rosell. "If you turn him down, I bet he's going to assume that you really are sick and follow through with his original plan to attack Fort Coumeire."

"That makes sense... And if that's true, then I should probably take him up on the offer. I'd like to avoid battle if I can, after all... But will I be able to make it through a meeting like that in the first place...?" I muttered.

My health was worsening by the day. I didn't know exactly when I would be meeting with Boroths, but it would surely be farther off than a day or two. If I was in a bad enough state that I couldn't even sit up on the day of the meeting, he'd know right away that my supposed recovery was a lie. It was a tough choice...but the fact that refusing the meeting would mean war for sure still felt like the most important factor.

"We cannot force you to push yourself any further than you already have, Lord Ars. I will begin preparations to bring our full might to bear against the enemy invaders. We will drive Seitz back, I swear," said Rietz. He was fully prepared to fight, and Rosell and Licia didn't object. Everyone was ready for that eventuality.

I took a moment to consider, then told them my decision. "No, that won't be necessary. I'll speak with him. I don't know if my health will hold for long enough, but if the alternative is certain war, then we'll be better off at least trying the option that might prevent bloodshed."

"But, Lord Ars..." Rietz began. I could tell that he was opposed to my decision—the panicked look on his face made that clear on its own.

"I knew you would say that, Ars. I would love to tell you to refrain, as well...but if you wish to accept this meeting, I will not oppose your decision," said Licia. She'd chosen to respect my wishes.

"You don't have to worry about me. It's just a meeting—I can manage that much. I'll have Boroths come to Castle Canarre so I won't have to exhaust myself going out to meet him. Considering his pretense is that he's apologizing to me, it would be strange for him not to be the one to make the trip."

I did my best to project an air of confidence as I reassured everyone. I was worried about all sorts of things, in truth, but I didn't feel like I had any other choice. I had a responsibility to do everything I could to avoid a war.

Rietz hesitated for a moment longer. "Understood," he finally said, looking like he'd made up his mind. "I will send a reply informing Seitz that we are willing to meet with them."

Just like that, the meeting was a go.

○

Our letter to Seitz was delivered without issue. I'd had it carried by a particularly skilled horseman who was ordered to deliver it with all due haste, and apparently, the trip had only taken a few days. I knew that traveling at a gallop was exhausting to both horse and rider, so I made a mental note to give the soldier who'd made the trip a bonus when I had the chance.

Our letter had specified that we were to meet with Boroths at Castle Canarre, and that their troops would have to halt their march immediately if they wanted the meeting to take place. There was a chance they would refuse that second condition, presumably under the pretense that they had to exterminate the bandits as soon as possible to spare innocent civilians in the vicinity from further harm. For now, though, all I could do was sit back and wait to see how

I WILL USE MY APPRAISAL SKILL TO RISE IN THE WORLD

they would reply.

A few days later, news arrived. It seemed that Boroths Heigand himself had shown up at Fort Coumeire, and was currently being escorted to Castle Canarre by Mireille. That surprised me, frankly. I'd expected him to send a letter before setting out, but apparently, he'd wanted to see me as soon as possible and left the moment we made it apparent I was open to meeting with him.

As for our condition that they stop their armies' advance, it wasn't entirely clear whether they'd followed through or not. The point was a bit moot, though—now that Boroths himself was within Canarre's borders, we couldn't exactly chase him out without confirmation that he was holding up his end of the bargain. Meeting with him was my only option, one way or another. I had to wonder if his unexpectedly quick departure was on account of him having seen through our intentions, in that respect.

Regardless, I was glad to meet with him as early as possible. The longer we waited, the higher the odds of my condition dramatically worsening. I'd already reached the point where just standing up took everything I had, though thankfully, I was still fully present in a mental sense. Whether or not the interview went well would entirely come down to my strength of will. I wouldn't know for sure if I'd be able to manage it until the actual meeting arrived, but if he'd been just a little slower, I might've ended up in such a bad state I couldn't even hold a proper conversation. That would have sunk the meeting then and there, so I couldn't have been happier to receive news of his haste.

Eventually, one of my retainers came to me with a report.

"Lord Ars? Boroths Heigand has arrived."

○

"I greatly appreciate your most gracious invitation, Count Ars Louvent of Canarre."

I met with Boroths in the parlor of Castle Canarre. He came flanked by a pair of guards, who it seemed were the only ones that'd accompanied him. Moving quickly with a large group was difficult, but it still struck me as a little careless to only bring two escorts along on a trip like this. We had absolutely no intention to assassinate him, of course—I had quite the grudge against him, yes, but exacting vengeance would do nothing to stop the war, so this really wasn't the time.

I, naturally, had brought guards as well. Trying to assassinate me in my own castle would be outlandishly reckless, but it never hurt to be cautious. After all, Seitz was by no means our ally. I'd chosen Rietz, Braham, Zaht, Ben, and a few other skilled fighters to accompany me.

The moment Rietz laid eyes on Boroths, a truly terrifying expression had come across his face. It only lasted for a split second, and he was back to smiling a moment later, but that contrast actually made the moment of fury even scarier. I was mad at Boroths too, but I had to suck it up for now.

"My name is Boroths Heigand. It is truly a pleasure to make your acquaintance," Boroths said as he gave me a deep, formal bow.

At a glance he looked like a rather kindly man—certainly not the sort of person who would hire assassins and start wars, judging by appearances. Rietz had told me that he had sent subordinates out to look for a killer to hire, though, so there was very little doubt that it had been his personal order, since I couldn't exactly see his subordinates independently deciding to sic the assassin on me after finding her. This was all just conjecture based on secondhand infor-

//# I WILL USE MY APPRAISAL SKILL TO RISE IN THE WORLD

mation, of course, and I didn't have any concrete evidence against him, so accusing him of masterminding the plot was off the table... not that I'd been planning to do so from the beginning.

To start, I appraised Boroths.

> Boroths Heigand
> Age: 36
> Male
> **Status:**
> LEA: 85/91
> VAL: 71/77
> INT: 75/80
> POL: 92/95
> Ambition: 20
> **Aptitudes:**
> Infantry: A
> Cavalry: A
> Archer: C
> Mage: C
> Fortification: C
> Weaponry: C
> Naval: C
> Aerial: C
> Strategy: B

He was as capable of an individual as I'd expect from the man who led a duchy's army...or at least that's what I thought at a glance, but then I remembered how the assassin he'd hired had falsified her appraisal's results. Boroths could know about the same technique she'd used. There would be no need to change his name, so I expected that was accurate at least, but I decided that it would be best not to take anything else I saw in his status screen at face value.

"It's a pleasure to see you whole and hale," Boroths continued. "I had heard rumors that you had taken ill, and was terribly worried."

"Your concern is most appreciated, but as you can see, I'm the portrait of health," I replied, doing everything I could to keep up the act. I wasn't healthy by any stretch of the imagination, but I thought I'd done a fairly convincing job of acting in a lively manner, somehow. Now I just had to get through the rest of the meeting without letting the act slip. My ample experience going into work sick during my past life as an office worker was actually coming in handy—I was a master at pretending to be happy and healthy when I was the opposite of those things.

"Well then, to start, allow me to offer my sincerest apologies for any concern that the movement of our troops may have caused for you and yours. I solemnly swear that our intentions were only to drive away the bandit menace threatening our people, and that invading Canarre was the last thing on our minds," Boroths said, once again bowing deeply.

If I hadn't known better, I probably would have wound up believing him without question. He came across just that convincingly—the man was an incredible actor. It was only thanks to the nature of the circumstances he was lying about that I could work up the skepticism to disbelieve him.

"There's no need to bow, Lord Boroths," I said. "All I ask is that we be informed in advance of any such bandit-related military operations in the future. Moreover...may I take your presence here as confirmation that your armies have ceased their advance?"

"You may," said Boroths. "I have sent the order to my men to hold their position. Although I would prefer to eradicate the bandits

I WILL USE MY APPRAISAL SKILL TO RISE IN THE WORLD

as soon as possible, I judged the delay to be an unfortunate necessity, the circumstances being as they are."

He really had halted his advance, then...or so he claimed. He didn't seem to be lying, from what I could tell, but then again, he was an individual who I couldn't afford to trust.

"Your understanding is greatly appreciated," I replied. I'd asked the question I needed to, and didn't want to probe any further for the time being. I was nearing the limits of my endurance, honestly, and wanted to end the meeting as soon as possible. Feigning health when I was just a step away from bedridden was turning out to be much more draining than I'd expected, both physically and mentally. "I hope that we will both strive to maintain the peace that we've managed to find," I added.

"But of course," Boroths replied with a smile that I returned.

I wanted to note that he had some gall to say that after trying to have me killed, but needless to say, I kept that quip to myself.

"I must admit," Boroths continued, "that when I heard that the newly appointed Count of Canarre was but a boy in his early teens, I took it as a jest. To think it was true! Rumor also has it that you have some manner of power that allows you to see an individual's strengths?"

Suddenly, we'd segued into small talk. I wanted to end the conversation as quickly as I could, but I couldn't be too obvious about it, or I'd draw suspicion. I had to at least make a token effort to engage with him.

"Oh, no, not in the least," I said. "If anything about me is remarkable, it's my own powerlessness. I would never be able to fulfill my duties if it weren't for the aid of my retainers."

"A modest man, I see. Believe me when I say that the ability to distinguish a capable subordinate from an incompetent one at a glance is something that anyone with experience reigning over a territory would desire. I must say, though, that the power they say you wield is a familiar one to me. They make it sound as if you are the holder of the Eye of Appraisal spoken of in ancient legends."

"The Eye of Appraisal...?"

He must be talking about my Appraisal skill, right? There are ancient legends about it...? Could that mean that other people have had the same skill in the past?

I had to admit that all things considered, I knew very little about my own skill. I'd read through countless books in the hopes of finding some reference to it, but had never gained any information that seemed at all relevant.

"Indeed," said Boroths. "It's said that long ago, three individuals in Summerforth bore powers in their eyes. There was the Eye of Warfare, the Eye of Foresight...and the Eye of Appraisal. Though the legends date back to before the founding of the empire, they say the three holders of the Eyes contributed greatly to the wars they were involved in."

I couldn't judge whether he was telling the truth or not, but considering he'd been entrusted with the whole army of Seitz, I could at least count on the fact that he was a very knowledgeable man. There were surely plenty of things he knew about that I'd never even heard of.

"I'm not familiar with these legends," I said, "but I most certainly don't have any power of the sort. I believe I have an unusual eye for talent, and I've been blessed with a number of truly exceptional subordinates, but luck played as much of a factor in granting me their service as my own abilities."

I couldn't just come out and admit that I possessed a fantastical power. Boroths had already plotted to assassinate me once. He

I WILL USE MY APPRAISAL SKILL TO RISE IN THE WORLD

was, to put it bluntly, my enemy, and it was in my best interests to tell him as little as possible. Though then again, Boroths probably wouldn't have brought the subject up if he wasn't very aware of my Appraisal ability already.

"And there's your characteristic modesty again! I've no means to say whether or not your power truly is the legendary Eye of Appraisal, Count Louvent, but I do believe that it lives up to the power depicted in those ancient stories. I wish I could have it for myself... though even the mightiest powers come with their drawbacks."

"What do you mean?" I asked.

"Well," said Boroths, "as the rumors have it, it seems a manner of fooling your appraisal's results has been discovered...and there's no telling what sort of villainy could be accomplished if the wrong person chose to exploit those means."

Hearing that from Boroths himself certainly got under my skin. It was all his fault that I'd had to go through that ordeal in the first place, and he thought he could talk down to me about it?

"What right do *you* have..."

A quiet but shockingly resentful mutter from behind me led me to glance over my shoulder. Rietz was emitting a palpable aura of rage-fueled bloodlust. He was still smiling, but I'd known him for long enough to know that he was the slightest nudge away from completely losing it. I really wouldn't have put it past him to leap at Boroths and throttle the man on the spot.

I mean, I don't think he'll literally go through with it, hopefully...

Anyway, having someone on my team be even more furious than I was actually helped me regain a bit of composure. This made me fairly certain that Boroths really did know how the assassin had managed to fool my skill—and given the tone he was speaking in, it almost felt like he was trying to use that knowledge as a threat? It was like he was declaring that whenever I went out to recruit new retainers, I'd have to be ready for any one of them to turn out to be another Natasha, dispatched by him to finish me off.

Not being able to trust my Appraisal skill's results would make it a very difficult power to use effectively. It would be a major problem if I was tricked into making another assassin into my retainer, or even recruiting a useless follower whose stats had been falsified to make them look exceptional. It seemed that whatever means Natasha had used to fake her stats had worn off over the course of time, so repeated appraisals would reveal someone's true stats in the long run...but still, I wouldn't be able to approach recruitment as casually as I had up until now.

I was starting to appreciate how troublesome of a situation this had become. I'd wanted to gather more mages for my army, but that wasn't looking likely anytime soon. Maybe I could make a deal with Boroths to learn how exactly my skill had been fooled? Or maybe I could focus on capturing Natasha and extract the method she'd used from her directly...?

"I appreciate your warning. It would certainly be a mistake to trust my own abilities too deeply, yes. The wrong person at the wrong time can indeed put you in a terrible situation if you drop your guard," I said, lacing my words with conspicuous sarcasm.

"While I am here, Count Louvent, I have a request that I would like to make of you, if you would be so kind," said Boroths.

A request? I definitely wasn't interested in doing him any favors, and for that matter, I wanted the meeting to be over with as soon as possible. I was feeling worse and worse with each passing minute. I felt sluggish, feverish, and a little nauseous. Rushing away now would look unnatural, though, so I chose to at least hear his request out.

"What would that be?" I asked.

I WILL USE MY APPRAISAL SKILL TO RISE IN THE WORLD

"I believe I've proposed this before, but would you consider cutting ties with Missian and entering into His Lordship the Duke of Seitz's service? The current circumstances strike me as quite different from those under which I made this offer previously, and I believe you'll find that there would be ample benefits to such an arrangement for both you and His Lordship the Duke."

Boroths's attempt at recruitment had come completely out of left field. Why on earth would a man who'd tried to have me killed make an offer like that? Maybe he was only saying it because he felt he had nothing to lose?

"As I've stated previously, I have sworn an oath of fealty to King Couran," I replied. "I'm afraid that serving Seitz is out of the question for me."

"But that's the rub, isn't it? *King* Couran. Missian has seceded from the Summerforth Empire, and that act of rebellion has earned it the empire's ire. His Highness the Duke of Seitz was beside himself with fury when he heard the news. It is by no means an act that he could ever approve of, and should he reach the conclusion that Missian declared its independence with the intent of invading its neighboring duchies, His Highness may very well choose to take action to stymie such an invasion in advance. If it comes to war, Missian will find itself at a grave diplomatic disadvantage—no duchy would ever openly support a rogue state. If ever you intend to forsake Missian, then I would recommend doing so with all due haste."

One minute Boroths was insisting that his intentions were purely peaceful, and the next, he spoke of how likely a future war would be. I had to admit that there was a certain logic to his argument. Couran's decision to declare independence was baffling to me in a number of ways. Although the likelihood of Missian being attacked from all sides was currently low, that situation could change at any time, and if Missian fell, there was no telling what would happen to House Louvent's standing. There was every chance I might be executed.

Couran had been good to me in a number of ways, and I wanted to keep serving him if at all possible, but if betraying him was what it would take to ensure the safety of House Louvent, then it was a measure I was willing to consider. There were indeed merits to joining up with Seitz, but there was also one major, deal breaking downside: I couldn't serve a faction that I couldn't trust. As such, I chose to turn the offer down outright.

"I'm sorry," I said, "but no number of solicitations will change my answer. I intend to remain in King Couran's service, and that is final."

"I see. I suppose it would be difficult to make a decision of such import on the spot. Know that if you change your mind, Seitz will always welcome you. Speaking as one who suffered a painful defeat at your hands in the last war, I could wish for nothing more than to have you as an ally in the future," Boroths said with a smile that struck me as forced. "And with that, I believe I've taken up more than enough of your time today. I bid you farewell, Count Louvent, and I apologize one more time for the matter regarding our troops' movements. I assure you it will not happen again."

"Thank you, Lord Boroths, for coming all this way to deliver that apology," I replied.

At long last, our meeting had come to an end.

○

Somehow, I'd made it through. Boroths had gone on his way, and I

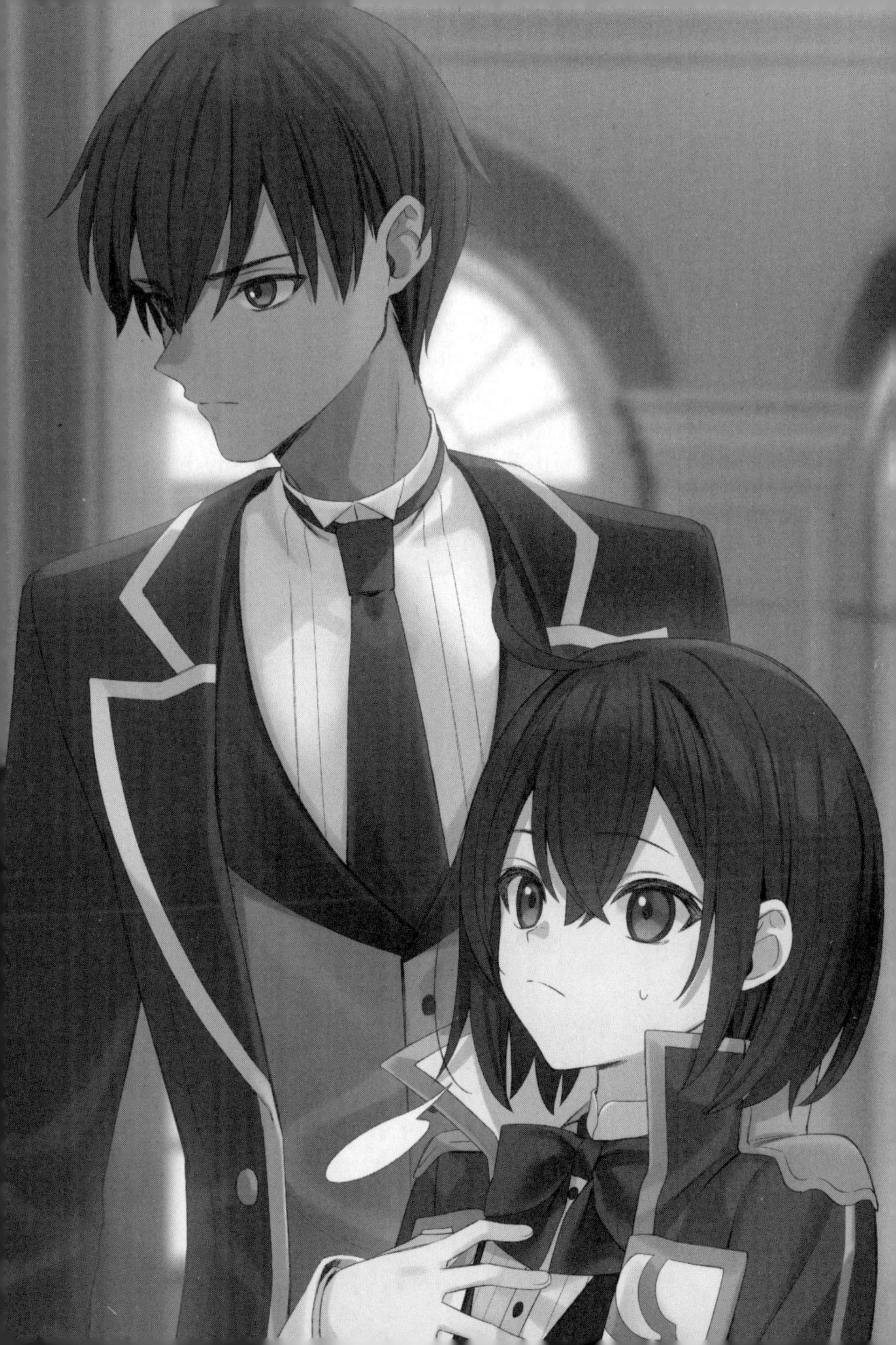

no longer had to act well in his presence.

"Do you think I managed to look like nothing was wrong with me, Rietz?" I asked.

"You played your part to perfection, Lord Ars. I only worry that I did a poor job concealing my own rage," Rietz replied.

"Honestly, I can't disagree with that."

Fortunately, it didn't particularly matter whether Boroths had realized how angry Rietz was. He knew exactly why my retainers would be upset with him, after all.

"For now, I'm a little worn out. I'll be heading back to my chamber..." I said.

"Ah, of course! Allow me to accompany you!"

I made my way back to my room, with Rietz accompanying me.

○

After his meeting with Ars was over, Boroths made his way back to Fort Purledo.

Has he fully cured himself...? No, I think not. Every once in a while, he let a sign of his suffering slip through. It does, however, seem to be true that he's mitigated his symptoms. Zetsu claimed he would be dead within the month, and at the very least, that most certainly has not happened. His condition is so minor that he can even hold a conversation.

As he rode along, Boroths mulled over the conversation he'd had with the young count.

If the poison hasn't been fully cured, there's a chance it could still finish him off...but, no, I suspect Ars Louvent will survive. There was still life in his eyes. Perhaps he's found a means to purge the poison for good. His followers certainly didn't seem shaken by his condition...

I WILL USE MY APPRAISAL SKILL TO RISE IN THE WORLD

Through meeting Ars, Boroths had come to accept that his plan had indeed failed.

Of course, hindering his use of the Eye of Appraisal was enough of an accomplishment for the time being.

During their discussion, Boroths had gone out of his way to make it seem that he knew everything there was to know about Ars's power. By doing so, he had hoped to instill a paranoia in Ars—to make him wonder whether every new talent he came across might just be a Seitzan spy, thus hindering his recruitment efforts. The truth was that Boroths had only briefly discussed the power with Zetsu. He knew very little about it, and he hadn't even learned how the assassin had fooled Ars's appraisal, meaning he couldn't send in disguised agents even if he wanted to.

For now, however...House Louvent's military might pose a clear and present danger. Their mages in particular are troublesome. They're bad enough in a field battle, but if it comes to a siege, one powerful mage can be all it takes to render a fort virtually unseizable. Their economy seems stable as well, and they're not lacking in resources. Claiming Canarre without a very good plan may well be a lost cause.

Boroths had finally reached his conclusion: Canarre would not fall.

I'll have to speak with the duke about this. War with Missian is inevitable, in all likelihood, and I'll have to have a strategy ready to propose for when the time comes.

○

A few days after my meeting with Boroths, the army of Seitz had withdrawn without a fuss. We'd asked them to do so, sure, but I was still a little surprised at how easily they'd abandoned their invasion.

I'd assumed that they'd use their bandit hunting pretext to stick around for a while longer.

I guess there wasn't any point to wasting time once they'd decided to withdraw. That'd just be a waste of rations.

In any case, the citizens believed that I was alive and well, and we'd successfully accomplished our goal of avoiding open warfare. It seemed like I could finally rest easy…if it weren't for the pressing issue of whether or not I could cure my poison, that is. I was feeling…well, pretty terrible, honestly. My condition was quite a bit worse than before, and standing was difficult. The pain was bad enough that I had trouble sleeping, as well, which wasn't doing my exhaustion any favors.

I could feel the limit of my endurance approaching. My willpower could only carry me so far, and if Virge didn't get back soon, I knew I might not make it. Still, I gritted my teeth and endured… and a few days later, Virge arrived back at Castle Canarre.

"'Kay, I'll cast the detoxification spell now," Charlotte said in a tone that struck me as a bit lackadaisical.

We were outside. Walking was beyond me, at the moment, so Rietz had carried me out of the castle. Charlotte would be using a large catalyzer to cast her spell, and we couldn't fit one of those into the castle, so the procedure would be occurring outdoors as a matter of necessity. It was still winter, and while I was dressed for the cold, I still felt a little chilly. Licia, Rietz, and my other retainers were all present as well, watching over us with bated breath.

Charlotte chanted her incantation, and the spell sprang into life. Magical light rained down upon me, and the poison's symptoms instantly faded, the sense of painful, paralyzing deterioration I'd been suffering from going along with them.

I WILL USE MY APPRAISAL SKILL TO RISE IN THE WORLD

"W-Well? How do you feel, Ars?" Licia asked nervously.

"I feel so much better... I can't remember the last time I felt this well, actually," I replied.

"T-Truly?"

I still felt like I'd lost a fair bit of stamina, and I didn't think I'd be walking around any time soon, but I could tell that mobility would come back to me with a little rest. My retainers, meanwhile, cried out with joy at their success.

"I-I hate to be a wet blanket about this, but we'll have to keep watch over him for a few days before we can say for sure he's been fully cured!" Rosell pointed out. He was the only one who'd kept his composure, and he was right. We already knew that the spell could mitigate the symptoms of the poison without curing it, so a degree of caution was necessary.

Judging by my intuitive sense for my own body, however, I didn't think we'd have any issues this time. The last time I'd had the spell cast on me, I'd still felt a slight sense of wrongness somewhere deep within me that was now no longer present. I believed that I really had been cured for good.

Still, I did as Rosell suggested and spent a week very carefully feeling out my own health. I grew healthier and healthier over the course of that week, and my symptoms showed no sign of making a comeback. My instincts had been correct: we'd successfully and completely rid my body of Natasha's poison.

Epilogue

After the poison was cured, the stamina that I'd lost gradually returned to me until I was all but good as new. I was still in my teens, so my recovery had proceeded remarkably quickly. If I'd been hit by that same poison in my thirties, I figured that the recovery process would have been much longer and more grueling.

It had been a long time since I'd been able to attend our regular meetings, and I was finally scheduled to make my return the day after tomorrow. I knew that my absence hadn't caused any major troubles, but as the head of House Louvent, it still felt wrong for me to not at least be present.

"Um, Ars? Are you really sure you'll be all right...?" asked Licia. She was still incredibly anxious about the possibility that the poison would rear its head again.

"Yeah, I'm fine," I said. "Just look at me! I don't look like I'm about to collapse again, do I?"

"Y-You don't, no... I'm sorry—forget I said anything. It's been so long since Charlotte cast her spell, and I know you've shown no sign of a relapse, but I still can't help but worry..."

I'd been bedridden so long with a hopeless prognosis that Licia was now finding it hard to believe that I'd really been cured. I could tell just how much I'd made her worry about me over the course of my illness. There was no objective way for us to test if I was completely recovered, so there was still a slight chance I could relapse, but after a week of wellness I felt safe in assuming I'd be all right. You'd think that if there was still poison somewhere in me, it would've shown some sign of itself over the course of a full week.

"I'll be okay. We used so much aqua magia, and Charlotte was the one who cast the spell. There's no way it'll come back," I said, speaking as confidently as I could to assuage her worries.

"Y-Yes, you're right... And there's no sense in me worrying, regardless..." said Licia. It seemed her concern persisted in spite of herself—she still looked as gloomy as ever. All I could do was hope that the passage of time would make her feel better in the long run. "You'll be returning to our meetings the day after tomorrow, won't you? I hope you'll be resting today and tomorrow, at least?"

"That's the plan... Ah, wait, no—there's one thing I wanted to do."

"What would that be?"

"I was thinking of paying a visit to my father's grave. I still have to thank him."

Even after regaining consciousness and having the poison cured, I still clearly remembered the time I'd spent outside of my body. It was thanks to my father's words that I was still alive, as far as I was concerned, and I owed him another thank you for what he'd done for me. I knew that his soul had probably moved on and was now living in a different person, just like mine had, so even if I spoke to him at his grave my words probably wouldn't reach him. Still, I wanted to try it anyway, just for good measure.

"I'm certainly not opposed to you visiting his grave...but what do you mean, you have something to thank him for?"

"I, uh... Okay, I know you might not believe this," I began, then went on to explain how I'd spoken with my father's spirit.

I WILL USE MY APPRAISAL SKILL TO RISE IN THE WORLD

"I-Is that really true...? He watched over you that whole time...? And if you were reduced to your spirit, doesn't that mean you really were just moments away from dying yourself?!" Licia exclaimed, the color draining from her face.

"Huh...? O-Oh, well, I guess... But my father saved me, more or less... I made it back to my body thanks to him, and now I'm alive and well again, so..."

"W-Well, you certainly do need to thank him, in that case," said Licia. She'd believed my outrageous story, which was nice on the one hand, but on the other, it seemed I'd just made her more worried than ever. "May I accompany you when you visit his grave?" she added.

"It's a little far away from here. Are you sure?" I asked.

"Of course! that's no issue at all!"

"In that case, we'll go together," I agreed. I didn't see any reason to turn her down.

My father hadn't been buried in Canarre proper. He'd been laid to rest in Lamberg instead. There'd been some talk of reinterring him in Canarre when I became the count, but since Lamberg was the land he'd lived in and ruled over for years on end, I'd felt it would be better to leave him there. I made a point of traveling to visit his grave every year on the anniversary of his death.

"Shall we get ready to leave, then?" I suggested.

"Of course!" said Licia. It seemed we'd be traveling together for sure.

As we were preparing to leave, Kreiz barged into our room.

"Ars, Licia! Let's play... Oh. Are you going somewhere?" he asked, full of energy. Wren and their pet, Rio, stepped into the room right on his heels.

"Yes, actually. I was going to visit Father's grave," I replied.

"You were? We'll come too!" said Kreiz.

"Would you mind?" Wren asked, following up his request.

"Hee hee! Why not? We'll all go together," Licia said with a smile.

"Hurray!"

Kreiz and Wren let out a synchronized cheer. With that, our party had grown to four—five, counting Rio, and even more when you factored the guards we'd have to bring. I picked Braham and Zaht for that responsibility.

We soon finished our preparations, and set out for my father's grave in Lamberg.

○

A few hours had passed since we set out from Castle Canarre. Lamberg was nearby, and we arrived on the same day that we'd left.

It felt like it had been a very long time since I'd been in Lamberg. I hadn't had many opportunities to visit lately, on reflection—I'd spent a long time bedridden thanks to the poison, and even before then, my work had kept me away from my homeland for a good long while.

My father had been interred near our old Lamberg estate, which I stopped by as well. It felt like it'd been ages since I'd seen my old home.

"Ahhh! Nothing like having a stiff drink while my lackeys are doing all the hard work for me! Now this is the good life!"

And, there she was: Mireille, flagrantly day-drinking where everyone could see her. She'd stepped up to prepare our troops for battle when it looked like we'd have to defend Fort Coumeire, but now that Seitz had withdrawn, she'd returned to her usual job as the acting Baron of Lamberg...not that it seemed she was actually *doing* said job at this particular moment.

"I'm going to have to make someone else the baron if you keep slacking off like this, Mireille," I said.

I WILL USE MY APPRAISAL SKILL TO RISE IN THE WORLD

"Huh? Oh, hey, kiddo! Nah, it's not like that—I'm not slacking off, truuust me! I just finished my work for today, so I'm taking a break!"

"For the record, I heard your little monologue a moment ago."

"Ugh! O-Okay…you got me. I'll take my work seriously. Starting tomorrow."

"Starting *today*."

"Fine, fine," Mireille grumbled. She sure didn't sound serious to me.

Maybe giving her this job really was a mistake…

"Also, wait—what're you doing in Lamberg, anyway?" Mireille asked belatedly.

"I'm here to visit my father's grave," I said.

"Oh? Why?"

I took some time to explain how I'd met with his spirit while I was unconscious.

"Huh! It's a weird, wild world out there," said Mireille. I wasn't sure if that meant that she believed me or not. "I never got the chance to talk with your dad, but I did see him once, back in the day. He had a real mean look in his eyes, so I didn't even think about getting close enough to talk to him."

"That's funny—my father said something very similar about you. He said that you used to be very unapproachable."

"Huh? As if! I mean, sure, I used to be a little prickly, but I was also a beauty who could turn heads just by walking down the street!" Mireille grumbled. "Anyway, I'd better head inside and get to work. And I mean that—I'm definitely not thinking of going in and slacking off again where you can't see me!" she added, then turned around and strolled into the estate.

She's definitely going inside to slack off.

"That woman never changes, does she…?" Licia said with a tired sigh.

We soon arrived at my father's grave.

"Father! We came to visit!" Kreiz shouted happily.

"Kreiz, don't forget the flowers!" Wren scolded.

I stood before the grave.

Thank you, Father. I swear that I'll do my utmost as the head of House Louvent to lead all of us into prosperity, I mused internally. I had every intention to keep that promise.

"My father-in-law passed away quite early, didn't he?" said Licia.

"He did, yes..." I replied.

"I trust that in that respect, you won't follow his example."

"I won't, I promise. I'll live a long life. I won't die before you, no matter what," I declared.

We spent the rest of the day taking it easy in our Lamberg estate, stayed the night, then returned to Castle Canarre the following morning.

○

The next day, I attended my first meeting in a very long time. I still felt like I was in perfect health, and since I'd spent so very long feeling terrible, the fact that I wasn't ill in any particular way was enough to make me feel as light on my feet as I'd ever been.

"Congratulations on your return to your duties, Lord Ars," Rietz said before the meeting started. He looked like he was almost tearing up a little—actually, no, he was straight up crying.

"I'm... I'm so, so glaaad! Ars, you're baaaaaack!" bawled Rosell, who was standing beside Rietz. It had been a pretty long time since I'd seen one of Rosell's classic breakdowns, and it almost felt nostalgic, in a weird sort of way.

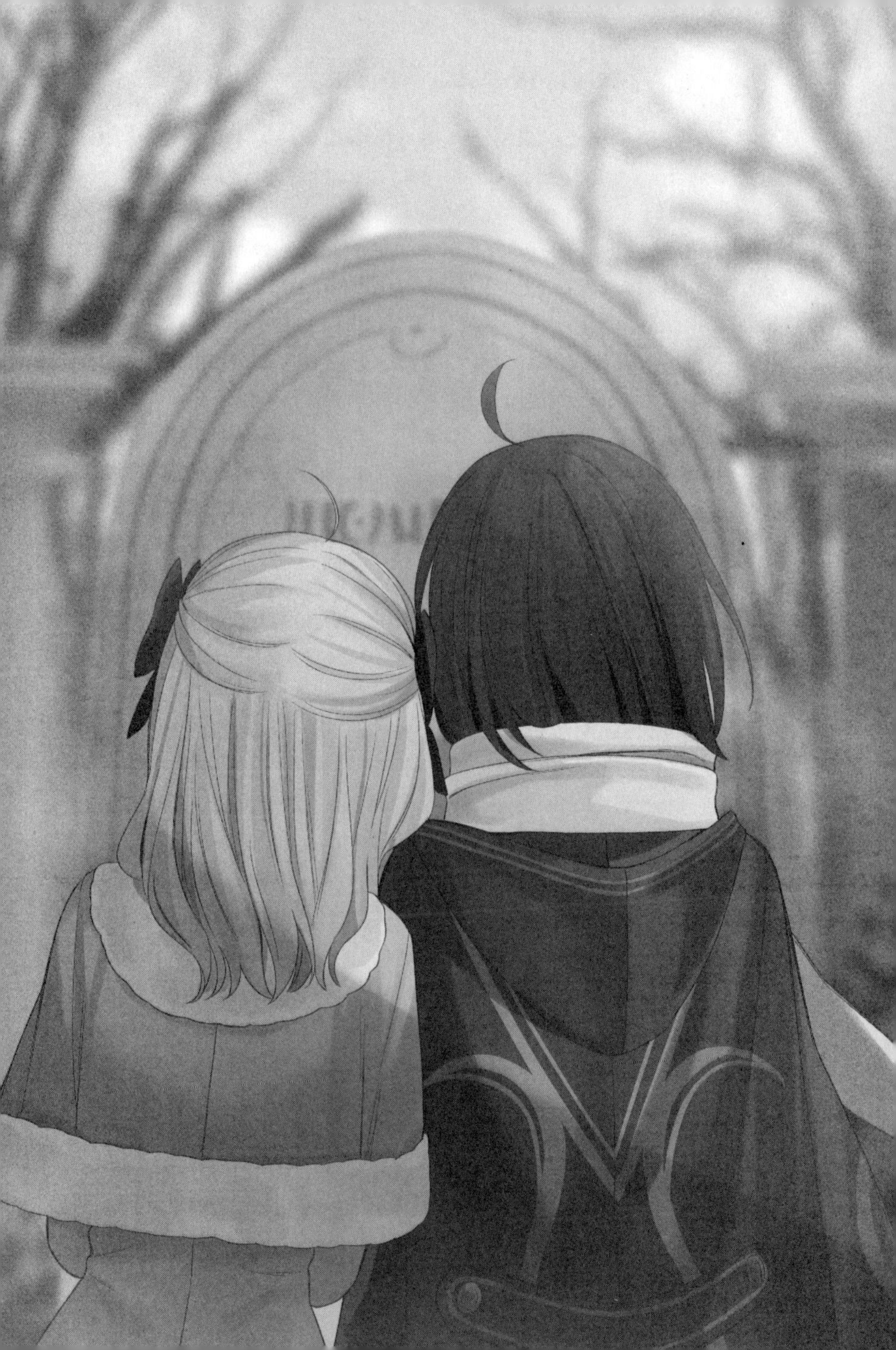

AS A REINCARNATED ARISTOCRAT

"You people were all way too worried. From the start, I knew there was no way he'd die. Of course, it *was* my spell that saved him, so you can give me credit for that," Charlotte said with one of her usual smirks. She'd earned it, this time—I really would have died without her. That went for Virge getting me the poison aqua magia that I'd needed as well, of course. I owed him my thanks too.

"I'm sorry I worried you, everyone," I said, "and I promise that I'll be more cautious from now on. I'll make sure that nothing like this ever happens again."

"I-It's... It's my responsibility to make sure that nothing like this happens, period! I swear that I'll never allow your life to be put in danger again, Lord Ars! I swear it!" declared Rietz.

He really must have felt responsible for what had happened to me. He had plenty of other responsibilities, of course, so I couldn't let him be too terribly preoccupied with guarding me. If I was going to get by in this world, I would have to learn to keep self-protection constantly in mind. Summerforth wasn't anywhere near as peaceful as Japan had been, after all.

"All right! Let's get this meeting started," I said.

With that, my first meeting in a very long time commenced. We covered all the usual topics, from the current issues facing the county to the appeals we'd received from our citizens. My retainers talked amongst themselves, gradually working toward the optimal solutions for each issue. There were many times when I just sat back and listened, though ultimately, it was up to me to make the final call in each case.

"By the way, what are the Shadows doing right now? Are they still searching for the assassin? What was her name...Zetsu?" Rosell asked Rietz.

Pham and his crew had spent a long time trying to track down the assassin who had poisoned me. My Appraisal skill had told me her name was Natasha, by the way, but apparently she went by Zetsu while working as an assassin. Plenty of people went by alternate names—Pham himself being one of them—and I'd decided to make a point of calling her Zetsu in the future.

"They're still carrying on their search, yes," explained Rietz. "To allow an individual who attempted to assassinate the head of House Louvent run free would be a stain upon our honor. Moreover, she was able to approach Lord Ars thanks to some sort of technique that allowed her to fool the results of his Eye of Appraisal. Being as there is a chance that Seitz has access to that technique, it is of vital importance that we learn its workings, lest his power become impractical to use. Apprehending Zetsu and forcing her to divulge her methods is the fastest and most effective option available to us."

I felt that Rietz was letting his grudge against Zetsu color his analysis maybe just a little, but he also had a point. Catching Zetsu might be hard, but if it let us learn how she'd managed to falsify her status screen, it would make my future recruitment efforts much easier.

"Hmm. Do you think we're gonna be able to catch her, though?" asked Rosell. "I guess it'd be best if we could for sure, so it makes sense to keep up the search. We don't want to have all the Shadows out and about and leave Canarre unguarded from enemy spies again, though, so I think we should probably cut down on how many people we dedicate to that job."

"Now that, I agree with. I'll give the order at once," said Rietz, accepting Rosell's suggestion without protest.

It would certainly be nice to find Zetsu, if we could manage it. Her stats had been very high when I appraised her after her disguise wore off, as well, so she was unquestionably capable. If I had a chance, I would've liked to recruit her as a new retainer...though I knew even considering that was dangerously naive of me.

The rest of our meeting proceeded more or less as usual, and ended without any major developments cropping up. I'd completely regained my former endurance, at that point, so I was able to last through the whole meeting without any difficulties—not that meetings like that required all that much stamina in the first place, I suppose.

And so, we at House Louvent managed to escape from the crisis we'd found ourselves in and returned to our usual daily lives.

A few days came and went.

The day started like any other. I got up in the morning, had breakfast, and was in the study, writing a reply to a letter from another noble house when Rietz burst into the room.

"Urgent news, Lord Ars!" Rietz shouted in a fluster. I knew in an instant what that meant: Rietz only lost his composure like that when the news was bad.

I was certain that something awful had happened. Had Seitz invaded? Had someone done something appalling, or had someone been poisoned like I had? A whole assortment of worst-case scenarios flashed through my mind, but as it turned out, I was wrong about all of them.

"We've received a report from Shin—he's completed his airship!"

○

In a corner of Ansel's capital—the Imperial Capital of the Summerforth Empire—was a certain pub. It was almost entirely unoccupied, at the moment, populated only by its owner and a pair of customers who were seated at the bar. Not that there was anywhere else for them to sit: the pub was so narrow that there wasn't room for anything other than a counter.

I WILL USE MY APPRAISAL SKILL TO RISE IN THE WORLD

One of the customers was a woman wearing a bulky hood that obscured her features. The other, who wore a mask, was the assassin Zetsu.

"It's quite the rare thing to see you fail to finish a job," said the hooded woman.

"It really isn't—these things happen, and the holder of the Eye of Appraisal would never be an easy target. He's been blessed with capable followers indeed," replied Zetsu. Her words were calm and calculating in a way that implied no frustration at all. She didn't seem upset in the least about her failure.

"And now those capable followers are after you?"

"So it seems. The Summerforth Empire is a big place...but I do believe they'll be making my work a little harder, for the time being."

"Careful not to let them catch you," the hooded woman said with a sneer. She made it sound like she was, to the contrary, hoping that her companion would be apprehended.

Zetsu shrugged. "Considering my reputation's taken a hit after this failure, I won't be getting many promising jobs for the time being anyway. This might be the right time for me to take a break. What about you, Raku? Has anything happened on your end recently?"

"Hmm. Nothing noteworthy. Work's been as steady as ever. Oh, but you've reminded me—you said you found the Eye of Appraisal's bearer, didn't you?" the hooded woman—Raku—asked.

"Right," Zetsu confirmed.

"Well, I've found a woman in the Duchy of Rofeille who seems likely to be the bearer of the Eye of Warfare. She's only sixteen, but she's absurdly capable in combat. They say she's carved her way through a hundred battles undefeated, and they're calling her the Goddess of the Battlefield. Not to mention that she's supposedly quite the beauty as well."

"How can you be sure you haven't just found a talented warrior?"

"I can't. That's very possible. But, while I don't know the details of what the Eye of Warfare does, it should allow her to see something that gives her an edge in battle, right? When a sixteen-year-old wins that many battles in a row, it's not hard to think she may have some special power backing her up."

"I see... Well, if she does have the Eye of Warfare, then we have both it and the Eye of Appraisal's holders identified. Maybe the Eye of Foresight's holder is out there somewhere as well," Zetsu said as she lifted her cup to her lips and took a sip of liquor. "I have a feeling that the day will soon come when all the infighting the Summerforth Empire's been plagued with comes to an end."

○

Couran had gathered up his retainers for a council of war in Castle Arcantez. He sat at a round table, with his followers arranged around its circumference. Their eyes were all fixed upon their new king, their expressions almost fearful. Couran was now the absolute and unquestionable ruler of Missian, and one wrong word on his retainers' part could cost them their standing in an instant. Their fears were far from groundless.

One of those retainers, however, remained undaunted by Couran's new royal status. His name was Remus, and he was one of the kingdom's most skilled generals. Although he had sided with Couran's brother Vasmarque in the civil war, he had been spared execution and allowed to serve Couran following its conclusion. That was as clear of a sign as there could be of how much Couran valued his abilities.

"The topic at hand today...is how we will go about dealing with Seitz in the near future," Couran announced. "The duchy's acts of aggression toward our kingdom have been flagrant, and demand an immediate response."

Couran had heard all about how Seitz's armies had moved to invade Canarre, only to pull back at the last minute. He had also learned that there was an overwhelmingly high chance that the duchy had orchestrated the attempt upon Ars's life.

"'Acts of aggression' hardly does their villainy justice. Their behavior has been outrageous, and cannot be overlooked! We should send our armies across the border and teach them a lesson they won't soon forget!" one of Couran's more hot-headed retainers proposed.

"I think not. There's no conclusive evidence that Seitz was behind the plot to take Count Louvent's life, and when all was said and done their move to invade amounted to nothing more than mere posturing," another retainer countered. A debate began to unfold.

"What say you, Lord Remus?" one of the retainers eventually asked.

A few seconds passed by in silence. The assembled retainers waited with bated breath for Remus to speak. Finally, he opened his mouth.

"Seitz's aggression is clear, but the wounds they suffered during their previous invasion of Canarre still pain them deeply. It will be no easy task for them to invade now, and I believe that they will be of no concern to us if left unprovoked," said Remus. "But, then again...I would hazard that His Majesty the King had chosen a course of action long before deciding to call this conference. Is that not so?"

"Well reasoned," said Couran. "Seitz is indeed in a weakened state. There is no telling whether or not they will try to invade...but their attempt to take Ars's life was an act that cannot be overlooked. No man who would allow his foes to murder his vassals with impunity has the right to call himself king," he continued, his words simmering with a deep-seated rage. "Seitz's actions are egregious, and demand swift and just retribution! I order all of you to prepare for war!"

Perhaps encouraged by Couran's willingness to act in the interests of one of his followers, the gathered retainers' spirits were raised in an instant. And so, Missian began preparations for open warfare with Seitz.

The council came to a close, and Couran's retainers departed from the round table. In the end, only Remus and Couran himself remained.

"You've always had a talent for firing up your men's fighting spirit," commented Remus.

"But not yours, it would seem," noted Couran.

"These old bones haven't much fire left in them. None to spare on matters of war, at the very least."

"And yet you jumped at the chance to provide Vasmarque with your council, did you not?"

"Not by my own initiative. I did nothing more than answer the questions that were posed to me," Remus replied dismissively.

A hint of sternness came across Couran's expression. "I see," he said. "Shall I take that to mean that you would not hesitate to offer me tactical council, should I ask for it?"

"But of course. I am now Your Highness's humble servant," Remus said with a nod.

"It seems you are opposed to the war I seek to start."

"As I said, I'm old, and haven't the energy to wish for bloodshed."

"Is that truly all there is to it? A matter of motivation?"

For a moment, Remus hesitated. "There is one other thing," he eventually added. "The question of whether or not we can win. Should we lose this battle, the whole endeavor would gain us nothing."

"Seitz's failure in the last war has instilled a fear of Missian in them. Moreover, they have given us all the justification we could need to march into war with our morale high. I do not believe we stand at a great risk of loss."

"I would not disagree. And yet, it has not been long at all since you took the momentous step of declaring Missian's independence. To invade Seitz now would be to prompt the suspicion and ire of all the other duchies, and in the worst case, to cause them to rally together and crush you."

"I will not deny that I had intended to delay this war until after our diplomatic ties with the duchies had had time to strengthen. Seitz's use of assassins, however, poses a clear and present danger to Missian. They have grown arrogant, and it is necessary for us to remind them of their place," Couran said with a wrathful scowl. When he said that Ars's assassination was an offense that could not be overlooked, he had meant every word of it.

"Did you not tell Count Louvent that you declared independence for the sake of peace?" asked Remus.

"I did, and I spoke the truth. I seek peace, in the long term, but peace can never be won without a fight. That's all there is to it."

"And yet…there is no guarantee that peace will await at the end of every fight. I, for one, have been fighting all my long life, and have yet to witness an age of peace at the end of it all," Remus replied, a look of resignation coming across his face.

"In any case, what's done is done," said Couran. "I've laid our course, and it cannot be altered. I will be relying on your talents when the fighting begins."

"But of course. What council I have to offer is yours."

Couran and Remus's conversation came to a close, and the two men left the council chamber behind them.

Author
Miraijin A

Thank you very much for purchasing the sixth volume. At long last, the anime has started airing! I sincerely hope that you watch and enjoy it! Thank you for your support!

Illust.
jimmy

Hi! I'm jimmy. The anime finally begins broadcasting this year! I hope you enjoy it, and of course, I hope you enjoy the light novel as well!